Books by Tom Hoffman

The Eleventh Ring

The Thirteenth Monk

The Seventh Medallion

Orville Mouse and the Puzzle
of the Clockwork Glowbirds

Orville Mouse and the Puzzle
of the Shattered Abacus

Orville Mouse and the Puzzle
of the Capricious Shadows

An Orville Wellington Mouse Adventure

ORVILLE MOUSE

and the Puzzle of the Capricious Shadows

by Tom Hoffman

With lots of love for
Molly, Alex, Sophie, and Oliver

A very special thanks to my
wonderful editors
Beth, Sophie, Oliver,
and Amanda
for their invaluable assistance
and excellent advice.

Table of Contents

"We shall not cease from exploration, and the end of all our exploring will be to arrive where we started and know the place for the first time."

−T.S. Eliot

"All that we see or seem is but
a dream within a dream."

–Edgar Allan Poe

An Orville Wellington Mouse Adventure

ORVILLE MOUSE

and the Puzzle of the
Capricious Shadows

Chapter 1

Mendacium

"I'm telling you, it's the same castle I dreamed about on Varmoran."

"Quiet, do you hear that?"

Orville Wellington Mouse stopped short, his ears perking up. "That pounding sound?"

"Yes, like a heartbeat."

"Um... that might be me. Not that I'm scared or anything, but sometimes if I get anxious, my heart starts pounding."

"It's not your heart, ninny, it's coming from down below, from the dungeons."

"Why am I dreaming about this creepy old castle again?"

"Don't ask me, it's your dream, not mine."

"You're the real Sophia, right? Not a dream Sophia I made up? You seem a little cranky."

"Pay attention, please. I already told you I was the real Sophia. I was having a lovely dream about Madam Dulcifer's Pastry Shop when I got pulled into your spooky castle dream."

3

"And that's why you're cranky?"

"I'm not cranky, Orville. All I'm saying is I'd rather be dreaming about a plate of yummy brimbleberry tarts than some moldy old castle with creepy pounding noises coming from the dungeons." Sophia paused, listening intently. *"It's muffled, but it sounds like a big machine, maybe an old fashioned steam engine. It could be a duplonium powered generator, but that seems out of place for an old castle like this. This is getting interesting, let's go see what it is."*

"Sophia, I don't think we should go poking around down there. In my dream on Varmoran it was weirdly dark in the dungeons. I woke up when the purple flowers started biting me, before I could see what was there."

"Remind me again what your inner voice said about three minutes ago?"

Orville groaned. *"Descend into the darkness and learn the true meaning of fear."*

"Let's go, then. Let's descend into the darkness. The stairs are over there. I'll lead the way." Sophia flicked her wrist and an orb of light shot out from her paw, illuminating the circular room. *"Look at the mosaic on the floor, a rabbit warrior in silver armor battling a blue lizard."*

"That was in my dream, too. We walked across it and went down a spiral staircase."

"Why is my light orb dimming? That shouldn't be happening."

"It's the same as my dream, it got really dark." Orville extended his paw and a sphere of radiant light appeared in front of him. Seconds later it had dimmed to the brightness of a flickering candle. *"Something is*

absorbing the light."

"Remember what the Thirteenth Monk told you? It's your dream, so you're the one creating everything in it, everything you see and hear."

"Why would I be making the orbs go dim?"

"Maybe there's something really scary down in the dungeons that you don't want to see."

"I feel kind of sick. Are you sure my inner voice is always right?"

"You know perfectly well it is. You have to keep going no matter how scared you get. It said you're learning the true meaning of fear."

Orville crept forward, his paw pressing against the rough castle wall, his heart pounding. When they reached the bottom of the staircase he sent his light orb around the perimeter of the room. *"It's not bright enough. I'm going to try something else."*

Orville concentrated deeply, creating a dozen dense thought clouds, then converted them simultaneously to brilliant orbs, shooting them out in all directions. The vast chamber was illuminated just long enough for Sophia to get a glimpse of the room.

"The chamber is about a hundred feet across in both directions. Stairs to the left. We have to go down to the lowest level. Something is waiting for us down there."

"What do you mean, something is waiting for us? What kind of something? Why would something be waiting for us?"

"It's just a feeling I'm getting, and I'm never wrong about my feelings. There is definitely something waiting for us down in the dungeons."

"This is the worst dream ever. Why does something have to be waiting for us?"

"We'll be fine. On our last adventure we had to jump into a volcano filled with molten lava. What could be scarier than that?"

Orville glared at Sophia. "Oh, I don't know, maybe something waiting for us in a dark creepy dungeon?"

They continued down the twisting irregular stairway, Orville leading the way, gingerly searching for the edge of each step with his foot.

"Okay, that was the last step. Creekers, that thumping sound is louder than ever. It's coming from the other side of the room. It does sound like a giant heart beating. That's not possible is it?"

"Go left, but whatever you do, don't go toward the giant evil beating heart."

"What?? Why did you call it that??"

Sophia snickered. "I'm being pulled to the left by my inner self. That's where we need to go. We're looking for two big doors."

Orville sent out another cluster of brilliant orbs. They vanished like the others, but not before Sophia had spotted two massive obsidian doors on the left side of the cavernous hall.

"Take my paw, I know where we have to go."

"I can't see you. I don't like this."

Sophia felt around for Orville's paw. "Let's go. Remember, this is just a dream. You can't get hurt in a dream."

Step by step the two mice crept across the dungeon floor, drawing ever closer to the monstrous pair of black doors. Sophia whispered, "Above the doors."

Orville looked up. He could just make it out, a shadowy gold medallion bearing the image of a coiled snake.

6

"I think I'm going to throw up. Do you think the thing waiting for us could be a giant snake?"

"You can't throw up in a dream."

"Why not?"

"You don't have a stomach, your body is just a thought. Focus, please. Let go of your fear. We need to understand the deeper meaning of what we're seeing. Remember what the Thirteenth Monk taught you about dreams, they have form and they have content. The form is the shape of the thing you're seeing, the content is the true symbolic meaning of the object."

Orville's observant mind flicked on, his eyes sharp. "Okay, we know it's the same castle I dreamed about on Varmoran, but I woke up before that dream ended because the purple flowers were biting me. I could be having the dream again because there's still something my inner self wants me to see down in the dungeons. It's probably something really scary, and that's why I'm making the orbs of light go out."

"Well done. What does the golden coiled snake on the door mean?"

"A coiled snake or serpent could symbolize great—" Orville never finished the sentence, his train of thought cut short by a low rumbling sound. The two massive obsidian doors had groaned open.

"What is that??" Orville's eyes were riveted on a shadowy form surrounded by an aura of purple shimmering light. *"It's really tall, taller than Proto. The light's getting brighter, I can see it!"*

Sophia was not easily frightened, but the sight of the spindly abomination filled her with an almost paralyzing sense of dread. The strange entity stood twelve feet tall, wrapped in a flowing purple robe, a long dark golden sash draped around its waist. Its face was shrouded in darkness, hidden within the nebulous shadows of a floppy hood, but there was no concealing its burning yellow eyes. The creature directed its gaze toward Orville. Sophia grabbed his arm. "Don't wake up, it's just a dream, we can't get hurt. Pay close attention to what it says."

"Why is it looking at me?" Orville jumped when a gnarled wooden staff topped with a fiery orb appeared in the creature's paw, sending wildly flickering shadows across the cavernous room. Three times the beast brought the great staff down with a thundering crash, shaking the castle walls. A sickening fear flooded through Orville, twisting and turning his insides until they squirmed like a hundred writhing serpents. This was worse than anything he ever could have imagined. He could not move, could not turn away from this hideous mesmerizing apparition, held captive in the unrelenting grip of its burning yellow eyes. This was magic, dark and deep, an impossibly powerful unyielding force that no shaper in this or any other world could hope to overcome.

A low hissing voice slipped and slithered from the creature's mouth. "Heed my warning, mouseling, for the fate of your world hangs in precarious balance. A great darkness shall vanish, taking with it a thousand worlds. Those left behind shall suffer my terrible wrath, forced to endure the endless horrors of my spectral demons. Fear my darkness with all your heart, for I am Mendacium, great and terrible wizard of ages long lost."

Something that felt like claws grabbed Orville's neck. He tried to speak, tried to tell Sophia to wake up,

8

tried to warn her this was the darkest of all magic. Much to Orville's surprise, the only thing that came out of his mouth was a horrific scream of unbridled terror.

Chapter 2

The Snake

Orville sat up in his bed, his neck still stinging from the dreadful grasping claws. His eyes darted across the shadowy room for any sign of Mendacium the Dark Wizard. "Creekers, that was the scariest dream I've ever had. I hope I didn't scream out loud."

Orville groaned when he heard the heavy footsteps running up the stairs, followed by a gentle tapping on his door.

"Orville? Are you all right?"

The voice belonged to Proto, the ten foot tall robotic rabbit he and Sophia had befriended while solving the puzzle of the clockwork glowbirds. Proto was the most advanced Rabbiton ever created by the Elders, a race of enormous rabbits who departed this universe fifteen hundred years ago for Mandora, a peaceful new world of their own creation. Proto was a pinnacle of engineered intelligence, a prototype Rabbiton equipped with the revolutionary Expanded L7 Sincere Friendship Simulation Package.

"Orville? I heard the most dreadful scream coming from your room. There wouldn't by any chance be a rather large yellow striped scaly creature in there with six legs and venomous fangs?"

"I'm fine, Proto, I just had a bad dream, that's all. Wait, why are you asking about a yellow striped scaly creature? Did you let something get through that photonic barrier thing?"

"Oh my, no, nothing like that. No need to worry at all, I'm just chattering on. Breakfast is almost ready. Tasty oatmeal with brown sugar and snapberries. Doesn't that sound delicious? Hurry down before it gets cold."

Orville shook his head. Proto's skill in the art of misdirection was unrivaled. "I'll be down in a couple of minutes. I have to get dressed." He glanced anxiously around his room. The last time he had a dream this scary he woke up to find his bedside table covered with six inches of snow. He scanned the table, looking for anything he might have shaped in his sleep.

"Nothing new. That's good, it was just a bad dream."

Unfortunately for Orville, when he hopped out of bed his foot had a sudden and extremely painful encounter with an unknown irregular shaped object. "AGGHHH!! My foot!! What in the world did I–"

A quick glance revealed the source of his foot's acute discomfort. Protruding out from under his bed was a hideous coiled golden snake. With a sharp yelp, Orville skittered backwards, tripping over his chair and tumbling to the wooden floor with a resounding thud, his eyes never leaving the ominous looking serpent. A powerful sphere of defense popped up around him, an impenetrable field of energy shapers use to protect themselves from malevolent forces, including uninvited golden serpents. The scaly reptile had not moved, its

11

eyes frozen on Orville.

Orville rose to his feet, studying the golden serpent warily, cautiously approaching it. He let out a nervous laugh of relief. The snake was not real, it was only a brass figurine.

Once again Orville heard footsteps on the stairs and a tapping on his door. "Orville? Are you quite certain you're all right? What was that dreadful crashing sound?"

"I'm fine, Proto, I just tripped getting out of bed and knocked my chair over. There's no big scaly yellow creatures in my room. I'll be right down."

"Very well. Don't dally, your oatmeal is getting cold."

"I won't, thank you!" Orville groaned, rubbing his leg. He ran his paw across the brass snake. This was bad. When he shaped something in his sleep it always held a deep significance, usually marking the beginning of a new and perilous chain of events. He had to talk to Sophia as soon as possible. He shivered, remembering the terrifying purple robed creature from his dream. Mendacium the Dark Wizard. Why had he dreamed about a frightening dark wizard of ages long lost, and what was the great darkness which would vanish? "Maybe Sophia will know something about this." He threw on his clothes, pushed the snake figurine under his bed, and ran downstairs.

"Morning, Proto. Where's Mum and Papa?"

"Papa left for the Metaphysical Adventurers headquarters already. He said he is working with Master Marloh to organize a great hodgepodge of journals left by past Metaphysical Adventurers."

"He mentioned that yesterday. It sounds kind of

interesting, some of those journals date back over five hundred years. It would be fun to read them, I bet they had some amazing adventures back then. Where's Mum?"

"She had to run some errands before work."

"This oatmeal is really good, different. What's that new flavor? It tastes almost like snapberries, but sweeter."

"How lovely of you to notice. I added a few tasty vegetables from my garden to the recipe."

"You put vegetables in my oatmeal?" Orville's spoon froze halfway between the bowl and his mouth.

"It's more of a fruit than a vegetable, I suppose, although it's quite difficult to determine exactly what it is. Most of the plants in my garden were started from ancient seed packets I discovered in the Cube, probably left there by the Elders, or perhaps the Anarkkians."

Orville's spoon did not move. "You put something in my oatmeal and you don't know what it is? It might be something the Elders or the Anarkkians left behind fifteen hundred years ago? That doesn't sound like a very good idea. Suppose it's a deadly poisonous plant?"

"You just said how tasty it was. I daresay you would not be saying such a thing if you'd just eaten a deadly poisonous plant. In fact, when I think about it, you wouldn't be saying anything at all. Ha ha ha ha!"

"You can't tell if a plant is poisonous by how it tastes!" Panic filled Orville, his arms and legs suddenly weak and shaky.

Proto gave another loud staccato laugh, slapping his leg. "Ha ha ha ha! Just one of my extremely humorous jokes. I wouldn't be much of a chef if I didn't scan the ingredients with a nuclonic wide spectrum screener to make certain there were no deadly toxins or venoms."

Orville lowered his spoon, eyeing Proto. He knew Proto prided himself on having a highly developed sense of humor, and some of his jokes were really funny, but an equal number of them were very perplexing. "Just so you know, it's really not funny to make someone think they may have eaten a deadly poisonous plant."

"I do apologize, I had thought it to be quite humorous, but clearly I misjudged the effect it would have on you. I shall store your negative response in my data repository, filing it under potentially non-humorous humor relative to the ingestion of deadly poisonous plants. Now, would you care for another non-poisonous flapcake?"

"Um… I'm kind of full, thanks. They were really good though. Hey, I just remembered, have you ever heard of someone called Mendacium?"

"That's a peculiar name. Where did you hear it?"

"I forget exactly, I was just wondering if you knew who he was."

"I'm afraid I can't tell you off the top of my head, but I shall be happy to research it for you. Only last week I set up a remote viewing port connecting me to the information storage crystals back at the Cube. By the time you get home from the Book Emporium I shall have identified this mysterious character. Is he up to no good? Are we off on another terrifying adventure fraught with deadly peril?"

"Umm, I don't think so. I was just curious about who he is." Orville tried to sound nonchalant, neglecting to mention that Mendacium was twelve feet tall and a dark wizard from ages long lost.

After breakfast, Orville grabbed his coat and headed for the front door. He checked to make sure Proto wasn't watching, then flipped open the big dictionary on the entryway table. Closing his eyes, he fanned through the pages, poking his paw into the book, randomly selecting one word.

"Today's word is *blustery*. I like the sound of it. Blustery, blustery. Its definition is 'weather characterized by strong winds, wind blowing in strong gusts'. On a windy day I can say, 'Quite a blustery day today, wouldn't you agree, Sophia?'" Orville grinned. This was going to work, Sophia would be impressed with his new vocabulary. He took out his note pad and wrote down the word and its definition.

"Bye, Proto! I'm off to the Book Emporium!" Orville stepped onto the front porch, slamming the door behind him.

Chapter 3

Orville's New Hat

Orville thoroughly enjoyed his daily walks to work. It was a pleasant and relaxing time, strolling down the winding country lane past three small farms and through a lovely forest. Each day was different, some days were hot, sunny and dusty, some frigid and snowy, or cool and crisp, the ground covered with crunchy orange, yellow, and red leaves. Or, like today, extremely windy, the sudden gusts swirling up clouds of dust.

"This is perfect, a blustery day! I'll send Sophia a thought cloud to meet me for lunch, then I'll use blustery in a sentence when I talk to her."

Orville strode down the road, the sporadic winds whipping up dust and leaves. As he strolled along, an imaginary conversation with Sophia was playing out in his mind.

"You have such a marvelous vocabulary, Orville. I wish I knew as many words as you do. You're really smart."

Orville's pleasant reverie was cut short by a brown

and purple blur flashing past him. He ducked down, afraid he was being attacked by a large bird, but when he looked up he saw this was not the case. The brown and purple object which had sailed past him was not an angry bird, but an errant hat, a hat which was soaring and whirling above him, carried to dizzying heights by the blustery wind.

"Someone lost their hat!" Orville looked behind him, but there was no one to be seen. "That's odd, I wonder where it came from?" He chased after the hat, watching as it soared higher and higher, finally descending into the top of a tall tree, trapped securely between two branches. With a shrug Orville continued on, then stopped and turned, looking up at the hat.

"That's an adventurer's hat, brown felt with a bright purple feather, the right brim folding up to the crown. It looks like a nice one, and they're not cheap. I should rescue it. Maybe Master Marloh will know who it belongs to."

Orville was well aware there were countries where the art of shaping, or using the mind to manipulate energy, was understood and well accepted as part of life. Unfortunately, Symoca was not one of those countries. The true nature of shaping was not generally understood here, many misinformed mice labeling it dark and dangerous magic, opinions stemming from age old superstitious tales, not based in the hard facts of science and deep physics. There were also a good number of mice in Symoca who did not believe shaping actually existed, mice who thought it to be nothing more than a whimsical tale created solely for the amusement of young mouselings. One consequence of this situation was the Symocan Shapers Guild and the

Metaphysical Adventurers were forced to keep their existence a closely guarded secret.

Orville glanced around to make certain he was not being watched. "It's wedged between those two branches. A small force beam at just the right angle should do it." He stepped ten feet to the left and aimed his paw at the hat. A brilliant beam of red light shot out, hitting the ensnared hat with just enough force to dislodge it from it's leafy prison. The hat tumbled down from the tree, landing on the dusty road in front of Orville. He scooped it up, looking for any clues which might identify the hat's owner. A chill shot through him when he turned the hat. Affixed to the front was a small brass medallion embossed with the symbol of a coiled snake.

Orville's eyes were wide. "That's the medallion from my dream, the one above Mendacium's chamber door, and it's the same coiled snake I shaped in my sleep."

He took a deep breath, trying to relax. "Maybe the castle dream was just my inner self telling me I was going to find this hat. That's not so scary. It's definitely not a new hat, but it's a nice one. It's old style, and the purple feather is amazing. You don't see hats like this anymore. I wonder if it fits me?" Orville flipped the hat onto his head and to his delight found it to be a perfect fit.

"This will impress Sophia. Maybe I'll get to keep it if we can't find the owner." Orville adjusted the hat to a jaunty angle and continued down the dusty road.

Wearing this new hat made Orville feel like a true rough and tumble adventurer. He raised one eyebrow. "Perhaps you have heard of me, I am Orville the

Adventurer." He ran his paw across the brim of his hat and snickered. He couldn't wait to show Sophia.

Orville attempted a casual demeanor as he swung open the front door and stepped into the Book Emporium. Master Marloh glanced up from the front desk, eyeing Orville's new hat.

"What a wonderful adventurers hat! Where in the world did you find it? I haven't seen an old style hat like that in many years. Quite dashing, I must say."

Orville ended the masquerade, unable to contain his excitement. "I found it on the way to work! The wind… um… is really blustery today and the hat blew past me and got stuck in a tree, so I rescued it."

"A marvelous hat. You have no idea who it belongs to?"

Orville sighed, reminded that the hat wasn't really his. "I don't know. I looked around but I didn't see anyone. I was hoping someone here might recognize it, since it's an adventurers hat."

"An excellent thought. Why don't you leave it on the counter and perhaps someone will be able to identify the owner. That medallion with the coiled snake should help. It looks oddly familiar, but I can't quite place it. Perhaps it will come to me later. We have two carts of new books which need to be placed on the shelves. That should take you a good portion of the day."

"I'll get started. I sent Sophia a thought cloud, she's stopping by at noon. We're going to have lunch behind the old barn, even though it's such a blustery day."

"Yes, quite blustery, indeed." A barely perceptible smile crossed Master Marloh's face. Yesterday Orville's word had been *lethargic.* "I'll let you know when she arrives."

The morning passed quickly, the first cart of books nearly shelved when Orville heard Sophia's voice coming from the front of the shop. He pushed the cart aside and darted through the racks to the front counter. He had decided not to mention his castle dream unless Sophia brought it up. He wanted to learn more about Mendacium before he said anything. He also knew Sophia's thoughts regarding magic. She had told him time and time again there was no such thing as magic, only science that we don't understand.

"Hi, Sophia, ready for lunch?"

Sophia gave Orville a hug. "Hi, best friend. Where should we go?"

Proto made us lunch. I thought we could eat behind the barn.

"That's sounds perfect. We'll be out of the wind."

Master Marloh called out to Orville. "Don't forget your hat." He tossed the adventurers hat to Orville with a wink.

Orville flipped the hat onto his head and the two friends strolled out the front door. The brisk wind was whipping up small clouds of dust around them.

"Quite a blustery day, wouldn't you say? I hope I don't lose my adventurers hat."

Sophia nodded. "It is windy out. We should be fine behind the barn though, and we'll have plenty of warm sunshine there."

"A blustery day, to be sure."

Sophia stopped, turning to face Orville, looking directly at him.

Orville's eyes widened. "What is it? Why are you looking at me like that?"

"Why are you saying blustery so much? Yesterday

you couldn't stop saying how lethargic you were, and today you can't stop saying how blustery it is. Let's hear it."

"I don't know, those words are just part of my vocabulary."

"Orville, it's me you're talking to, Sophia Mouse, your best friend in the world. We've linked our minds twice. We know everything about each other. Spill it."

Orville gave a painful sigh. "Fine. Every morning I pick a word out of the dictionary and write it down in my notebook and try to use it at least ten times during the day. Yesterday's word was lethargic, today's word is blustery."

"Why are you doing that?" She could barely hear Orville's mumbled reply.

"Umm... I was trying to impress you?"

Sophia said nothing, but took Orville's paw, leading him to their lunch spot behind the barn. She sat on the wooden bench and motioned for him to sit next to her. "Why are you trying to impress me?"

"I don't know, maybe because you're so smart and I wanted you to think I was too?"

Sophia squeezed Orville's paw. "Let me explain something to you. There are many different ways to be smart. I learned all about it in my science classes on Quintari. A long time ago they used to think a mouse was either smart or not smart, but it doesn't work like that at all. There are actually sixteen different ways you can be smart. Some mice are smart in music, some in art, some in writing, some in math, some in understanding how mice think, some in understanding how the universe works. I could go on and on. Do you remember that big set of blue encyclopedias in the school library?"

"Yes."

"Would you say they're really smart?"

"Huh? Books can't be smart."

"Exactly. Just because a mouse has a lot of facts stored in their head doesn't mean they're really smart, it just means they have a good memory. Memory is important, but it doesn't make you smart. Look at Mirus Mouse, he can't remember what he told us five minutes after he said it, but he's a brilliant inventor. He's a genius. I know a lot of facts and big words and a lot about science and I do happen to be really smart, but in some ways you're smarter than I am. Sometimes I'm jealous of how smart you are."

"Huh? What do you mean?"

"You see things most mice would never notice, you find hidden connections between things that don't seem to be connected. You find puzzles and mysteries everywhere. You noticed the clockwork glowbirds, you noticed your papa's marble rolling uphill. It was you who suggested we feed Proto's tasty little cakes to the sticky green ball creatures on Periculum. That saved our lives. I never would have thought of that. There's a big difference between knowing lots of things other mice have already discovered, and discovering things no other mouse ever thought of. That's what you do, Orville. You're an amazing mouse and you don't need to use big words to impress me. I'm already impressed."

Orville looked down at his feet, trying to fight back the tears. "I always felt like kind of a dimmer next to you. Thanks for saying those things. It's the nicest thing anyone has ever said to me."

Sophia squeezed Orville's paw again. "I like your new hat. It makes you look really adventurous. You should keep wearing it."

Orville grinned. "I found it on the way to work. I think it's really old."

"Can I look at it?"

Orville took off the hat and gave it to Sophia. She ran her paw over the coiled snake medallion, closing her eyes.

"What is it?"

"Nothing, it's just a nice old hat. You should wear it. It makes you look handsome."

Orville's eyes narrowed slightly. There was something Sophia wasn't telling him. He gave a silly grin. "You're really jealous of how smart I am?"

Sophia rolled her eyes and groaned. "Give me my lunch, ninny."

Chapter 4

Red Snackles

Orville ran all the way home from work, eager to find out if Proto had discovered anything about Mendacium the Dark Wizard. He dashed up the front steps and flung open the front door.

"I'm home!"

Proto's head popped out from the kitchen doorway. "Just in time, I'm preparing dinner. Papa is upstairs and Mum will be home shortly. I need you to pick a few vegetables from the garden for the salad. I'm trying a new recipe. I like your new hat, very rugged and adventurous."

"Thanks, I found it on the way to work. You're sure all those weird vegetables you're growing are safe?"

"Ha ha ha ha! Worried about eating a deadly poisonous salad?"

"Um... I think I mentioned that's not really something to joke about? Some plants are very poisonous. You have to be careful what you eat."

"Yes, you are quite right, some plants are very deadly indeed. I've read quite extensively about them. Very frightening. Perhaps one day I shall plant an entire garden of deadly poisonous plants and study them more closely. No need to worry about the plants in my garden, I have scanned them all and found them to be quite safe and very nutritious."

"Well, that's good. What do you need me to pick?"

"The name on the seed packet was impossible to read, so I'm calling them red snackles, a fanciful name that popped into my head. I'll need ten of them. They're red, three inches long, slightly tart and very crunchy. If you have trouble picking them just give a loud shriek, something resembling the cry of the Gnorli bird should do nicely."

Orville laughed politely. This was one of those times when Proto's sense of humor eluded him. "Okay, cry of the Gnorli bird. Got it." Orville grabbed the vegetable basket from the kitchen table and trooped into the backyard.

"Proto really has done a nice job with his garden. It's huge, with lots of different plants. This won't be so bad, the wind has died down and it's nice and sunny. Not blustery anymore." Orville grinned to himself, running his eyes across the array of brightly colored vegetables. He spotted the red snackles at the far end of the garden near the tall wooden fence. He adjusted his hat and flopped down on the ground next to the snackles.

"Okay, ten red snackles it is." Orville grabbed one of the red vegetables and tugged at it gently. "I wonder if these are ripe enough? Vegetables should almost fall off the vine when they're ripe." He pulled harder on the snackle. It felt strange, as though the plant was resisting him, fighting back. Orville let go, staring at the plant with a frown. "Why can't Proto grow normal vegetables like everyone else?"

He stood up and grabbed a snackle with both paws, giving it a sharp tug. The plant made a hissing noise and a bright green mist spewed out of it.

"AGGHH!! My eyes, it burns!" Orville staggered over to the wooden rain barrel next to the back porch and stuck his face in the water, rinsing his eyes. He stood up, glaring angrily at the red snackle plant. "I'm not going to be outwitted by a vegetable. Wait, cry of the Gnorli bird. Maybe Proto wasn't trying to be funny."

Orville stepped over to the red snackle plant, looking around to make certain no one was watching. "I can't believe I'm doing this." He put both paws to his mouth and let loose a loud shriek, the closest he could come to the raucous cry of the Gnorli bird when it spots a giant carnivorous centipede, its favorite meal. Much to his surprise, one of the red snackles dropped off the plant, plopping onto the ground.

"That's weird. Oh, well." Orville picked up the red snackle and dropped it into the basket. "One down, nine to go."

He was preparing to give the great cry of the Gnorli bird for the eighth time when he heard a noise coming from behind him. A mouse was clearing its throat. Orville whipped around to see the face of old Ebenezer Mouse peering over the fence. Orville groaned to himself. Ebenezer was their neighbor, a cranky old mouse who never had anything nice to say.

"What in creation is all the wild ruckus about? Have you gone loopy in the nutter? Practice your dang bird calls some other time, I'm trying to take a nap! One more crazy screech out of you and I'll be over there talking to your papa and we'll see what he has to say about it, you furry little mumkin!" Ebenezer's face dropped down behind the tall wooden fence.

Orville gave a long sigh. Why was everything so difficult? Even picking vegetables for dinner had become a struggle. Seven red snackles would have to do. He took off his hat and tossed it down next to the vegetable basket.

"At least it's nice out." He raised his face toward the brilliant afternoon sun, basking in its warmth. "Mmm... so toasty. Feels good. Nothing like a warm sunny day."

A minute later he opened his eyes, glancing back at the fence to make certain old Ebenezer Mouse wasn't watching him. He eyed the basket of vegetables. As he was counting the red snackles an odd thing happened. Orville began to feel dizzy, off balance, as though the world had suddenly become crooked, lopsided.

"Whoa, why am I feeling like this? Maybe it was the green mist from the snackles. It could have been poisonous. Oh, no, maybe Proto didn't–"

It was at that moment Orville realized the true reason for his peculiar unbalanced sensation. He squinted, trying to make sense of what he was seeing. This couldn't be. It simply could not be. The shadow from his new adventurers hat and the shadow from the vegetable basket were going in opposite directions.

"That's not possible. The sun is in the west, shining on the basket and forming a shadow that points east. The hat's shadow is pointing west, toward the sun." Orville felt sick. This was like the clockwork glowbirds, like his papa's blue marble rolling uphill. It could not be, and yet it was. He could not deny what he was seeing.

He grabbed the adventurers hat, twirled it around

and plopped it down on the ground again. The shadow was still pointing west. "Urrghh! This can't be happening."

He snatched up the hat and ran to the front yard, tossing it on the ground. The shadow was pointing toward the sun.

Orville flopped down next to the hat, his chin resting on one paw. He studied it closely, but no matter how hard he thought about it, he could not come up with a reasonable explanation for the shadow's unruly behavior.

"That's it. It's time to tell Sophia about my scary castle dream and this crazy hat. I know she won't believe there's dark magic involved, but even Sophia doesn't know everything. Wait, I never asked Proto what he learned about Mendacium!"

Orville grabbed the hat, jumped up and raced back to the garden for the basket of red snackles. He dashed into the house to find his papa and mama seated at the kitchen table. Proto took the basket from Orville, counting the red snackles.

"Seven will be perfect." Proto chuckled to himself, giving Orville a wink.

"Wash your paws and have a seat. Proto has a delicious dinner for us. How was work today? I love your new hat. Where did you ever find an old style adventurers hat like that?"

"I found it on the way to work. Master Marloh said I could wear it until they find the owner." Orville stepped over to the kitchen sink and began scrubbing his paws. His chat with Proto would have to wait.

Dinner seemed to last forever, although Orville did enjoy hearing about the old Metaphysical Adventurer journals his papa was organizing. The early adventurers had gone on some extraordinary missions, but Orville was anxious to find out what Proto had learned about Mendacium.

Orville helped with the dishes, but by the time he was done Proto had gone up to his room.

"I'm kind of tired, I think I'll go to bed early tonight."

"Okay, good night, sweetie. Pleasant dreams."

Orville nodded, hoping his dreams would not include Mendacium, the great and terrible dark wizard of ages long lost. He ran up the stairs, but instead of going to his room he went up to the third floor. Years ago his papa had converted their attic into a spare bedroom, now Proto's room. Orville was raising his paw to knock on the door when he heard a low growling, followed by curious slithery, scratching noises.

"What in the world is that?" Images of a long yellow scaly creature with venomous fangs popped into Orville's head. He lowered his paw and crept silently back down the stairs. It didn't seem like a good time for a chat with Proto. He'd talk to him at breakfast.

Orville tossed his hat onto the top shelf of his wardrobe and flopped down on his bed. "It's going to be a busy day tomorrow. I'll talk to Proto about Mendacium, tell Sophia about my scary castle dream and show her the weird hat shadows." Five minutes later he was asleep.

Chapter 5

Orville's Wardrobe

Orville had a restless night, tossing and turning in his sleep, visions of Mendacium's burning yellow eyes flickering through his dreams. He finally sat up in his bed with a groan. "Why am I dreaming about that crazy wizard? What time is it? How can it be morning already?" Orville squinted at the rays of sunlight coming through his window, but was suddenly disoriented. The light was not from his window, it was coming from his wardrobe. Beams of sunlight were streaming through the cracks of the wardrobe door.

Orville froze, stunned by the eerie light, his mind scrambling for a logical explanation. "My wardrobe is on fire!"

He leapt out of bed and flung open the wardrobe door, a bucket of water appearing in his paw. The good news was his wardrobe was not on fire, the bad news was his adventurers hat was glowing brightly, the light flooding into his room.

"This is bad. It's dark magic, I know it is." Orville searched his room for movement, terrified of what he might find. He slammed the wardrobe door shut and jumped back into bed, pulling the covers over his head.

"Okay, it's not that bad, the hat is just glowing. Maybe it's made from some kind of special material that glows in the dark. Not so scary. It's not like there are spectral demons with big claws crawling around trying to eat me. Drat, why did I think of that?"

Orville drifted off to sleep but woke with a start when he had another dream about Mendacium. He peeked out from under the covers, relieved to see the light from his wardrobe was gone. He lay his head down with a sigh, falling at last into peaceful slumber.

The following morning he awoke exhausted, but did manage a grin. "I'm feeling so lethargic today, I hope it's not blustery out." He crawled out of bed and pulled on his clothes, gingerly opening the wardrobe door.

"Whew, that's good, still not glowing. I need to tell Sophia about this, but first I have to ask Proto about Mendacium."

He ran downstairs, finding Proto in front of the stove flipping snapberry flapcakes on the heavy iron griddle.

"Proto, did you learn anything about Mendacium?"

"And a fine good morning to you. Tasty snapberry flapcakes with a hint of red snackles for breakfast today. As a matter of fact, I did glean some fascinating information about this Mendacium fellow. Quite interesting, indeed. Not at all what I was expecting." Proto turned back to the griddle, humming softly as he flipped the flapcakes.

"Proto! What did you find out?"

"One moment, there's nothing worse than an overcooked flapcake, I always say. Although, I suppose *two* overcooked flapcakes would be worse." He chuckled to himself.

"I love overcooked flapcakes. What did you find out?"

"Very well, I discovered a character named Mendacium did indeed exist, but over three hundred years ago."

Orville gave a low gasp. "Three hundred years ago?"

Proto laughed. "You probably weren't aware of it, but I made quite a clever little play on words when I called Mendacium a character. He was indeed a character, but a character in a book, a rather scary tale written for mouselings. The book was quite popular for a number of years, the author being a native of Lapinor."

"He was a character in a book? Mendacium didn't really exist?"

"Quite correct."

"What was the story about?"

"He was a dreadful dark wizard from a distant realm, commanding a vast army of ferocious spectral demons. Even worse, he hatched a nefarious plan to destroy our world and every mouse in it. How terribly frightening! Mwa ha ha ha!"

Orville stared blankly at Proto. Why would he be dreaming about a character from a three hundred year old book he had never even heard of? Orville shook his head and took a seat at the kitchen table.

"Flapcakes are nice and crunchy, just the way you like them."

"Thanks. Just a few, I'm not feeling very hungry."

After breakfast Orville headed to the living room, flipping through the dictionary to select his word for the day.

"Today's word is *capricious.* I've never heard of that one. It's pronounced *kuh-PREE-shuss.* Not too hard, *kuh-PREE-shuss.* It means, 'given to sudden and unaccountable changes of mood or behavior'. " Orville grinned, hollering out to Proto, "Hey, Proto, quit being so capricious!"

"Oh dear, do you really think my behavior is capricious? I always think of myself as being quite steadfast and predictable."

"Just kidding! I was trying out a new word. It's capricious. I'm off to work. See you later!" Orville darted out the front door, slamming it behind him.

As he strolled along the narrow winding lane, Orville found himself hoping someone would stop and admire his adventuring hat. He imagined them calling out, "A marvelous hat, young sir! Quite dashing!" He adjusted the hat's angle slightly, then stopped in his tracks, staring at his shadow, a shadow which did not include the hat perched on his head. He looked around, discovering the hat's errant shadow on the opposite side of the road. A shiver ran through him. "I probably shouldn't be wearing this. It might have dark magic in it." Orville tucked the hat under one arm.

When he stepped through the door into the Book Emporium, Master Marloh was nowhere to be seen. Orville set the hat on the front counter and headed to the back of the shop where he had left the carts of new books to be shelved.

Four hours later he was placing three copies of *The Invisible Mouse and the Rabbit Who Saw Him* on an upper shelf when he felt the claws on his neck. A fearful shriek burst from his lips as he whirled around. Unfortunately, his leg collided with the cart of books and he tumbled backward into the shelf. The fearsome creature who grabbed his neck proved to be none other than Sophia Mouse, her silly grin vanishing when he collided with the book shelves and tumbled to the floor.

"Are you all right? I didn't mean to scare you so badly. Sorry!"

"You're not supposed to sneak up on a mouse like that! And you didn't scare me, I was just surprised, I knew it wasn't Mendacium."

Sophia looked puzzled. "Mendacium? Who's Mendacium?" She paused, furrowing her brow. "Wait, I've heard that name, and recently. I know, it was in a dream I had! You were in it, too. We were in that creepy dark castle you dreamed about on Varmoran. It was really scary, Mendacium said he was a dark wizard, and said something about darkness vanishing and taking a thousand worlds with it."

Orville jumped up, trying to regain some semblance of dignity. "We need to talk. This is really serious, I discovered something very strange about my new adventurers hat."

Chapter 6

The Experiment

"Show me."

Orville set his hat on the ground in front of Sophia. "See? The shadow is going in the wrong direction. The sun is over there, but the shadow is going this way."

"I thought you said the hat's shadow pointed toward the sun? This shadow is going sideways, ninety degrees off from where it should be."

"It was pointing at the sun before, but now it's different."

Sophia said nothing. Her eyes were focused on the hat and its errant shadow.

Orville could not stop himself. "I have no idea why the shadows are being so capricious."

Sophia put her paw to her forehead and closed her eyes.

"What's wrong?"

"Is your word for today *capricious*?"

"What, I can't use big words without you thinking it's my word for the day? I know a lot of big words."

"If you say capricious again, I will pound you."

"Okay, you were right, it's my word for the day, but just so you know, I was using it correctly. The shadows are being… that word you don't want me to say."

"I need to think." Sophia leaned forward, putting both paws over her eyes. Orville sat silently. He could almost feel Sophia's mind ratcheting and clicking and spinning, a hundred billion synaptic connections flashing simultaneously.

"What do you think it means?"

"Quiet."

"Sorry."

Four very long minutes later Sophia rose up from the wooden bench.

"I think I understand what is happening, but before I say anything we have to conduct an experiment, then pay a visit to Madam Molly, the Astromechanistic Deep Physics Scholar at the Symocan Institute. She's the only one who can help us."

"What do you mean conduct an experiment? What kind of experiment?"

"It will take both of us."

"I'm not exactly a scientist, you know."

"Do you know what a sundial is?"

"A sundial? Isn't that something mice used a long time ago to tell time, kind of like a clock?"

"Exactly. Before they had clocks, mice needed some way to tell the time of day and the time of year. It works like this, if you poke a stick into the ground, the stick's shadow will change as the sun moves across the sky. If the sun is directly overhead, the stick's shadow will be really short, if the sun is low in the sky the shadow will be really long. The length and direction of the shadow changes throughout the day and also throughout the year. For a specific time on a specific day of the year, the shadow's position is always the same. Mice used to mark the position of a shadow for special days, like the day they started planting their crops. When the shadow returned to that exact position the next year, they knew it was time for planting."

"Clever, but I don't get what it has to do with my hat?"

"The hat's purple feather will be our sundial. I want you to put the hat in your backyard on a big flat board, then every fifteen minutes make a mark showing exactly where the tip of the feather's shadow is."

"Every fifteen minutes? For how long?"

"We need to do it for one complete day, or until the feather's shadow returns to its original position. Start at midnight and measure the shadow for twelve hours. I'll take over for the next twelve hours, or however long it takes. Write down the exact time you mark the shadow, and make sure to indicate which direction is north. You don't work tomorrow, so you can start tonight. Whatever you do, don't move the hat, not even an inch."

"This sounds kind of tedious. You're sure we have to do it?"

"Yes, I'm sure. This is really serious, and I mean *really* serious. I don't want to say anything else until we meet with Madam Molly."

"Okay, I'll start tonight."

"I'm sorry I snapped at you about your word for the day. Your hat has me kind of worried. I think it's wonderful that you're learning new words."

"Thanks. Oh, I found out something about the spooky castle dream we had. Proto told me the only

Mendacium he could find was a character in a three hundred year old book who was a dark wizard and had an army of demons from another planet and was trying to destroy our world. Why do you think I'd have a dream about that? I've never even heard of the book."

"Neither have I. I really don't know why you'd dream about it. Papa always said we have to let a chain of events unfold at its own pace. That's the only way to discover its deeper meaning."

Orville hesitated to ask the next question. "Do you think it's possible Mendacium might be real? That he might be alive and... be a dark wizard who uses dark magic?"

"You mean an evil dark wizard who could cast a spell and turn you into a big warty toad?"

"I didn't say anything about turning me into a toad, Sophia. I was just concerned that–"

"There is *no* magic, dark or otherwise. There is only science. Magic is the word we use for scientific processes that we don't understand yet. Before mice knew the science behind electricity, they thought lightning bolts were magical spears thrown by giants who lived in the sky. Whoever or whatever this Mendacium is, I can tell you with one hundred percent certainty he is not a dark wizard and is not using dark magic, because there is no such thing as either one."

Orville nodded, now more certain than ever that Mendacium was an evil wizard using dark magic who was planning to destroy the world with his army of spectral demons. Despite his fears, he headed home after work and began preparations for Sophia's sundial experiment.

During dinner Orville told his papa that he and

Sophia were going to measure the length and direction of shadows over one full day.

"You mean like a sundial?"

"Exactly, but she wants me to measure it during the night, too."

"There aren't any shadows at night. It's dark out."

"Umm… well… if there's a full moon there could be shadows."

Orville's papa gave him a curious look. "Did she say why she wants to measure shadows?"

"It's just something she was interested in."

"Probably for a class at the Institute. Well, Sophia knows what she's doing. She's smarter than both of us put together. Let me know if you need any help."

In preparation for his nocturnal vigil, Orville placed a large sheet of wood on the grass in the backyard. He set his hat in the center, resting several heavy stones on the brim to keep it stationary.

At exactly midnight Orville took his first measurement. It was pitch black out, but one side of the hat was glowing in bright sunlight, the hat casting a long shadow across the sheet of wood.

"Creekers! Where is that light coming from?" Orville looked all around but could not find the source. He checked his pocket watch, marking the time and the location of the purple feather's shadow. One quarter hour later he made a second mark. The length and direction of the shadow had changed slightly.

By the time Sophia arrived the next day Orville could hardly keep his eyes open.

"How's the experiment going?"

"So hard to stay awake. The shadow from the hat keeps changing. It's like there's another sun shining on it, but a sun I can't see."

Sophia said nothing. She stepped over to the board and studied the marks indicating the movement of the feather's shadow.

"Interesting. Good job. Get some sleep, I'll take over."

"What do you think it means? Why is it scary?"

"We'll need to talk to Madam Molly. Once I know for sure I'll tell you everything."

Orville gave Sophia his watch and trudged back to the house. "So tired."

Sophia called out, "Hey, Orville, how come you're so *lethargic*?"

"Unnh." Orville disappeared into the house.

Sophia's experiment ended precisely twenty-one hours, four minutes and thirteen seconds after it began. The tip of the feather's shadow had returned to the same spot it had been at midnight. She studied the markings on the board, tracing the shadow path with her paw.

"It's true, just what I was afraid of. Madam Molly might be the only mouse alive who can save our world from total annihilation."

Chapter 7

Handsome Mortimer

The next morning Orville awoke to the sound of Sophia's voice coming from downstairs. He threw on his clothes, darted down the stairs and into the kitchen. Sophia was seated at the table with Orville's mum and papa. Proto was wearing his brightly flowered apron, setting bowls of steaming oatmeal on the table.

"You're just in time for breakfast. I have prepared some delicious oatmeal with brown sugar, cinnamon, and a smidgeon of blue pindragon feathers from my garden. Let me know how you like it. It's a new recipe I'm trying out."

Orville had no idea what blue pindragon feathers were and didn't want to ask. "Sounds tasty, thanks."

"I was just telling your mum and papa about us blinking up to my school so I can give you a tour. It's time you saw it, I've been going there for over a year."

Orville nodded. "It sounds fun. Maybe I can meet some of your teachers."

"I have to talk to Madam Molly about a project I'm working on, so you'll meet her. We should leave soon.

Sometimes it's a little challenging to find her."

"I hope she's not as hard to find as Ollo the Rock Mouse was when we were solving the puzzle of the shattered Abacus."

Sophia gave him a curious smile.

With breakfast finished and the dishes done, Orville and Sophia stepped into the living room. Sophia took Orville's paw in hers and called out, "We'll be back before dinner." The two best friends disappeared in a flash of blue light.

Before Orville realized what was happening he was perched on the top of a nine thousand foot tall mountain peak, a bitterly cold wind howling past him. He was about to tell Sophia how cold he was when they blinked again. This time they were standing next to a thundering river, great swells of foaming white rapids roaring and pounding through a field of massive gray boulders. A gargantuan snow bear stood scant yards from him, occupied with a wriggling silver fish it had snatched from the raging river. A split second later they left the snow bear behind, arriving in a brilliant flash of blue light behind a tall brick building at the Symocan Institute for Mechanistic Studies.

"Here we are! It only takes three jumps to get here. I use the mountain peak and the river as stops, since we can't be in thought cloud form for more than two seconds. Master Marloh told me about them. Did you see the size of that snow bear? Wasn't he amazing? I've seen him once before, but not that close."

"He was enormous. I'm glad he was eating that fish instead of chomping on me."

Sophia snickered. "Let's look for Madam Molly. She might be in the Stellar Observatory, but probably not. We should check, just in case."

The pair of adventurers strolled across the campus, Sophia pointing out the various buildings to Orville, including a magnificent gray stone building. "All the first year students live here, it's called Old North. I spend a lot of time in that red brick building, too. That's where the science labs are and where we build a lot of our experimental mechanical devices. The technology here is primitive, but Mirus said I should learn all the basics of mechanistics first. Once I graduate he'll teach me more advanced technology, including everything he knows about designing flying machines and everything he knows about the high tech devices stored in the Metaphysical Adventurers headquarters."

"Is everyone here as smart as you are?"

"I don't know, there's a lot of smart mice here. Oh, here comes Mortimer Mouse. I'll introduce you. You'll like him."

Orville looked up to see an extremely handsome mouse approaching, a mouse who was at least six inches taller than Orville, and a mouse who looked remarkably athletic. Mortimer's face lit up when he saw Sophia.

"Hi, Sophia! You're looking more beautiful than ever. What are you doing here? I thought you were back in Muridaan Falls?"

Orville's brain was suddenly on fire, his neck burning. *"You're looking more beautiful than ever??* Who *was* this mouse and why was he talking to Sophia like that? Why didn't she tell him that was unacceptable behavior? Unless... unless she liked it, unless..." Orville's stomach twisted into a painful aching knot. "Was Mortimer Mouse more than just–"

"Orville? This is Mortimer Mouse?"

Orville looked up. "Hi, Mortimer, I'm Orville. Pretty nice school you have here. Have you been friends with Sophia for very long?"

Sophia's eyes narrowed.

"Oh, not too long. We met in a deep physics class and Sophia helped me with some of the harder calculations. All the students here help each other. That's how we learn."

"Well, nice meeting you. Sophia and I need to be going. We have to talk to Madam Molly."

Mortimer nodded. "You might have a hard time finding her. I think she's off campus for three days, up at her cabin in the mountains. Sophia, do you know where it is? I can show you if you'd like."

Orville answered for Sophia. "No need for that, we'll find it. Shouldn't be a problem." He pointedly adjusted his adventurers hat.

Sophia glowered at Orville. "Mortimer, if you could draw us a little map, that would be wonderful. I've heard it's out of the way and hard to find."

"You're right about that. Madam Molly is an odd one, to be sure, but she could be the smartest scholar at the school. She's brilliant." Mortimer set his pack down and pulled out a sheet of paper and a pencil. A few minutes later he handed Sophia a carefully drawn map. "Shouldn't be too hard to find, especially for a genius like you." He gave Sophia a wink and patted her on the shoulder.

Orville's eyes almost burst into flames.

Sophia smiled brightly. "See you later, Mortimer. Thanks so much for the map. Good luck on your exam!"

44

"I'll need it. Nice meeting you, Orville. Hope you enjoy your visit to the school."

"See you later." Orville gave a thin smile as he watched Mortimer Mouse walk away.

Sophia stood with her paws on her hips, glaring at Orville.

"What? Why are you looking at me like that?"

"You know perfectly well why I'm looking at you like this. Why were you so rude to Mortimer? He's a very nice mouse."

"Oh, well, maybe because he said you were looking more beautiful than ever and he winked at you and patted you on the shoulder?"

Sophia stared blankly at Orville. A light of understanding blinked on in her eyes. "Are you jealous? Jealous of Mortimer Mouse?"

"I'm not jealous, I just don't think some mice should be calling other mice beautiful and winking at them and patting them on the shoulder."

A huge grin spread across Sophia's face. "You're jealous. Orville Wellington Mouse is jealous of Mortimer Mouse."

"I didn't say anything about being jealous. I just don't think–"

"For your information, Mortimer says that to every girl in the school whenever he sees them. He says it to all of them, Orville. He always says they're looking more beautiful than ever. He pats everyone on the shoulder. He's a nice, friendly mouse."

"Oh, well, do you… um… like him very much? He's sort of handsome, if you like that kind of a look. And sort of tall."

"Now that you mention it, he really is very tall and

45

handsome, and there's only one reason why Mortimer isn't my best friend in the world and the mouse I care more about than any other."

Orville felt sick. "What's the reason?"

"He's not you. You're my best friend in the world and the mouse I care about more than any other."

Orville felt weak. "Oh, I... um... I'm sorry I was rude. You're right, I was jealous. I've never felt like that before. I don't like it. It's awful. It makes my insides hurt."

"You never need to feel like that again. I thought you knew how much I love you."

"Um... I love you, too."

"Good. Now let's go find Madam Molly. I hate to tell you this, but we have to save the universe from total destruction and I have no idea how we're going to do it."

Chapter 8

Mysterious Madam Molly

"The map says it's a twelve mile hike to Madam Molly's cabin. Can't we just blink there?"

"I've never been there before, so I don't know where to land. I don't want to blink onto the side of a steep ravine or inside a snow bear cave or something. When we're in thought cloud form we don't have time to search around for a safe landing spot."

"Good point. Wait, you said there are snow bear caves near her cabin?"

"Relax, Madam Molly is way older than your mum and she walks from her cabin to the school all the time. She hasn't been eaten by a snow bear yet."

"The map says we head south toward the mountains on Sun Blossom Lane. That sounds safe enough, better than Ferocious Snow Bear Lane."

Sophia snorted. Sometimes Orville could be so funny.

A short walk found the two adventurers strolling

along Sun Blossom Lane, a lovely winding dirt road leading toward the mountains. "This is nice, the wild flowers are pretty and smell really good. The spruce trees are a lot taller on this side of the mountains. They must get more rain here."

An hour later Orville was panting, trying to catch his breath. "Why do they call this Sun Blossom Lane? They should call it Steepest Hill in the World Lane."

Sophia laughed. "Not much farther. We should reach the ravine in about half an hour. Mortimer's map says there's a bridge across it."

"At least there's a bridge, that's good news."

The last half mile of Sun Blossom Lane was painfully steep, Sophia and Orville scrambling on all fours up the rugged mountainside. Sophia called out when she reached the top. "The bridge is just ahead."

Orville stared silently, a deep frown appearing on his face. "That's not a bridge, it's four big ropes with a bunch of narrow wooden boards tied to them. That doesn't look very safe at all, Sophia. Look at the ravine, it's a two hundred foot drop to the bottom."

"It's not that bad. Madam Molly crosses it all the time and she's really old, probably at least sixty."

"You also said she's really eccentric. No normal mouse would cross a wobbly old rope bridge like this one."

"Well, I'm going to. It looks like fun." Sophia adjusted her backpack and stepped out onto the bridge, grasping the ropes on either side of her. She began walking forward, the bridge swaying slightly. "It's not bad. The view of the ravine is amazing. There's a little whitewater river way down at the bottom. I don't see any snow bears, though."

Two minutes later Sophia was standing on the other side of the ravine. "Come on, just pretend Mortimer Mouse is watching you." Sophia gave a cackling laugh.

That was all it took. Orville adjusted the strap on his hat. "I'm not scared, I was just waiting for you to get across." Orville stepped out onto the rope bridge. It wasn't quite as terrifying as he had imagined, even though the bridge was swaying back and forth in the brisk wind. He was careful not to look down, and also shaped a powerful sphere of defense around him, although he wasn't sure how much it would help if he fell two hundred feet onto the jagged rocks below.

Three very long minutes later he stood next to Sophia doing his best to look calm and collected. "Nothing to it."

Sophia gave him a hug.

"What was that for?"

"Because you're the bravest mouse I know."

Orville grinned. "It was a little scary, I guess. Which way to Madam Molly's?"

"The map says we follow the left trail until it forks, then veer right, going uphill until we reach the cabin."

"I like all the spruce trees. Hey, look through those ones, you can see all the way back to the school."

"We're pretty high up. I can't believe Madam Molly hikes this trail three or four times a week. I hope I'm that active when I'm her age."

"You will be. Let's go, I'm kind of anxious to meet her, after everything you've said about her."

Sophia hiked up the rocky mountain path. "Oh, one thing I didn't mention, don't make eye contact with her. It makes her really uncomfortable. Just look at her shoulder or something."

"Huh? Why?"

"I don't know, it's just what everyone does. Nobody looks directly into her eyes. I guess it makes her really nervous. She's probably shy or something."

"I can understand that. I was really shy when I was a mouseling. It was hard for me to look mice in the eye."

"I've never been shy."

"I'm so surprised to hear that, I never would have guessed."

Sophia rolled her eyes. "Hurry up, ninny, we have a world to save."

"You keep saying that, but you won't tell me what we're saving it from."

"Here's the fork in the trail. Veer right."

"Creekers, the path goes almost straight up. How are we supposed to get up there?"

"See that big ledge up there?"

"I see it."

Sophia flicked her wrist and vanished in a flash of blue light. A split second later she was standing on the ledge waving down at Orville.

Three blinks later Orville spotted the cabin. "That's it? It's not much of a cabin. I thought it would be a lot bigger than that."

Sophia eyed the little log cabin. It was only fifteen feet wide and ten feet deep, nestled up against the side of the mountain, surrounded by a lush garden filled with colorful wildflowers and pink rose bushes. "It's beautiful, but you're right, the cabin is a lot smaller than I'd expected." Sophia stepped down the narrow pathway leading to the front door of the cabin. She nudged Orville. "Remember, no eye contact."

Sophia rapped gently on the door, calling out,

"Madam Molly? It's Sophia Mouse, I need your help with a project I'm working on."

There was no answer.

"Maybe she's not here."

Sophia knocked again. "Madam Molly?"

A moment later the door swung open, a spry old mouse looking at them with surprise.

"Sophia? What on earth are you doing here? I thought you were back in Muridaan Falls. Who's your handsome young friend?"

"This is Orville, he's my best friend. I have a question, and you're the only one I know who can answer it."

"Gollywogs, it must be quite a question to bring you all the way up here. If it's about romance, you've come to the right old mouse." Madam Molly gave a great boisterous laugh, slapping Orville on the shoulder.

Orville laughed but didn't make eye contact. He was confused. Madam Molly didn't seem shy at all, quite the opposite in fact.

"Just joshing you, I'm the last mouse to be dishing out romantic advice. Both of you come inside, and tell me about this mysterious question you have."

The two adventurers followed Madam Molly into a cluttered and cozy cabin. She motioned for them to sit on a small stuffed couch.

Sophia slid her pack off and pulled out a rolled up sheet of paper. She spread it out on the small table in front of Madam Molly.

Madam Molly gazed at it, her eyes bright. "Shadows, you're here to ask me about shadows."

"That's exactly right. This chart shows the length and movement of a shadow from an eight inch tall object for one full day."

Madam Molly nodded, eyeing the chart. "And you want to know what planet it is."

"Exactly."

Orville glanced over at Sophia. What was she talking about? What planet?

Madam Molly paced back and forth across the cabin floor, one paw rubbing her furry chin. She glanced at Orville several times, then at Sophia. Finally she picked up a small wooden stool, setting it down in front of them. She sat down facing the two mice.

Orville was being careful not to make eye contact.

"You're not telling me everything, that much I do know. Orville, I want you to look directly into my eyes."

"What? Um… Sophia said I…"

"It doesn't matter what Sophia said, look into my eyes."

Orville looked hesitantly into Madam Molly's eyes. He'd never seen eyes that green before. And they had small gold flecks in them, flecks that were swirling like a lazy whirlpool. The flecks were mesmerizing and Orville was lost, his thoughts whirling around like autumn leaves in a wind storm. He was remembering something that happened when he was a mouseling. He'd wandered out of the yard and lost his way, ending up in the center of Muridaan Falls. It was Ebenezer Mouse who had found him walking through town and brought him back home. He remembered how kind and funny Ebenezer had been, telling Orville not to worry, that he was safe. He'd forgotten that day, forgotten how different Ebenezer was back then. Madam Molly looked away and Orville was suddenly back in the cabin.

"What was that? What just happened? Where was I?"

Madam Molly rose to her feet, gazing at Orville. "You're a shaper, and a powerful one, a Metaphysical Adventurer. I should have known it, the violet aura surrounding you gives it away. I'm glad your papa is home again. You're lucky. You're in for rough times. Rough times ahead. There's an old castle. You'll learn the true meaning of deep fear. Not a bad thing to learn, but it won't be easy. Darkness, a vanishing darkness. Confusing. At the center is a tall and powerful entity, not what it seems to be. The end of all things unless you stop it. Sophia will be with you. Trust her always. You have been friends far longer than you know. Sophia is from Quintari, also a powerful shaper. No surprise. That explains a great deal. I will help you."

Orville's jaw dropped. Madam Molly picked up Sophia's shadow chart, studying it carefully. "The planet rotates once every twenty-one hours, four minutes and thirteen seconds. That's what we need. Both of you, follow me."

Madam Molly stepped over to an ornate wooden bookcase on the far wall. She grasped one side of it and swung it open. The bookcase was a door, and behind the door was a long dark tunnel leading into the mountain.

Orville gulped. Who *was* this mouse?

Chapter 9

The Book of Shadows

Madam Molly grabbed a small white cube from the rocky ledge next to the door. She waved her paw and the cube glowed brightly, emitting a warm yellow light. She strode forward down the tunnel, motioning for the two adventurers to follow her.

Orville looked at the cube curiously. "What's that cube? How does it work?"

"Not certain, but I think it draws energy from the surrounding environment. It's Thaumatarian, very old."

Sophia gave a start. "You have an object made by the Thaumatarians?"

Madam Molly grinned. "I've been known to collect a thing or two." She walked briskly down the long tunnel, pointing to a narrow vein of dark metal in the rock. "This was an old mine, abandoned hundreds of years ago. I discovered it when I was hiking and decided it was just what I needed, out of the way and private. I can get a lot of work done here."

"Your eyes, the gold flecks, the way you knew Orville's mind. Do you read thought clouds?"

"Not the same. Where I come from all the mice do what I do. No one has any secrets there, not a bad thing."

Orville asked, "Where do you come from? I've never seen anyone do that before. Sophia and I have linked minds, but what you did is different."

"Not so different from that. I link to your mind but you don't link to mine. It's just how we evolved."

"We?"

"The mice where I'm from."

"And you're from…"

Madam Molly smiled. "Here we are." She stepped into a dark cavern. She clapped her paws and a hundred brilliant overhead lights flared on, illuminating the vast chamber.

"Whoa, you have a lot of books and… other stuff." Orville's eyes were scanning the floor to ceiling racks holding thousands of books, and the rows of long wooden tables packed with gleaming mechanical devices. He recognized some as early telescopes. "You collect old telescopes?"

"I collect any technology relating to astronomy and the deep mechanistics which lie beneath it."

"I don't recognize a lot, just the telescopes."

"Many of these devices were made by Thaumatarians. They're old, very old. The Thaumatarians left a lot of things behind when they moved on."

"Where did you find all this stuff?"

Madam Molly weighed her answer, then shrugged. "I've been to Thaumatar. I traveled there with some friends of mine who located the planet a few years back. They took me through a spectral door and I spent almost a year there. Brought all these trinkets back with me."

Orville gazed across the tables. "Who took you there?"

"You're a curious one aren't you? That's a good trait. A couple of mice, treasure hunters of the best kind. Good friends of a pair of very adventuresome rabbits I know."

Sophia raised her paw. "About the shadow chart?"

Madam Molly grinned. "Back to business. Follow me." She stepped across the room to a towering rack of books along the wall. "Hmm... twenty-one hours, four minutes and thirteen seconds. That should be volume six, I think. I'll need some help lifting this. Not as strong as I used to be."

Orville stepped over and helped Madam Molly carry the enormous volume to a reading table, setting the book gently down. "Whew, that's heavy!"

Sophia examined the well worn maroon cover of the dusty old tome. "How old is it? What kind of book is it?"

Madam Molly ran her paw gently over the book. "It's Thaumatarian. Not sure about the age, but it's a lot older than I am." Orville wasn't sure if he was supposed to laugh or not.

Sophia gingerly opened the book and pressed her paw against one of the pages. "It doesn't feel like paper."

"It's not, it's something else. Not sure what. I found this entire set in an ancient library on Thaumatar."

"What do these symbols mean?" Sophia pointed to a group of golden hieroglyphs on the front cover.

"Roughly translated from the Thaumatarian, it

means, *The Book of Shadows*. You're not the first one to think of using shadow charts and planetary rotational times as a way to identify stellar bodies. These volumes chart thousands of planets visited by the Thaumatarians. If we're lucky, they'll have the one you're looking for."

Sophia unrolled the shadow chart and set it on the table.

Madam Molly opened the enormous tome, running her paw down rows of incomprehensible hieroglyphs, slowly turning the pages. "Should be somewhere in this section." Sophia studied the book. Each page was filled with the peculiar hieroglyphs, but also held several shadow charts resembling the one Sophia had made.

Madam Molly gave a victorious squawk. "Got it! That was easy. The universe has smiled upon you, Sophia Mouse. This chart is identical in every way to yours. I had to make a few conversions, since your hat's feather was a different height than the standard height they use, but more importantly the rotational period of Tectar matches your shadow chart exactly. The shadows you're measuring are cast by sunlight shining down on a little planet called Tectar. See this symbol here? That means Tectar supports life. Not sure what this other symbol means, haven't seen it before."

Orville was completely baffled. How could the sun from some other planet be shining on his adventurers hat? It made no sense, and yet Madam Molly seemed to have found irrefutable proof in *The Book of Shadows*, and Sophia did not seem at all surprised by this revelation.

"This is wonderful, exactly what I was looking for."

"You're not going to tell me how you obtained this shadow chart, are you?"

"I can't, not just yet. Orville and I have a few things to do first. I'll tell you after we understand exactly what's happening."

Madam Molly reached out with one paw, gently turning Sophia's head toward her, gazing into her eyes. "You're a Metaphysical Adventurer too. I should have guessed. I won't go any deeper, but whatever you're looking for, I wish you both the best of luck. I know a little about Metaphysical Adventurers. Please give my fondest regards to Master Marloh." She turned away, giving Orville a wink.

Sophia and Orville stayed for tea, chatting with Madam Molly about her adventures on Thaumatar, then bid their farewells and blinked back to the Symocan Institute.

"I'm telling you, she winked at me when she said it. I think she was more than friends with Master Marloh. You didn't see the wink. I saw the wink."

"Maybe she was winking at you. You are kind of cute, you know. Not all dreamy and handsome like Mortimer Mouse, but–"

"You think he's dreamy and handsome?"

"Orville, I was teasing you. Didn't you learn anything when Master Marloh formshifted us into beautiful mice? No one cared what kind of mice we were, they only cared that we were beautiful. That's wrong. Your physical form doesn't matter, what matters is your character, the kind of mouse you are. That's what I love about you, you are true and sincere. To be honest, Mortimer Mouse is friendly and outgoing, but he's a bit on the shallow side. He doesn't think about things the way you do. He would never have noticed the clockwork glowbirds or the capricious shadows from your hat."

"I used to worry a lot that you wouldn't want to be friends anymore."

"I won't tease you then. Do you really think Madam Molly and Master Marloh were more than friends?"

"I'm sure of it. She had a funny smile on her face when she winked. We should mention her in front of Master Marloh and see how he reacts."

"That's kind of devious, I like it. Let's go, it's time to head back to Muridaan Falls. I need to ask Master Marloh about the World Doors. I've heard there's a set of them in a place called The Swamp of Lost Things, but it's a long way from Muridaan Falls, in southern Lapinor."

"Wait, are you saying we have to visit the planet Madam Molly told us about? Tectar? I don't understand what's going on. How could the sun from Tectar be shining on my hat?"

"I'll tell you everything I know. Let's sit under that shade tree." Orville and Sophia plopped down on a long wooden bench.

"Okay, remember how the Thirteenth Monk sent us home from Periculum through the Void?"

"That's the dark space that separates all the worlds."

"Right. It's hard for most mice to imagine, but there are many worlds simultaneously occupying the same space. They're called parallel worlds. Scientists on Quintari have known this for a thousand years. Parallel worlds would not be possible without the Void, the dimension between all the worlds, the dimension that keeps all these parallel worlds separate. I think something is shrinking the Void. If the dimension between parallel worlds vanishes, the worlds will overlap." Sophia waited for Orville's reaction.

"Uhh... what does that mean exactly, the worlds overlap?"

"It's not good. In fact, it's very, very, bad. Your adventurers hat is a tiny indicator that the process is underway. The hat is in Tectar and the Tectar sun is shining down on it, but that small portion of Tectar's universe which contains your hat is overlapping with our world. Your hat isn't really here, Orville, it's on Tectar."

"That sounds a little crazy. Even if it's true, who cares? As long as I can wear it, who cares where it really is?"

Sophia gave a groan. "Orville, the Void is vanishing, the space between the parallel worlds is disappearing."

"Wait, Mendacium said the great darkness shall vanish, taking with it a thousand worlds. Do you think he was talking about the Void?"

Sophia grabbed Orville's arm. "You're right! That has to be it, that has to be what he meant."

"Why would it be taking a thousand worlds with it?"

"That's what I'm trying to tell you, if the Void goes away, all the parallel worlds will be forced to exist in one universe. Thousands of separate parallel universes will be jammed together into one single universe. What do you think will happen?"

"A lot of planets will bash into each other? Suns will collide?"

"That's just the beginning. What comes after that is unimaginable. Gravity would destroy everything. Right now our universe is expanding, space itself is expanding. Think of two black dots on a balloon. As you blow up the balloon, it expands, the space between the two dots increasing. The two black dots are not moving, but the space between them is growing larger. Space has been expanding since our universe began, the distance between stars growing. If all the parallel worlds were combined into one universe, the additional mass of all the new stars and planets would be so great that not only would this expansion stop, it would reverse. The gravity we feel on Earth is the result of the planet's mass warping space around it. The mass of all the new stars and planets from the other universes would drastically warp space, pulling everything together until it was all compressed to a single tiny point called a singularity, a mysterious object even the scientists on Quintari don't completely understand. Everything we know would be gone, thousands of universes gone, infinite lives on an infinite number of planets, all gone."

Orville's jaw dropped. "Creekers. Are you sure about this?"

"I'm sure. We have to find out why the Void is shrinking and we have to stop it. Your adventurers hat is just the beginning. Other objects and worlds will begin to appear as the overlapping increases. Things could get very bad, very quickly."

Chapter 10

Haukesworth Mouse

Master Marloh's eyes were on Orville's hat. "This news is most disturbing. I've heard rumors over the years that the Void was changing, but I dismissed them as the product of overactive imaginations. This hat and Sophia's shadow chart have changed all that. The state of the Void is now a prime concern of the Metaphysical Adventurers, and it doesn't sound like we have much time before things get very bad."

Orville looked up at Master Marloh. "What will you do? Who can stop something like that?"

"The universe has already given us the answer. You discovered the hat and its capricious shadows, you and Sophia dreamed about Mendacium, and uncovered the hat's connection to Tectar. These events were not accidental. It is you and Sophia who must prevent the worlds from overlapping."

Orville glanced at Sophia, then back to Master Marloh. "Sophia and I are responsible for the fate of all those worlds?"

"We'll take Proto with us. That should even the odds."

Orville gave a weak smile. He knew even Proto

could not protect them from a terrifying wizard wielding impossibly powerful dark magic.

Sophia nudged Orville. "Master Marloh, I forgot to mention that Madam Molly said to give you her fondest regards. She seems like a lovely mouse."

Master Marloh's face was unreadable. "Please give her my best regards also, when you see her again."

Orville snickered, slapping his paw over his mouth. Master Marloh furrowed his brow, about to make a reply when they were interrupted by a new voice.

"Very nice, lovely work, quite accurate."

The three mice turned to see Amanda Mouse strolling past them, her eyes motioning toward Orville's new hat.

Sophia looked at Amanda curiously. "What do you mean, it's quite accurate?"

"The hat on the counter, it's quite accurate."

"It's accurate? I don't understand."

Amanda looked befuddled. "The detail and workmanship of the hat. It's all quite accurate for the time period. Well done, indeed."

"I'm so sorry, Amanda, I'm still uncertain what you mean about the hat being accurate. Have you seen this hat before?"

Amanda's eyes darted from Sophia to Orville and back to Sophia. She blinked several times, then spoke slowly, clearly enunciating her words. "The hat that is sitting on the front counter is a very accurate recreation of the hat worn by Haukesworth Mouse over three hundred years ago. It is a highly accurate replica of Haukesworth Mouse's hat. A copy of his hat. An accurate copy. Of his hat. Well done."

The three mice stared blankly at Amanda as she

stepped over to the main desk and picked up the adventurers hat, her paw brushing the long purple feather.

"Lovely feather. I recognized it immediately from a photograph I saw three years ago in Pileus Mouse's controversial treatise, *A Thousand Years of Hats, Volume IV*, page 612, I believe. This is a rather stunning replica of the adventuring hat worn by Haukesworth Mouse, the Metaphysical Adventurer who disappeared on his third visit to Tectar, one of the twelve worlds accessible through the Thaumatarian World Doors. The workmanship is exquisite, even the stitching is..." Amanda's voice trailed off as she flipped the hat over, examining it closely. She pulled a large magnifying glass from her coat pocket and studied the stitching. "Oh, my heavens, this is astonishing. Remarkable."

"What? What do you see? Did you find something?"

Surprise was etched across Amanda's face. "I'm afraid I misspoke myself, this is not a replica of Haukesworth Mouse's hat after all."

"Whose hat is it?"

"Oh, it is most certainly Haukesworth Mouse's hat, but it's not a replica, this *is* Haukesworth Mouse's hat. It's clearly the original hat worn by Haukesworth Mouse. Look at the style of stitching and the manner in which the snake medallion was molded from brass, attached to the hat with three square copper rivets. Look at the natural wear patterns on the sweatband. This hat is hundreds of years old, of this I have no doubt."

Orville said, "Do you know anything about that coiled snake medallion? Is it scary?"

"Scary? Why would it be scary?"

"It's a snake, snakes are scary."

"It's not scary at all. Such an odd question. Every historian knows before we had a united Shapers Guild, there were a multitude of isolated local guilds, each with its own secret symbol. Members wore the symbol on a pin or a brooch as a way of identifying themselves to other guild members. Haukesworth Mouse belonged to a guild whose chosen symbol was a coiled snake. The coiled snake historically represented great power, power which could be unleashed in an instant, like the sudden deadly strike of a serpent."

Sophia's mind was spinning. "You said Haukesworth Mouse disappeared on Tectar? Is that what I heard you say?"

"Quite correct, Haukesworth Mouse disappeared on a planet called Tectar. There was a short caption next to the image of his hat stating he never returned from his third visit to Tectar."

Amanda left three stunned mice standing at the front desk.

Sophia clutched Haukesworth's hat tightly in her paws. "This is vitally important information, but we have to use logic. We know someone named Haukesworth Mouse traveled to Tectar three hundred years ago, and it was his hat which appeared in our world when it began to overlap with Tectar. It seems clear that whatever is causing the worlds to overlap must be located near where Haukesworth Mouse lost his hat, since it's the first sign of the two worlds overlapping."

Orville snorted. "You're saying we need to find out where Haukesworth Mouse went on Tectar, and where he lost his hat? That's impossible, how do we even begin to–"

Orville was cut short by a sudden exclamation from Master Marloh. "The journals! That's where we'll find it! Your papa and I have been sorting through thousands of old Metaphysical Adventurer journals down in the archives. If Haukesworth Mouse was indeed a Metaphysical Adventurer, and if we can find his journal, it could answer all these questions. Members almost always leave a detailed entry before they leave on a mission, in case a rescue party needs to be sent out. We'll start today. I'll bring in some of the other members to help us. There are thousands of journals to sort through."

It took four days to find Haukesworth Mouse's journal, and it was Orville who found it, surrounded by towering stacks of weathered and worn volumes, many with barely legible pages, some written in cryptic cyphers or unrecognizable languages. Orville pulled a heavy journal off the pile, his eyes blurry from long hours of searching.

"I found it!!" He jumped to his feet, holding the heavy gray volume over his head. In faded brown ink on the cover of the old journal was the drawing of a coiled snake, beneath the snake lay the words they had been searching for.

Haukesworth Mouse
His Journal of Adventuring

Cheers rang out from a dozen weary Metaphysical Adventurers. Orville's papa clapped him on the shoulder. "There is no doubt now that the universe has chosen you for this mission."

Master Marloh nodded in agreement. "Take a few days off and read Haukesworth's journal. Let us know as soon as possible what you learn."

Sophia said, "We need to know how he was planning to get to Tectar. One of the twelve World Doors leads to Tectar, but I think the existence of the World Doors was unknown to mice three hundred years ago."

Orville's papa agreed, saying, "You're quite right. The doors weren't discovered until long after Haukesworth Mouse disappeared on Tectar. If we can find out how he got to Tectar, it might give us the precise location of his arrival."

Orville set the massive journal on the floor. "Whew, that's heavy." He gently lifted the front cover, examining the first page. "There's at least three hundred pages of tiny cursive writing and a lot of it is faded, hard to read. It's going to take a really long time to get through all this."

The room was strangely silent.

"So, um, I guess I'd better go home and get busy reading."

Sophia snorted, whacking Orville's arm. "Come on, I'll help you carry it home."

Chapter 11

Haukesworth's Journal

It is my fervent hope that on this, my last expedition to Tectar, the location of that lost mythic land, the deepest held secret of Tectar, shall be revealed to me. In my bones I have felt it, I am closer than I have ever been to success in this endeavor, my inner voice speaking words of inspiration and encouragement."

Orville stopped reading and set the journal down on his desk.

Sophia frowned. "That was his last entry? It doesn't really tell us what he was looking for."

"He was looking for a lost mythic land."

"That still doesn't help us much. Was there anything about his other trips to Tectar?"

"That's the good news. I found out how he got to Tectar, and you were right, it wasn't through the World Doors. I'll read it to you, I bookmarked the page."

Orville opened the tattered journal again, running his paw down the page until he found the entry.

"Great fortune has smiled upon me this day, for within the journal of the brave and stalwart Parzifal Mouse I have found clear mention of a waypoint, a path to Tectar. He has made mention of an island far below the southernmost point of Symoca, a journey of ten days by sail during the months prior to the setting in of the frigid snows of winter. It was Parzifal himself who discovered this island, and Parzifal who so named it the Isle of the Serpent, for the island's uncanny resemblance to a writhing serpent. His choice of name bodes auspiciously for my journey, filling me with great expectations, as it echoes the symbol of my own guild, a coiled serpent. In the snake's eye shall be found a cave, coming and going with the tides of the day. Woe to he who is caught unawares by the inward rushing sea, but in the darkest recesses of the cave lies an ancient gateway to Tectar, a passage created eons ago by noble architects unknown. There is no safe return for the adventurer who takes this path. If the timing be misjudged, the unfortunate soul shall return, only to perish beneath a thousand tons of sea, never again to witness a setting sun."

Orville stopped reading, looking up at Sophia. "What do you think the lost mythic land was that Haukesworth was looking for?"

Sophia shook her head. "I don't know. It must have been something really important. It sounds like he spent most of his life trying to find it. It's strange, I'm starting to care about him even though I know he died three hundred years ago. I hope he found it, whatever it was. He seems true, sincere."

"I know, I like him, too. He must have been a good Metaphysical Adventurer. There's more in the journal.

This is the part that kept me awake last night." Orville opened the journal and began to read.

"The name of Caligari has been given to me by those dwelling to the west of the murderous Forest of Thorns, bordering the great Obex Range. The once resplendent Castle Caligari now lies abandoned, in aging disrepair and decay. It is Castle Caligari I seek, my inner senses directing me to this rumored edifice, the spot on which I have pinned my hopes, where the question shall find its answer. Despite such glad tidings, I am filled with grievous concern regarding this perilous undertaking, questioning my own abilities, whether or not I may possess the fortitude to pass through the Forest of Thorns and safely journey across the frigid Obex Range, even with such powers of shaping as I possess. Only time shall reveal the outcome of this, my last great adventure."

Orville stopped reading, flipping several pages ahead in the journal. "Look at this drawing." Orville held the book up for Sophia to see.

"It's the castle from our dream! You found it, this is it, this is where we have to go. Your dream was about Castle Caligari, the mythical location Haukesworth Mouse was searching for."

"I'm not the first one to dream about it. Look what he wrote underneath the drawing."

Sophia hunched over the book, squinting to read the faded brown cursive writing.

"I have sketched to the best of my limited ability a likeness of Castle Caligari, shown to me by a favorable and near miraculous dream. I shall not rest until such time as I stand before this dark and forbidding edifice in the land of the dead."

70

"Land of the dead? What does that mean?"

Orville closed the journal. "I don't know, but I don't like the sound of it. Do you think he ever found the castle? What do you think the murderous Forest of Thorns is? A forest with a lot of stabby thorns doesn't sound so bad. You could just pop up a sphere of defense and that would take care of it."

"There must be more to it than that. He was a shaper, he would have known how to create a sphere of defense. We really have no idea what kind of lifeforms we'll encounter on Tectar."

"Maybe Master Marloh will know something about Isle of the Serpent. We should ask him." Orville did not mention Mendacium the Dark Wizard, something notably missing from Haukesworth Mouse's journal. He found himself wondering if Mendacium the Dark Wizard and his horde of spectral demons had brought Haukesworth Mouse's life to a tragic and untimely end.

"Orville, you're worrying again. What is it?"

"I'm not worried, I was just wondering what happened to Haukesworth."

Sophia nodded, but she knew Orville's thoughts were haunted by visions of Mendacium. "Okay, first we need to formulate a plan. We know Haukesworth traveled by sailing ship to the Isle of the Serpent. We have something a lot better, we can take a Dragonfly and be there in eight or nine hours, maybe less. No need to sail there on the autumn winds. Once we land, we'll find the cave and go through the gateway, more than likely it's an ancient spectral doorway."

"He said we had to be careful about the tides, that they flood the cave."

"Proto can check the tidal charts before we leave.

The important thing is we know to keep our eyes on the rising tide. Once we get to Tectar, Haukesworth said we travel east through the Forest of Thorns, then cross the Obex Range to Castle Caligari. Once we reach the castle we figure out what's causing the Void to disappear and put a stop to it."

Orville smiled. Sophia could make the most insurmountable obstacles sound like insignificant little bumps in the road. She had a natural confidence, and it was infectious. Maybe that's why he liked her so much, she always made him feel hopeful. "I'd say we have a plan. I'll pack tonight and have Proto check the tide charts. He'll be thrilled when I tell him we're off on another adventure." Orville heard a small cough outside his bedroom door. "Proto, have you been eavesdropping on our conversation?"

The bedroom door swung open and Proto poked his head in. "Oh, good heavens no, that would be dreadfully rude, quite inappropriate. I just happened to be dusting the picture next to your door and couldn't help but overhear your discussion regarding Haukesworth Mouse and his journeys to Tectar. I fear Sophia might be quite correct, the Forest of Thorns may not be at all what it seems, perhaps it is not inhabited by trees at all, but by hordes of slithering creatures covered with long deadly poisonous thorns."

Orville gave a mock look of terror, well aware of Proto's penchant for frightening creatures. "Great heavens, with creatures like that we'll certainly need you there to protect us. You'd better pack tonight, tomorrow is going to be a busy day. We have to tell Master Marloh what we learned about Castle Caligari and the doorway to Tectar, then pay a visit to Mirus

Mouse to requisition a Dragonfly for our trip to the Isle of the Serpent. We can leave tomorrow afternoon."

Proto rubbed his silver hands together. "Tectar sounds simply dreadful, far worse than Periculum or Varmoran."

Chapter 12

Red Sea Rising

"What's wrong with you, mouse? How many times do I have to remind you to oil the duplonium motors before a flight? Do you want your Dragonfly to burst into flames and go down in the Vesarak Sea?"

Orville stared blankly at Mirus Mouse. Mirus was also known as the Mad Mouse of Muridaan, the greatest inventor in all of Symoca and arguably Symoca's most eccentric mouse. His memory, or lack of it, was legendary among Metaphysical Adventurers. "Oil the duplonium motors? They need oil?"

"What?? They need oil??" Mirus' eyes were bulging. "You're a copilot in the Dragonfly Squadron and you don't know a simple thing like that? How old are you, mouse??"

"Sorry, I know you must have mentioned it, but it slipped my mind somehow. Sophia, do you remember anything about oiling the motors?"

Sophia shook her head. "I'm sorry, Mirus, I don't recall any mention of that. Could you remind us again how to oil them?"

Mirus gave a great screech. "That was a test, and

you both failed miserably! You *never* oil duplonium motors! Never! I've told you that twenty times! Your ship would burst into flames and you'd go down in the Vesarak Sea."

The pair of adventurers stood mutely before Mirus. Orville was staring at his feet, afraid to look at Sophia, afraid he might start laughing.

Mirus exploded in laughter, a raucous sound quite similar to the screeching of the wild East Symocan Kukululu bird. "Ha ha ha ha! Ha ha ha ha! You two mice are all right! Oil the duplonium motors? Ha! I use that one on all the new pilots!" He slapped Orville on the shoulder. "Let's go, mouse, time to hit the clouds!"

Proto stepped out from behind the Dragonfly. "I believe the ship is ready to go, Captain Orville. I have thoroughly oiled both duplonium motors." He gave a loud snort and poked Orville in the ribs with a long silver finger.

Orville glared at Proto. "Yes, very funny, Proto, even funnier than your poisonous vegetable jokes."

Sophia eyed the gleaming ship, a thirty foot long iridescent green flying machine resembling an enormous dragonfly, capable of vertical take off and speeds up to one hundred and ninety miles an hour. She hopped into the cockpit. "Come on, Captain Orville, the Isle of the Serpent is calling our name!"

Proto's eyes lit up and he scrambled into the rear seat of the craft, maneuvering his enormous backpack into the ship's storage compartment.

Orville jumped into the ship, giving Mirus a wave. "Ready to go!"

"It's about time, mouse! Let's get this bug in the sky!" Mirus stepped over to the hangar doors and swung them open.

Orville slipped on his flight goggles, one of Mirus' many amazing inventions. Turning a dial on the left side of the goggles magnified his vision up to eight times, and pushing the silver tab allowed him to see in the dark.

"Engines on!" Orville flipped the main switches, listening closely to the sound of the two duplonium motors as they whirred to life. Duplonium is a rare element which reacts violently with water, causing it to boil instantly, with no decrease to the mass of the duplonium. In a closed system like the one on the Dragonfly, it provided virtually unlimited steam power for the ship. As Mirus Mouse put it, "She'll fly till her wings fall off!"

Sophia slipped on her goggles. "Engines sound good. Let's take her up."

Orville pushed the left stick forward, watching as the four sparkling transparent wings became a blur.

"Wings look good. Lifting off." He pushed the stick forward and the ship rose ten feet above the hangar floor. "Taking her out."

Sophia grinned. She loved this part. "Let's go, Captain Orville. I hope you're not going to fly this bug like an old grandmum."

Orville snorted, "Not unless a grandmum flies like this!" He slapped the right stick forward and the engines roared, the Dragonfly shooting out of the hangar above the long grassy runway. Within seconds they were streaking down the field at eighty miles an hour, the three adventurers pressed back against their seats.

"Hold on to your hats! Here we go!" Orville jammed

both sticks forward and they shot up into a brilliant blue sky at one hundred and sixty miles an hour.

Sophia raised both arms above her head and shrieked, "Whoo hoo! That's what I call flying!"

Orville slowed the ship down as they circled a thousand feet above Mirus Mouse's vast complex. Sophia was still grinning when she pulled a map from its storage tube, spreading it out in front of her. "Mirus marked our route on the map. It looks simple enough, we head due southwest until we spot the island. It's seven hundred and twenty-three miles so it will take a while, even cruising at a hundred miles an hour. We shouldn't have any trouble finding it, the island is over twenty miles long and it's the only island in that section of the Vesarak."

Several hours later the ship was winging its way across the Vesarak Sea, Proto in the middle of a seemingly endless reminiscence of his early years, back when he was known only as Prototype Model 10E Deluxe Rabbiton with the Expanded L7 Sincere Friendship Simulation Package. Proto had been created by the Elders, a race of very tall and technologically advanced rabbits who made a sudden exodus at the end of the Anarkkian War, moving on to Mandora, a peaceful new world of their own creation. Prior to their departure they had played a vital role in the war against the brutal Anarkkian invaders.

Rabbitons were a ubiquitous fixture in the world of the Elders, tireless workers capable of performing any number of tedious and mundane tasks, but they were incapable of experiencing feelings or emotions.

At the end of the Anarkkian war there was a great clamoring by the public for Rabbitons who possessed emotions, kind and gentle Rabbitons who could assist in the care and raising of their young postwar families. Proto was the first friendly Rabbiton ever created by the Elders, a basic prototype for all others to follow. Trial runs for the new and revolutionary Sincere Friendship Simulation Rabbitons began with Proto's placement into a family of two adult Elders and three rambunctious young bunnies. He often said these had been some of the happiest days of his life.

"And then, on his fourth birthday, the idea just popped into my head out of nowhere that the party should have a thrilling space pirate theme. What young bunny doesn't like space pirates? I made the cutest costumes for all the guests, twenty-two bunnies in total, quite a considerable undertaking, I assure you. It was a lovely party, and the look on their faces when I appeared as the infamous bloodthirsty Dread Pirate Blackbones was a moment I shall never forget. Those dear little bunnies were so overwhelmed by the time and effort I had spent creating my costume that they burst into tears at the very sight of me. It was a deeply moving experience, and one I shall treasure to the end of my days. Their parents had to assure them over and over that I was not the *real* Dread Pirate Bones and I was not going to cook them and eat them. So delightful, those sweet little bunnies, such fond memories I have of them. Of course I baked a lovely cake, six tiers, each one a different flavor, decorated with little bones made out of…"

Sophia's eyes were drooping, her head resting against the cockpit door as Proto's voice droned on, merging with the hum of the ship's wings.

Orville was listening absently to Proto's story while

78

scanning the broad sea ahead. It was a glorious day for flying, not a cloud in the sky and barely a ripple on the water. Orville squinted, focusing on an area of the sea several miles distant with a peculiar red hue to it.

"What in the world is that? Why is the sea red?"

He twisted the dial on his goggles, magnifying his vision. "That's weird." Not only was a large irregular shaped section of the sea red, but it was filled with towering waves and stormy windblown whitecaps.

"Sophia, wake up! There's something strange going on ahead of us."

Sophia was instantly alert, her eyes on the tumultuous red sea. "What is that?"

Orville shook his head. "I don't know, I'm going to fly over it to see what's causing the waves. Maybe it's an underwater volcano or something. It's not windy at all."

"I don't think there are any active volcanoes in this area. You'd better be careful, I'm getting a bad feeling."

Orville slowed the ship down, cautiously approaching the peculiar stretch of sea. "It doesn't look too scary. The water is all red and there's lots of waves, but I don't really see anything that– wait, look over there! That ship just came out of nowhere!"

Proto poked his head forward to get a glimpse of the ship. "It's an enormous three masted sailing ship, fully rigged with thirteen sails. Curious that such an archaic vessel would be roaming the Vesarak."

"I'm going to fly over it and get a good look. This is amazing, I've never actually seen a three masted sailing ship, just pictures of them in books."

"Orville, wait, I don't think you should–"

Sophia's warning came too late. Orville had crossed into the red stormy sea. Later, when he described it to his papa, he said it felt like a giant hand had grabbed their ship and flung it across the sky. The furious maelstrom they entered rocked the ship wildly, twisting and spinning it as they careened through the sky above the stormy sea. Orville shrieked, popping up a sphere of defense around the tumbling craft.

Sophia cried out, "Everyone hold on!"

"We're going down!" Orville screeched in terror as a furious blast of wind flipped the Dragonfly over and sent it shooting toward the churning red waves, flashing scant yards above the great three masted sailing ship. He grabbed the right stick and pulled it back, simultaneously jamming the left stick forward. The Dragonfly righted itself and began to gain altitude, blasting across the border of the violent red sea, once again above the calm waters of the Vesarak.

Orville drew in a deep breath. They were safe. "Whoa! What was that? Where did that wind come from?" He looked behind them, his eyes on the tempestuous sea raging behind them.

Sophia's eyes were wide. "Did you see it? Did you see the ship?"

"I didn't get a chance, I was trying to keep us from going into the sea. Did you get a good look at it?"

"I saw sailors on the deck, some of them up in the rigging."

"Were they old fashioned sailing mice? What kind of clothes were they wearing?"

"They weren't mice. They were nothing at all like mice. They were tall, with shiny blue bodies, and they had four arms."

Orville stared at Sophia. "What? Are you sure?"

"Yes, I'm sure, we were only twenty feet above the masts when we passed over the ship. I could see their eyes. They had orange eyes."

"Who do you think they were?"

Proto poked his head between the seats. "I believe we just witnessed a rather dramatic confirmation of your hypothesis regarding overlapping worlds. The section of red sea we passed through was not of our world, but was a portion of another world which is now overlapping ours. It could be Tectar, but it could also be any one of a thousand other worlds."

"That has to be it. Master Marloh was right, more sections of the worlds are beginning to overlap."

Sophia's face was grim. "The overlapping process will accelerate rapidly as the Void grows smaller. We have to get to Tectar before that red sea spreads across our world."

Orville jammed the right stick forward, the duplonium motors responding with a deep roar. The Dragonfly flashed through the sky toward the Isle of the Serpent.

Chapter 13

Isle of the Serpent

"I see it!" Sophia pointed to a dark speck on the horizon, a barely visible island.

"Right on schedule." Orville adjusted the ship's course slightly. "It won't be long now."

Twenty minutes later the adventurers were circling high above the Isle of the Serpent.

"Haukesworth was right, it does look like a snake. That end is narrow, like the tail, and the other end looks like the head."

Proto scanned the island. "Most of the island appears to be covered with dense jungle, clearly it supports life."

Orville knew what was coming next.

"I'm curious as to what sort of creatures would live on such a remote island? In such an isolated environment I suppose they would have to become excellent hunters, quite fearsome, I should imagine."

Orville nodded, poking Sophia's arm. "Probably have lots of poisonous fangs and claws, that sort of thing."

Proto rubbed his silver hands together. "Oh, dear, do you really think so? We should probably land before it gets dark. Who knows what sort of nocturnal predators may be skulking about."

Sophia snickered, and Orville was about to laugh when he realized Proto might be right, there could be deadly creatures inhabiting the mysterious island.

"I see a clearing near the head of the snake. I'm going to land there. We can set up camp, have dinner, and get a good night's sleep. In the morning we'll get up with the sun and search for the cave."

Proto put down a small booklet he had been reading. "Low tide is just before noon tomorrow, which means we'll have approximately two hours to safely search the cave before the tides rushes in and drowns us."

"Thanks, I feel better now." Orville was hovering the ship a hundred feet above the island, surveying the landing area.

"What are you looking for?"

"Just getting a feel for the terrain."

"You're looking for Proto's scary creatures, aren't you?" Sophia whacked Orville on the arm.

"Even if I was doing that, there's no harm in being cautious. I don't want to land in a giant pit of carnivorous centipedes or something."

"Take us down, nervous ninny, I'm starving and I'm tired of flying."

"Fine." Orville frowned, but set the ship down in the wide sandy clearing. Proto hopped out, scanning the area.

"Nothing untoward so far. I hear tropical birds squawking, but no roaring or growling or slithering."

"Cheer up, I'm sure we'll find hordes of dreadful

creatures on Tectar." Orville jumped down onto the white sand. "Let's set up camp on that hill. We'll have a good view of the island and the sea. We can have a nice relaxing dinner and watch the sun go down."

Sophia smiled brightly. "Now you're talking. That sounds like a lovely idea. This is turning out to be a rather pleasant adventure. Orville, in your honor I will shape a delicious snapberry pie for dessert, and I'll save at least one small piece for you." Sophia gave a cackling laugh.

"Very funny. This must be Pick on Orville Day. Let's head up the hill. I'll shapes tents and sleeping bags in case it gets chilly after dark."

The sunset was glorious, far exceeding their expectations, and Proto had prepared a delicious dinner over a roaring campfire, after which they had tasty snapberry pie. The three adventurers warmed themselves by the fire, making their plans for the following day.

Once Sophia and Orville were safely snuggled in their sleeping bags, Proto took a stroll down to the white sandy beach running around the island. A brilliant yellow moon had risen, casting its sparkling reflection across the Vesarak. Proto gazed up at the glowing orb. "Quite lovely indeed. It's curious how a gigantic ball of rock flying through dark space can be transformed into a thing of glowing ethereal beauty simply with the addition of a little sunlight." Proto stopped abruptly, his silver ears rotating. "What in the world is that crunching sound? It's coming from the direction of the campsite. I'd better check."

Proto ran back to the camp and found Sophia and Orville still sleeping soundly. "Odd, I was certain I heard something. Perhaps it came from farther down the island."

He trekked down the hill toward the clearing where they had landed the Dragonfly, stopping short. The crunching, grinding sound had started up again. He crept forward, peering through the trees, flipping on his enhanced night vision system, quickly spotting the source of the mysterious sound. "Oh dear, this is most unfortunate, Sophia and Orville are not going to like this even one tiny little bit."

Proto crept forward through the trees for a better view, watching closely as the Dragonfly was dragged into the sea by a monstrously large dark blue speckled crab. The ship's fuselage had been crushed beyond recognition by the beast's titanic claws. Proto stepped into the clearing. "What do you think you're doing? Put that ship down this instant!"

The gargantuan crab paid no heed to Proto's warning. Moments later the ship was gone, vanishing beneath the waves in a bubbling white froth.

"Oh dear, this is going to make our return to Muridaan Falls most problematic."

"Proto! What's all the hollering about? Is something wrong?" Orville dashed out from the trees, peering into the moonlit shadows. "Proto? What was all the– wait, where's our ship? Where's the Dragonfly??"

Proto eyed Orville nervously. "There is a lovely full moon tonight, such a glorious shade of yellow, and look how its reflection sparkles like Nirriimian white crystals across the sea. Quite beautiful, wouldn't you agree? Almost magical."

"Lovely. Where's the ship, Proto?"

"Might I suggest that you don't go for a dip in the

sea, no matter how enticing it appears beneath the soft moonlight?"

"I'm not going to be mad at you. I just want to know what happened to our ship."

"I'm afraid a rather enormous blue crab crawled out of the sea, grabbed the Dragonfly with one claw, crushed it, and dragged it back into the sea."

"What?"

"I'm afraid a rather enormous blue crab crawled out of the sea—"

"Stop. You don't need to repeat it, I was just having a hard time processing what you said."

Sophia darted out of the trees. "Where's our ship??"

Half an hour later Sophia and Orville were curled up in their sleeping bags next to a roaring campfire.

"Can crabs climb hills?"

Sophia groaned. "Quiet, I'm trying to sleep. We have a big day tomorrow. Proto is standing guard. If the crab comes back we can just climb a tree."

"Wait, did you hear something? A rustling sound?"

"Go. To. Sleep."

"Fine, good night. You don't have to be so crabby. Get it? Be so crabby?"

Chapter 14

The Cave You Fear

"Proto, it's not your fault the crab destroyed our ship. Besides, if you think about it, it doesn't jeopardize our mission at all, because we can't take the Dragonfly to Tectar, and we don't want to risk coming back through the spectral doorway because of the tides. We really only needed the ship to get to the Isle of the Serpent." Sophia slung her backpack onto her shoulder, giving Orville's sleeping bag a substantial nudge with her foot. "Wake up sleepy bones, we have a cave to explore. Time and tide wait for no mouse."

Orville groaned, crawling out of his snuggly cocoon. He stood up, stretching his arms and yawning. "What's for breakfast?"

Sophia flicked her wrist and a snapberry muffin appeared in her paw. "One freshly shaped snapberry muffin. Eat it on the way to the cave, we're on a tight schedule. Proto, you said you found the cave?"

"Quite so. Last night while I was patrolling the beaches keeping a wary eye out for monstrous crabs, I explored the section of the island which represents the serpent's eye, the cave's location according to Haukesworth Mouse. The cave I discovered is not a natural formation, and appears to be extremely old."

Orville converted their camping gear back to thought clouds and the trio of adventurers headed south toward the eye of the serpent, the lush tropical growth soon replaced by flat rocky terrain.

"Where's the cave? All I see is black jagged volcanic rock."

"It's not so much a cave as it is a circular shaft descending into the earth."

"It goes down into the island? How far?"

"I am uncertain, but there is a rather crude metal ladder bolted to the shaft wall."

"This is starting to sound a little creepy."

"It's on the other side of this rise."

Orville clambered over the piles of shifting black rock, spotting a wide circular depression. He slipped and slid his way to the bottom, to a twelve foot wide circular hole in the ground. Creeping cautiously to the edge, he peered down into the darkness. "Creekers, it goes down really far. That ladder looks kind of rickety. Do you think it's safe?"

Sophia studied the structure. "It's covered with barnacles and seaweed but it looks sturdy enough. It's a good thing Haukesworth warned us about the tide. At high tide the seawater would flood the bowl and pour down the shaft. We don't want to be down there when that happens. Let's go, we have another hour until the tide starts to rise, which gives us about two hours to find the doorway to Tectar." Sophia stepped over to the ladder and began her descent into the mysterious eye of the snake.

"It's dark down here." She flicked her wrist, creating a glowing orb of light. The brilliant sphere descended another fifty feet, revealing the floor of the shaft. "Not too much farther."

When they reached the bottom Sophia hopped off the ladder, followed by Orville and Proto.

Orville eyed an arched black opening on the far side of the circular shaft. "I guess we go that way." He did not sound entirely enthusiastic about the idea.

Proto stepped ahead of him, flicking on his ear lights. "Ah, much better." He strode through the opening into a massive rectangular underground cave, a good portion of it occupied by an irregular shaped pool of seawater with a great barnacle encrusted boulder sitting in the center.

Orville peered out from behind Proto. "That's kind of weird. Why would there be a big pond down here?"

"A more correct term would be tide pool. After the high tide floods the cavern, most of the seawater drains off, but the depression in the cavern remains filled."

"Where does the water drain to?"

"I am uncertain, possibly an underground river."

Sophia nodded. "That would explain it. There's a door on other side of the tide pool. It must lead somewhere. Let's go."

Orville was about to reply when he saw the boulder in the middle of the lake shudder. He gave a shriek, realizing what was happening. "Run for the door! Giant crab!" He pointed to the pool, watching as the massive crab rose up from the water, revealing two black beady eyes. Proto gaped at the creature's gigantic claws.

The trio of adventurers raced around the edge of the tide pool toward the doorway. The mammoth crustacean had spotted them, turning with a clanking, scraping sound. Sophia let out a yelp. "It's coming after us!"

The great beast scuttled out of the tide pool toward them, Orville and Sophia simultaneously popping up spheres of defense.

Proto was the first to reach the heavy metallic door. "Oh dear, I do hate to be the bearer of unfortunate news, but it appears the door has been securely locked with a–"

Orville screeched, "Out of the way!" A brilliant blast of purple light shot out from his paw, hitting the rusted padlock. The lock vanished and Proto slammed the heavy door with his shoulder. It squealed open and they darted into the inky blackness beyond. Orville looked back just in time to see a huge blue claw reaching through the doorway. He grabbed Sophia, pulling her safely out of the crab's reach.

Proto eyed the massive claw, strangely mesmerized. "Quite fearsome, I must say." He gave a curious grin and stepped toward the huge appendage, watching as it slowly opened. He could see the crab's gigantic black eyes peering at him through the doorway. Proto stretched one arm out, touching the huge glistening claw. "This is called the dactylus, the part of the claw which moves up and down, and these are the razor sharp teeth of the claw... quite deadly I would imagine." He ran his silver fingers along the white gleaming teeth.

"Proto, what are you doing?"

Three things happened in the blink of an eye. First, Proto jerked his hand back, second, the massive claw snapped shut with a dreadful crunching noise, and third,

90

Orville gave a shriek and skittered backwards, tumbling into a dark shaft.

"Orville!" Sophia dashed toward the rectangular opening.

Orville's voice rang out from below. "I'm okay! I had my sphere of defense up. You should see all the stuff down here. You might want to use the ladder though."

Sophia scrambled down to the room below, blinking up a bright sphere of light. "This is old tech, maybe pre-Anarkkian."

Proto slid down the ladder, still grinning from his close encounter with the gigantic crab. "Fascinating beast. You're quite correct, this is pre-Anarkkian technology. Certainly less advanced than the Mintarians or Quintarian, but quite a marvel in its day. I'm uncertain precisely who may have constructed this complex. The seawater has taken a toll on the interior, but this appears to have once been a waypoint, something akin to a train station. Look at the rows of chairs bolted to the floor."

Proto strolled over to one of the chairs and took a seat. "It fits me quite well. Whoever built this must have been as tall as I am. This very well may have been an early creation of the Elders. It does have a vaguely familiar feel to it."

"Look at those weird panels on the wall with all the controls. Most of it's covered with barnacles and algae and seaweed. Those look like pictures, but it's hard to tell." Orville stepped over to the wall, a broad beam of orange light flashing out from his paw. The slimy green algae and seaweed vanished beneath the orange light, revealing a colorful image beneath.

"Rabbits! Tall rabbits carrying luggage. You were right, this must have been built by the Elders."

Sophia called out, "We need to keep moving. This is interesting, but I don't want to be here when the tide comes in."

"Through that exit into the big corridor."

The three adventurers hurried down the long hallway, coming to a halt in front of a pair of tall narrow yellow doors. Orville pushed them open. "Another room filled with chairs. This room is in better shape than the first one."

Twenty minutes later they stepped into an enormous circular rotunda. The walls were covered with images of smiling rabbits carrying suitcases and backpacks, pointing at a variety of spectacular scenic attractions.

"It's just like the train station in Muridaan Falls with all the travel posters."

Sophia pointed to the center of the room. "I think we found our gateway to Tectar."

Orville studied the thirty foot tall wavering translucent disk, stepping around the periphery of the room until he faced it directly. "It looks like a big flat circle of water, like the spectral doorway in Mount Ianua, except this one is green instead of orange. This has to be what Haukesworth Mouse was talking about, he just didn't know they were called spectral doorways. This one must lead to Tectar."

"Look above the door."

Orville turned, eyeing a beautifully rendered mural portraying four smiling rabbits. The adult rabbits were carrying suitcases, the two bunnies pointing at a structure in the distance. Orville gulped. The bunnies were pointing at the silhouette of a dark castle. "It looks almost like Castle Caligari. This has to be it, if we step through this gateway we'll be on Tectar." He didn't mention he had no idea how they would get home again.

Sophia insides turned to ice when she heard the dull roaring sound. "Water! Seawater coming down the corridor! It's too soon!"

Orville let out a wild shriek. "Through the spectral door! Hurry!"

The three adventurers dashed toward the tall shimmering green disc. "Everyone hold paws!" Orville turned to see tons of foaming seawater pounding into the room just as they leapt through the shimmering disc into Tectar.

Chapter 15

The Farmhouse

Orville had never experienced a world of such beauty and clarity. The skies were a brilliant azure blue, dotted with soft puffy clouds, the trees tall, green, and majestic, the ground carpeted with soft verdant grass flowing like water in a warm luxurious breeze. Great swaths of vibrant orange, gold, pink, and violet wildflowers painted the landscape.

"Creekers, this is like a dream, how could anything be so beautiful?"

Sophia nodded, soaking in the magnificent vista. "The fragrance from the wildflowers is heavenly."

Proto surveyed their surroundings. "There's a small yellow house poking up from behind a stone wall on the other side of the woods. Perhaps we should investigate, I'm curious to discover what the local inhabitants look like."

"They live in houses, that much we know."

"We should probably find out exactly what's living there before we go barging in. Haukesworth never actually described the inhabitants of Tectar. I hope it's not those weird blue creatures with the four arms you saw on the sailing ship."

The adventurers kept low, creeping silently through the trees and tall grass toward the stone wall.

Orville whispered, "Whoa, the wall is a lot taller than I thought. I'm going to climb up and take a peek."

Paw over paw, Orville silently scaled the wall, peering over the top. "It's a farm, probably about twenty acres." The wall itself was an imposing bit of architecture, fifteen feet tall and four feet thick, completely encircling the farm. "This wall must be a mile long. I wonder why it's so big?" He eyed the rustic yellow farmhouse, watching for any sign of movement. His patience was rewarded several minutes later.

"Rabbits! Rabbits live here. Their fur is green though, and their ears are really short." Orville had spotted two giggling young bunnies running around the side of the house chasing a fat waddling bird. The taller of the two bunnies caught the bird, picked it up and gave it a hug, then set it down, watching as it scurried off into the fields. What happened next was not what Orville was expecting. The rabbits turned slowly until they were looking directly at him.

"They saw me! How could they spot me from so far away?" Orville ducked down behind the wall.

A thought popped into his head. "We saw your thought clouds. Don't worry, you and your two friends will be safe inside the wall."

Orville poked his head back up. One of the bunnies waved at him. They could read thought clouds? They'd be safe inside the wall? Safe from what? The taller bunny pointed toward the main gate, motioning for Orville to head in that direction. He climbed back down the wall, running over to Sophia and Proto.

"You're not going to believe this. Green rabbits live

here, and they read thought clouds. They said we should go to the front gate, that we'd be safe inside the wall."

"Safe from what?"

"I don't know, but they seem friendly. I have a feeling we should do what they say."

"Maybe they can point us toward Castle Caligari. I'm certain we can handle whatever creatures they're afraid of. This appears to be a simple world, with very limited technology. It's also incredibly beautiful." Sophia gazed across the glorious rolling forests and hills. "Sometimes I think we'd be better off without all our technology."

Orville was also studying the landscape, looking for whatever it was they would be safe from inside the huge stone wall. "We should go, we don't want to keep them waiting."

"Is Orville Wellington Mouse getting nervous?"

Orville frowned. "I'm not scared, I'm just being cautious. Whatever they're afraid of must be huge if they need a fifteen foot wall to keep it out. I know everything looks lovely, but something monstrous could pop out of nowhere."

Proto's ears perked up at the word 'monstrous'. "I certainly hope it will be scarier than that big clunky crab on the Isle of the Serpent."

Orville couldn't think of an appropriate response. He headed down the narrow path, soon standing beneath a massive spreading shade tree next to the stout iron gate. He noticed the tree had inch long thorns on the branches. Maybe this was the kind of tree found in the Forest of Thorns. He shrugged. Not so scary after all. Orville eyed the gate's two inch thick metal bars.

"Creekers, this could stop a herd of charging Nadwokks."

The two young rabbits darted out from behind a small shed and ran to the gate. Together they lifted the heavy latch and the great iron door squealed open.

Sophia smiled brightly at them. "Aren't you two just the cutest little bunnies ever! You probably have no idea what I'm saying, do you?"

A thought cloud flashed out from the taller bunny. Sophia drew the thought cloud to her, hearing the rabbit's voice in her mind. "Your mind will convert our thoughts to whatever language you speak. Just use thought clouds, there's no need to talk."

Sophia nodded, turning to Orville. "You're right, they communicate with thought clouds. I'm not even sure they have a spoken language."

Orville smiled at the two young rabbits, watching as they pushed the great iron gate closed, fastening it securely with the heavy latch. Orville sent out a cloud. "You said we would be safe here. Safe from what?"

The two bunnies looked at each other, a flurry of thought clouds flashing back and forth between them. The taller one sent a cloud to Orville. "Please come and meet our parents. They have invited you to share a meal with us. We don't often have guests and they welcome your company." The two bunnies ran off toward the farmhouse.

Orville turned to Proto and Sophia. "We just received a dinner invitation, their parents would like to meet us. They seem nice enough, but wouldn't tell me what the wall is for."

The bunnies held open the front door as the adventurers stepped inside. Orville scanned the interior the home. It was clean and simple, sparsely furnished with handcrafted wooden chairs and tables. He noted a number of cute little paintings on the wall, clearly the work of the young bunnies. A lovely dark green rabbit wearing a white apron stepped out from the next room. She smiled at each of them, giving them warm hugs. Their gracious host showed no apprehension toward Proto.

Thought clouds flashed out to Orville and Sophia. "You are welcome guests in our home. Dinner is almost ready. I know your Rabbiton friend does not eat food or read clouds, but he is more than welcome to join us at the dinner table if he wishes. I am Gemma, wife of Aelric, our two bunnies are Edric and Elgar. Aelric will be in shortly. He has been working in the fields. We grow all our own food inside the wall. All the plants we grow are quite gentle."

Orville and Sophia both had the same thought. Gentle plants? Orville remembered Master Marloh telling him it could take years to understand the thought processes and culture of otherworldly inhabitants, given the infinite variety of beliefs they held. Whatever Gemma meant, dinner smelled delicious and Orville was starving. He sent a cloud to Gemma. "How do you know about Rabbitons? Have you seen one before?"

"Only in a book. Aelric bartered with a traveling merchant years ago for a book titled *The Dark Anarkkian Night,* a historical record of the great Anarkkian wars. There are many photographs of Rabbitons to be found within its pages."

Proto was pleased to join them at the dinner table. Soon after they were seated a weary Aelric Rabbit stepped through the back door. He sent out a thought cloud. "Gemma said we had guests. Our closest neighbors live a good distance away, so guests are a welcome respite. I am Aelric, and you may stay with us as long as you wish."

Sophia smiled. "Thank you for your kind offer, Aelric. As you may have guessed, we have traveled far and are quite unfamiliar with this area. You have the most darling little bunnies. You must be very proud of them."

Gemma laughed. "They are a pawful, I will say that, but they are the love of my life. Along with my dear Aelric, of course."

Orville sent out a thought cloud. "This soup is delicious. Gemma mentioned you grow all your own vegetables. She said the plants are quite gentle?" Orville was still curious about Gemma's odd description of their crops.

Aelric nodded. "Quite gentle indeed. They are serene, content with their lot in life, much as we are."

"The plants are content?"

"Quite so. There is no need for worry."

Orville smiled pleasantly, glancing over at Sophia, her expression unreadable. Orville knew she couldn't send him a thought cloud without the others seeing it. He wondered what Aelric meant by 'no need for worry'.

A thought cloud floated out from Sophia. "Perhaps you might be able to help us. It was our good fortune to find your lovely farm, but our true destination is called Castle Caligari. I'm afraid we have no idea where it is."

Gemma's thought cloud was gray. "Why would you wish to visit such a place as that?"

Orville sensed Gemma's unease. "We are searching

for a lost member of our village, and that was the last place he was seen. We don't really know anything at all about the castle."

Aelric took Gemma's paw. "Most admirable, but you should not travel to the far side of the mountains, to Castle Caligari. It is a dark abomination filled with malevolent creatures who worship the Beast of Castle Caligari." He leaned toward Orville and Sophia, sending a small blood red thought cloud to them. "Its name is Mendacium and it wields the darkest of magic. The Beast is the source of a thousand grisly and gruesome tales."

A thought cloud popped out from Elgar, the younger of the two bunnies. His eyes were wide. "What kind of gruesome tales, Papa? Are there ghosts there? Do they eat rabbits?"

"Such tales are not meant for young ears."

Orville's heart was pounding. The Beast? Dark magic? This was far worse than he'd imagined.

Sophia said, "I'm so sorry, I didn't mean to bring up such a dreadful topic. We're simply trying to locate a missing friend. It's very important that we find him."

Aelric sighed. "Your thoughts tell me you will not be swayed, despite my efforts to warn you away from that dark place. I have never traveled to the other side of the mountains, but I do know the way. It is an arduous, perilous journey, I cannot stress that enough. You must head east for three days until you reach the Forest of Thorns. There are tales told of rabbits passing through the forest, but I have never met one who did. You could circumvent the forest, but such a detour would add many long months to your journey. If you find your way through the Forest of Thorns, you will have reached the Obex Range, its jagged peaks rising over seven thousand feet. You will need heavy winter clothing and sturdy climbing gear to traverse the range, the weather being brutally cold, the terrain harsh and demanding. I have heard tales of full grown rabbits being swept away by the monstrous winds at the upper altitudes. When you reach the far side of the range, follow the great winding river for three days and you will come upon Castle Caligari. Take great care, trust no one, trade clouds with no one, keep hidden at all times. The creatures there are not like us."

Orville clamped his knees together, trying to keep them from shaking.

Sophia knew they could shape warm clothing and climbing gear, but said nothing. She had no idea if Aelric or Gemma knew what shaping was, and she didn't want to frighten them, saying instead, "Thank you so much for your kindness. You have helped us more than you can know. Do you have any advice which might help us pass safely through the Forest of Thorns?"

Aelric glanced at the two mouselings. He thought for a moment, then sent a cloud. "There is a deep and simmering anger within the forest. It is not a safe place to be. Some have said you must sleep during the day and travel with all haste during the night, though none I know have passed through the forest."

Proto noticed the slight frown on Sophia's face. He whispered, "What is it? Is he talking about some kind of dreadful creature?" He did not sound the least bit worried.

Dinner conversation turned to more pleasant topics, including a number of humorous stories about the two young bunnies, Edric and Elgar. After helping to clear the table and wash the dishes, the adventurers retired for the night, Aelric and Gemma providing them with pillows and blankets. Orville had also decided it would be best to keep their shaping skills hidden. Not all mice were comfortable with such things, and he had no wish to frighten their gentle hosts.

Orville fell asleep in minutes, exhausted from the long journey, but was abruptly awakened in the middle of the night, his slumber disturbed by a curious sound floating across the night air. It was a peculiar noise, like something being dragged along the dirt road outside the wall, something very large. He peered out his window into the darkness, his gaze finding only formless shadows.

Orville's nerves were tingling. Whatever was making the sound could be what the two bunnies had warned them about, the reason for the great wall surrounding the farm.

"I should look. Whatever it is, we should be aware of it so we can protect ourselves. I'll just take a quick peek over the wall." Orville pulled his clothes on and slipped out the open window, creeping silently across the yard toward the stone wall. The dragging, scuffling sound was louder now, directly outside the wall.

"So creepy, I can't imagine what it is." He silently scaled the stone barricade, gingerly feeling for footholds in the dark. When he peered over the top of the wall it was too dark to identify the source of the sound. He decided to send out an orb of light. It was risky, but hopefully everyone in the farmhouse was sound asleep, as it would be hard to explain to Gemma and Aelric where the bright light had come from. With a flick of his wrist a brilliant light sphere shot out from his paw.

The scuffling sound stopped the instant he shaped the light. He looked up and down the dirt path running along the wall, searching for a great lumbering creature, but saw nothing. There was no movement, no sound, no creature. "It's not possible. I couldn't have been mistaken, there was something moving out here." A powerful wave of dread rolled through him. There was only one logical explanation, Tectar was inhabited by gigantic invisible beasts.

Chapter 16

Proto's Discovery

Sophia gave Gemma a warm hug. "Thank you so much for sharing your home and your food with us. You have been more than kind."

Aelric shook Orville's paw. "I wish you well on your journey. Take great care in the Forest of Thorns. I'm sure your Rabbiton will be of invaluable assistance to you. I have some feeling for these things." Aelric studied the trio of adventurers. "I know there is much you have not revealed about your true purpose here, but I sense your motives are true, your intentions good, and that is all I need to know."

Orville smiled. "You are a perceptive rabbit, and one who has made three new friends by your kindness and generosity. I hope we shall meet again. I do have one last question. I was awakened last night by a strange sound coming from outside the wall. Do you know what that might have been?"

"Just the wilderness, I suspect."

Orville nodded, but still did not have the answer to his question.

Sophia hugged Edric and Elgar, secretly shaping small boxes of chocolate creams in their coat pockets. "It was lovely to meet you, you're both so *sweet*." She grinned at her little play on words.

Aelric wrestled open the ponderous iron gate and the three adventurers stepped through, leaving behind the comfort and security of the walled farm. Orville turned to give one final wave, but realized something was wrong, he felt off balance, just as he had when he noticed the errant shadows from Haukesworth's hat.

"Come on, Captain Orville, no time for dawdling!"

"I'm not dawdling, there's something not right about the gate. I'm not sure what it is, though."

"Think about it while we're walking. Aelric said it will take us three days to reach the Forest of Thorns."

"That place sounds creepy. Why do you think he said we should sleep during the day and travel at night? That doesn't make sense. If you travel during the day you can watch out for scary creatures who live in the forest."

Proto replied, "If the scary creatures are nocturnal, hunting only at night, it would be safe to sleep during the day, but not safe to sleep at night."

Sophia nodded. "That makes sense. Aelric was right, it's a good thing we have you standing guard at night, watching for all those dreadful creatures who want to eat Orville."

Orville frowned. "Very funny. Suppose the creatures in the forest are different from anything we've encountered before? Suppose they're weird and ghosty or have dark powers beyond our comprehension? Or maybe they're invisible?" He waited to see how Sophia would react to the idea of invisible creatures.

105

She gave him a look of mock terror. "Invisible creatures with dark powers beyond our comprehension? You mean dark magical powers? Like creepy old wizards who will turn you into a big warty toad?"

"Stop talking about big warty toads! I didn't say anything about them turning me into a toad. I'm just saying there could be something to all those stories about dark magic. You know, like that book about Mendacium the Dark Wizard. You heard what Aelric said about the castle, about all the gruesome and grisly tales."

Sophia thwacked Orville's arm. "I also heard him say he'd never been to the other side of the mountains. Stop worrying about imaginary invisible creatures. Relax and enjoy this lovely walk. The wildflowers and the trees are beautiful."

Orville gave a yelp. "The trees! That's what was wrong! The first time we walked through the iron gate there was a big shade tree next to it. This morning the tree was gone. That's what threw me off balance."

"I don't remember a tree being there."

"I'm telling you, there was a big tree next to the gate when we walked in, but not when we left. It had thorns on it."

"Maybe Aelric cut it down for firewood."

"We would have heard him chopping it down. Besides, we were only there for one night so he wouldn't have had time. I told you about those weird noises in the night, like something really big was being dragged down the road. Maybe someone cut the tree down and stole it."

"Who steals big trees?"

"I don't know, maybe someone needed firewood, or

106

timber to build a house. All I'm saying is, the tree was there and then it was gone."

Sophia looked extremely dubious, but did not argue.

The narrow lane they were on eventually converged with a wide dirt road. "Look, wagon wheel ruts. Probably from farmers taking their crops to market. Maybe the creatures here aren't as scary as I thought. It must be safe to walk around during the day."

Sophia called out when she crested a steep hill. "I see a little town!"

Orville darted to the top of the hill and slipped on his flying goggles, twisting the silver dial to magnify his vision. "It reminds me of Muridaan Falls. It has a wall around it, but it's not nearly as big as the one around Aelric's farm. Some of the houses have thatched roofs and there's a bunch of little wagons being pulled by rabbits."

Sophia smiled. "I like this world. It's simple and it's beautiful."

"Do you think we should stop at the village? They might have more information about Castle Caligari, or the Forest of Thorns."

"We don't have time. The overlapping of the worlds is accelerating. Think about the stormy red sea we flew over. If that spreads across the Vesarak it could destroy Muridaan Falls. Besides, I guarantee most of the rabbits in that village have never even heard of Rabbitons, much less seen one. I don't want to frighten them or cause a big stir."

"You're right. I just wish I knew why Aelric and Gemma built that big wall around their farm."

The answer to Orville's question arrived that night, long after he and Sophia had curled up in their sleeping bags. Proto was resting in a comfy green chair shaped by Orville, gazing up at the heavens, musing over a pale yellow crescent moon floating through the night sky.

"A lovely moon tonight. I've always been drawn to crescent moons, more so than full moons. There's something quite beguiling about them, an intriguing and mysterious quality, the way they peek out from the shadows, hiding the true depth of their being." Proto chuckled, imagining a shy and reclusive moon darting about in the night sky. His lunar musings were interrupted by a curious shuffling sound, his bashful crescent moon slipping behind a tall tree. It took Proto a moment to realize the moon had not moved behind a tree, but a tree had moved in front of the moon.

"Great heavens!" Proto leapt to his feet, flicking on his night vision optical system. His eyes grew wide. With its roots acting like great spindly spider legs, an enormous tree was ambling across the road toward Proto. It stopped twenty feet in front of him.

Proto was stunned, never having encountered a tree capable of mobility, but was intensely curious about its nature. Perhaps the tree was not a tree at all, but was a sentient being, an intelligent creature who bore only a coincidental resemblance to a tree.

Proto stepped closer to the tree and introduced himself. "Good evening, sir or madam, I am Proto the Rabbiton. It is a great pleasure to make your acquaintance."

The enormous swaying tree shuffled forward, its branches rustling as it walked. When it was almost upon him, a slender branch reached down, running its soft leaves across Proto's face, as though it was trying to determine exactly what he was.

"As I previously had mentioned, I am a Rabbiton, created by the Elders over fifteen hundred years ago."

The branch pulled away from him, the tree motionless.

Proto waited a moment, then rapped his long silver fingers gently on the tree's wide trunk, but there was no response.

"How peculiar. It would appear the trees on Tectar have gained the rather uncanny ability to move about at will. Quite remarkable, I've never heard of such a thing, other than those purple flowers on Varmoran who tried to eat Orville. They were mutations caused by the Anarkkian greenstones dropped on Varmoran during the war. It's possible the Anarkkians dropped greenstones on Tectar, drastically altering the physiology of the trees. I will need to research this when I return to Muridaan Falls."

Proto decided this remarkable discovery was cause enough to wake Orville and Sophia. "Orville! Sophia! I have solved the mystery of Aelric and Gemma's great wall!"

Orville's eyes were barely open when he crawled out of his sleeping bag. "What? What is it? It's the middle of the night. Why did you wake me?"

Seconds later a bleary-eyed Sophia emerged from her sleeping bag. "I was having the best dream. What about their wall? Why are you smiling?"

Proto was looking extremely pleased with himself. "I am delighted to announce I have personally discovered Tectar's greatest secret. It is my pleasure to inform you that the trees which grow on Tectar are quite mobile, our tall leafy friends able to ambulate about at will, to walk around, take a stroll, go for a hike, meander about in the dark of night."

Orville groaned. "It's not very funny to wake someone in the middle of the night and try to trick them. Trees don't walk." Orville was suddenly wide awake. "Wait, if they could walk, that would explain the disappearing shade tree at the iron gate and the weird shuffling sounds I heard!"

Sophia rubbed her eyes and yawned. "I think you're mistaken, trees possess highly developed systems specifically designed to convert sunlight into—"

One thing Orville admired about Sophia was her ability to take the most astonishing events in stride. No matter how extraordinary, she would logically analyze the situation, make a carefully considered and accurate risk assessment, then proceed to act on it. This, however, was not one of those times. Sophia gave a piercing shriek when a large branch reached down from above and ran its leaves across her face and shoulders. She skittered wildly backwards, the branch jerking away from her. With the same strange shuffling noise Orville had heard at the farmhouse, the tall tree lumbered back across the road into the woods.

Sophia gaped at the tree, then at Orville. She rubbed her eyes. "I'm going back to bed. I'll need a lot more sleep before I can face a world filled with walking trees."

The following morning Sophia emerged from her tent to find Orville cooking snapberry flapcakes over a small fire. She flopped down next to him. "We need to use logic. First, we all know photosynthesis is how trees make their food."

"Um, what is photosynthesis again? I remember something about it from school, but I'm a little hazy on the exact details." Orville's voice trailed off into awkward silence. He had no idea at all what photosynthesis was. Sophia gave him a disapproving look.

"Why are you looking at me like that? I can't know everything. I know I didn't do very well in science class, but it was because my science teacher didn't like me. Master Osterous always asked me really hard questions on purpose."

"Then pay attention, because this is important. Trees use a process called photosynthesis to convert sunlight energy into chemical energy, which they store in a special kind of sugar they use for food. Animals have to run around to find their food, but trees don't, all they need is sunlight and water."

"I don't need to run around to find my food, I can shape anything I want." Orville flicked his wrist and a large oatmeal cookie appeared in his paw. "Mmm, I love oatmeal cookies."

"Focus, please. This is exactly why you don't know what photosynthesis is. Plants need sunlight to live because they use it to make food, which allows them to grow. Now, since you're so good at noticing things, what did you notice about the trees besides the fact that they can walk?"

Orville finished his cookie, brushing the crumbs off his chin. "So tasty. They only move around at night, not during the day."

"Brilliant! Exactly right. Why do you think that is?"

"You're just like Master Osterous, always asking me really hard questions."

"Orville Mouse, would you please stand and tell the class how Proto's discovery makes trees on Tectar different from the trees found on Earth?"

"Certainly, Scholar Sophia, I'd be happy to. Unlike the trees on Earth, the trees on Tectar like to sneak up behind little mice in the dark and choke them into oblivion with their long creepy branches."

Sophia burst out laughing. "Very good, Orville, you may be seated. Class, Orville is quite right. The trees on Tectar remain motionless during the day because they are busy absorbing sunlight and producing sugar. The sugar they make during the day provides the energy they need to walk around during the night, choking little mouselings who don't pay attention in science class."

"Wait, what about the trees in the Forest of Thorns? If they walk around during the night, it changes everything."

"You're right, we need to rethink our plans. The trees we've encountered so far seem harmless enough, ambling around at night, but I have a strong feeling the trees in the Forest of Thorns will not prove to be so friendly. You heard Aelric's warning about a deep simmering anger in the forest."

Orville shivered, imagining a horde of angry trees chasing after him, trying to stab him with long venomous thorns.

Chapter 17

Forest of Thorns

Rounding a curve in the dusty road at the top of a rolling hill, Orville had his first glimpse of the Forest of Thorns.

"Creekers, look how big it is!" Half a mile away stood a massive wall of dark trees, the outer edge of a forest stretching to the horizon. "It must go on for a hundred miles."

Proto scanned the forest with his wide spectrum optics. "I see nothing unusual other than the extremely close proximity of the trees to each other. There does not appear to be sufficient space for us to pass between them."

"What do you think we should do?"

Sophia eyed the dark wall of trees. "We should study them before we try anything, learn what we can about them, watch their behavior, maybe we'll discover a weakness."

"Maybe they're not as scary as Aelric thought. Sometimes stories get exaggerated."

"That's true. We'll camp here and get some rest. Proto, why don't you wake us after dark and we'll pay a visit to the forest. The moon is out so we'll be able to see what they're doing. Maybe they spread out during the night, far enough for us to pass through."

After a quick dinner, Orville and Sophia took a nap in preparation for their nocturnal expedition to the forest. Orville woke with a start when something pinched his foot. Proto's voice rang out. "Giant crab!!"

"Proto! Scaring a sleeping mouse is another thing that is not funny. Remember what I said about your poisonous vegetable jokes? Some things are not funny. And just so you know, I didn't think a giant crab was biting my foot."

Proto gave his loud staccato laugh. "Ha ha ha ha! Rise and shine, adventurers! Time to meet our leafy ambulating neighbors. I do hope their thorns aren't venomous. I don't wish to alarm you, but I have read about a species of flying creature native to Nirriim who spray a caustic chemical mist capable of eating through a sphere of defense in seconds. We must keep a wary eye out for unknown terrors such as these."

Orville crawled out of his sleeping bag with a groan. "Do we really have to do this? I'm so tired."

Sophia was up and ready to go. "Come on, Captain Orville, you can sleep all you want after we save the universe. The forest is blocking our path and the only way to get past it is to understand it and find a weakness, just like Proto did with the Anarkkian attack spiders on Varmoran."

Orville popped up a powerful sphere of defense. "Okay, I'm ready. Unless they spray us with that weird venom Proto was talking about."

The three adventurers trekked down the long hill toward the Forest of Thorns, small bushes and scrubby trees darting out of their path. "This is so creepy.

114

Bushes aren't supposed to be running around, traipsing all over."

"It's normal in this world, and I kind of like it." Sophia grinned as two little saplings dashed past her, one chasing the other. "Look at those little ones playing! So cute."

Orville's eyes were on the dark forest standing in front of them, the trees packed together so tightly it resembled a massive impenetrable wooden stockade. He stopped twenty feet from the wall of trees. "Whoa, look at the thorns on their branches, they must be a foot long. This is bad, really bad."

Sophia inched closer to the forbidding trees, a powerful sphere of defense around her. "I'm going to try something." She sent out a large pink thought cloud to the nearest tree. "A pleasant good evening to you, tree."

Much to her surprise a puffy thought cloud floated back from the tree's branches.

"Pleasant evening as well. Mouse out for moonlight stroll? Seldom seen. Lovely moonlight makes us still sleepy, quite lethargic."

Sophia turned to Orville. "It sent me a thought cloud. I can talk to it."

"I'm getting a dark feeling, I don't trust this forest at all. Aelric was right, it's really angry."

Sophia sent a cloud to the tree. "We mean you no harm. We are travelers making our way to Castle Caligari. We are trying to reach the Obex Mountains, but I'm afraid your magnificent forest stands in our way."

"Many unsavory tales surrounding Castle Caligari. Why shall a little creature be interested in dreadful places?" Sophia felt deep simmering suspicion in the tree's thoughts. It shuffled toward her, its enormous branches rustling noisily.

Orville stepped back. "What's it doing??"

"Relax, we're just having a conversation."

The tree was now scant feet from Sophia. "Little mouses be careful not to poke yourself on the thorns. They are long and deadly. Purpose of thorns to clean our bark, destroy pesky insects, destroy little things which annoy us."

"You've heard stories about Castle Caligari?"

The tree leaned down, sending a small gray thought cloud to Sophia. "Darkest presence."

"A dark presence lives there?"

"Creature wields powers past thought. Creature to be feared beyond all."

Sophia decided not to share this bit of information with Orville. "Would you allow us safe passage through your great forest? We mean you no harm."

"No creatures pass. We are many trees, one forest, our thoughts many, our thoughts one. No creatures pass."

"Are you saying each tree knows what the others are thinking?"

"We are many, we are one."

Sophia eyed the tree. This was not going as well as she had hoped. "You're certain a mouse did not pass through your forest three hundred years ago? A mouse named Haukesworth?"

"We are certain no mouse passed. We remember such a dreadful annoyance. Not allow such things."

Sophia attempted a bright smile. "Thank you for your help. We won't trouble you again." She turned and walked back to Orville and Proto.

"What did the tree say? Can we get through?"

Sophia motioned for Orville and Proto to follow her. When they were a good distance away from the forest she told them what the tree had said.

Orville frowned. "If Haukesworth didn't pass through the forest, how did he get to the Obex Mountains?"

Sophia shrugged. "Maybe he flew over it. He could have had a blinker ship or something."

"He didn't mention anything like that in his journal. I don't think his guild had flying machines. Creekers, why is everything always so difficult?" Orville kicked a small stone, watching it bounce across the hard packed rocky terrain.

"Orville, there's no need to–" Sophia stopped, her eyes on the wide flat rock where Orville was standing. She fell to her knees, brushing away a thin layer of dirt and debris.

Orville dropped down next to her. "Is that what I think it is?"

"It is. Someone carved the symbol of a coiled serpent into the rock."

"Why? What does it mean?"

"It means Haukesworth Mouse stood on this very spot three hundred years ago, probably trying to figure out how to get past the Forest of Thorns."

Orville held the gold coiled serpent medallion on his adventurers hat next to the one carved in the rock.

"They're not quite the same. The carved serpent on the stone has its head and neck extending out from the spiral."

Proto had been studying the carving. "Perhaps it is

meant to be a signpost, pointing us in the right direction. The head of the snake points to the east, along the outer edge of the forest."

"That's it! Haukesworth marked the trail for other members of his guild to follow. You may have just saved our lives, Proto."

Orville grinned. "It's Proto to the rescue!"

The trio of adventurers made their way back to camp, Sophia and Orville crawling into their sleeping bags. Orville woke up an hour later, his sleep disrupted by three small trees who were scampering about, leapfrogging over him.

"Unnghh! Knock it off, you crazy little trees!" He swatted at the rambunctious saplings and they dashed off into the night. "I guess they're a little bit cute." He burrowed back down inside his sleeping bag and was soon fast asleep.

Chapter 18

Down Under

"There's another one of those stone huts. I wonder who lived in them? They're really small."

"It looks like they've been abandoned for centuries, there's nothing in them. Maybe they were rest stops for travelers, a safe haven from the weather."

"Or a safe haven from the thorn trees."

The early morning sun found the three adventurers trekking along the outer perimeter of the Forest of Thorns, scouting the area for spiral serpent carvings left by Haukesworth Mouse.

Orville was having a difficult time staying focused. Something about the Forest of Thorns was bothering him and he couldn't figure out what it was. It wasn't until they stopped for lunch that the answer came to him. Sophia sat down on a boulder and began shaping lunch. "Orville, water or lemonade with your lunch?"

"Water, I guess." He gave a yelp. "Water! That's it! That's what's wrong. There are hundreds of thousands of trees in the Forest of Thorns, but it hasn't rained once since we've been here. Where do they get their water?"

Sophia furrowed her brow. "That's a good point. So many trees in close proximity would require a vast supply of water to survive. Even if Tectar has a rainy season, it wouldn't be enough to support a mammoth forest year round."

Proto nodded. "Quite puzzling. If by some chance the trees didn't need water to survive, they would not have such extensive root systems."

After lunch and a lengthy discussion regarding the trees, they were no closer to understanding how the forest could survive without water. They continued on, skirting the edge of the dark forest.

Orville spotted another stone hut. He approached the small edifice, peering in through a narrow rectangular opening next to the door. "I don't think these buildings had windows, just that narrow vertical slot to let light in. Maybe they had wooden shutters or something to keep bugs out, if they even have bugs here."

Sophia glanced inside the hut. "It's just like the others, a solid stone hut with a heavy wooden door. I just thought of something, where did they get the wood to make the doors?"

"From trees, where else would they get it?" A look of horror crossed Orville's face. "Oh, I see what you mean, the trees here aren't like the ones at home. Um… maybe they waited till the trees died before they, you know, got the wood. That's sort of creepy, like building a house out of old mouse bones."

Sophia grimaced. "Eww."

Proto grabbed Orville's shoulder, pointing mutely to the wide stepping stone in front of the wooden door.

"A coiled serpent! You found one!"

"The serpent's head is pointing to the doorway. It's directing us into the hut."

"That doesn't make sense. Why would Haukesworth send us in there? Unless he's saying it's a safe place to sleep?"

"Let's find out." Sophia grabbed the heavy door with both paws and pulled. "I'm going to need some help, it's jammed shut." Proto reached over and grasped the iron latch, giving it a sharp tug. The door gave way and Sophia stepped into the hut's interior.

"There's lots of cobwebs and dust, but not much else."

Proto's eyes glowed brightly with an orange light. "I am using my wide scan spectrometer to identify any anomalies within the building." The orange light panned across the building's interior. "Interesting." Proto sank to his knees, brushing away a thick layer of dirt and debris on the floor, revealing a sheet of iron with a large ring bolted to one end.

"Please don't tell me that's a trapdoor."

Proto grasped the iron ring and pulled. With a loud squeal of rusted metal he raised up the heavy iron plate.

"Since Orville requested I not tell him what I have discovered, I will tell you, Sophia, I have discovered a trapdoor leading down into a rather ominous and forbidding darkness."

Orville groaned. "Trapdoors are worse than caves. They always go down to scary dark places with creepy monsters that grab you with long slithery tentacles, then stab you with thorns and stuff you into their big chomping mouth."

Sophia burst out laughing. "You're such a ninny, you have absolutely no idea what's down there. It could be a treasure chamber filled with gold, silver, and Nirriimian white crystals, or a bakery giving away free brimbleberry tarts and back rubs. Besides, it doesn't matter what's down there, Haukesworth sent us here and we need to find out why."

"I never thought of that, it really could be a treasure chamber. Proto, you can carry all the gold." Orville scampered down the ladder. "I hear water, maybe a river. How could there be a river down there?" He sent an orb of light down to the base of the ladder. "It goes down pretty far. The ground looks really smooth. Nothing scary so far."

"Do you see any pastry shops?"

"Very funny, ha ha." Orville reached the last rung of the ladder and hopped off, studying the curious floor. "This is weird, the ground is really smooth and flat. There's a few pebbles and some dust, but that's it."

Sophia and Proto hopped down from the ladder. Sophia sent out a group of light orbs. "This place is enormous, and it's definitely not a natural formation, someone built it. Your river is not a river, it's an aqueduct."

"What's an aqua duck?"

Sophia's eyes narrowed. "What did you just say?"

"I said what's an aqua duck? How could a river look like a duck?"

Sophia took a deep breath. "It's called an aqueduct, not an aqua duck. It's not a kind of bird, aqueducts are how ancient mice moved water from one place to another. They constructed great stone channels or pipes which carried water to their towns and cities. The water had to flow downhill to get there, so they would find a river or lake at a higher elevation, then divert water down the aqueduct to their town."

"Oh. I guess I missed that in school."

"Now you know. What we don't know is why there is an underground aqueduct, and what all the stone huts are for."

Proto said, "Perhaps the stone buildings were entrances to a vast underground world. I don't wish to cause undue alarm, but it is possible a race of creatures is living below the surface of the planet, and they are the ones who created all this."

Orville knew what Proto was thinking. He was imagining scaly lizard creatures who loved to snack on plump little mice. "I don't think scary creatures would be smart enough to build aqueducts, Proto, just in case that's what you were thinking."

"You're quite correct. They would more than likely be an advanced race, like the Anarkkians, armed with deadly particle beam weapons capable of obliterating a mouse in a single—"

"Proto! That doesn't help. It's scary enough down here without that kind of talk."

"I do apologize, but we must remain vigilant. It's just good common sense."

Orville sighed. "I suppose you're right."

Sophia pulled a two inch brass sphere from her pack and tapped a blue tab, watching as a tiny beam of light spun around, finally coming to a stop. "I know why Haukesworth Mouse sent us here. My compass says the aqueduct is flowing directly east. If we follow it we'll be traveling beneath the Forest of Thorns. Haukesworth didn't go through the forest, and he didn't fly over it. He went under it."

"Whoa, that's good news! Let's take a look."

The adventuring trio made their way to the edge of the roaring aqueduct. Sophia sniffed the water. "It smells okay." She dipped her paw in and tasted it. "It tastes fine, it's fresh, clean water."

"Fresh water! This is how the Forest of Thorns gets the water it needs. Their roots must go down into the aqueduct."

"That might explain it." Sophia ran her paw along the smooth stone of the aqueduct wall. "It's definitely not a natural formation. Someone built this entire underground complex."

"How could it be so big? The Forest of Thorns is at least a hundred miles across."

"I don't know. I've never seen anything like this. Not even in books."

Proto said, "The aqueduct goes through that large arched tunnel in the side of the cavern. There's a narrow ledge running along both sides but it's not wide enough for us to walk on."

It was Orville who spotted the three gray metallic domes lying on the ground next to the cavern wall, each dome twelve feet across and four feet tall. "I wonder what these are?" He leaned over, rapping one of the domes with his paw. "It sounds hollow." He pushed the dome, surprised when it slid several inches across the ground. "They're really light. I wonder what they're made of?"

"What are they?"

"We shall soon find out." Proto flipped over one of the domes.

"It looks like a large metal bowl, but it is exceptionally light and strong, apparently made from a synthetic composite material."

Sophia had a wide grin. "It's more than just a big bowl, it's our ticket past the Forest of Thorns. We don't have to walk, we can ride this down the aqueduct."

Orville gaped at Sophia. "Are you serious? Shooting down a roaring aqueduct in a big wobbly bowl seems like a very, very bad plan. Suppose there's a giant waterfall, or the aqueduct comes to and end and we go down a big gurgling drain?"

"I suppose you could walk along that narrow ledge next to the raging rapids if you'd rather do that."

Orville eyed the precarious ledge, imagining himself slipping and plunging into the rushing torrent of foaming water. "Maybe the boat isn't such a bad idea. How would we launch it? The water is moving really fast."

A long wooden pole blinked into Sophia's paws. "Proto, you position the boat on the edge of the aqueduct. Hold it steady while Orville and I climb in, then you hop in and use this pole to launch us into the water."

Proto soon had the small craft balanced on the outer wall of the aqueduct, holding it still as Sophia and Orville climbed in. He scrambled in after them, the long wooden pole in one hand.

"Hold on, I'm going to push us off! Keep a sharp lookout for mutant fish who might leap out of the water and drag us overboard."

"Wait, what?? Why do you think there are mutant fish?"

Proto gave a staccato laugh as he pushed them into the turbulent rapids with the wooden pole. Seconds later they were barreling down the aqueduct toward the dark opening in the cavern wall.

"Whoo hoo!!" Sophia raised both arms into the air. "This is amazing! We're flying!"

Orville was clutching the side of the craft, peering into the roaring foamy water. "Why did you say mutant fish might drag us out of the boat? Did you see something?"

Before Proto could reply they were shooting through the long dark tunnel. Orville was clutching the outer rim of their makeshift craft as they raced madly down the roaring aqueduct, rocking and swaying wildly.

It took several minutes for Orville to get used to the rolling motion of their oddly shaped vessel. The good news was they hadn't tipped over, and the craft wasn't taking on any water. Even better, no mutant fish had leapt out of the aqueduct and grabbed Orville.

"This isn't so bad. It's a lot better than walking along the ledge, that's for sure." Orville slid down into the boat, leaning back against the smooth curved surface. "I kind of the like the way the boat bobbles and sways. It's a little like riding in the back of a hay wagon. I bet I could stand up. It's not as rough as I thought it would be."

"Orville, standing up is a very bad idea."

"It's not that hard, I stood up in the boat when Papa took me out in the Vesarak Sea. It just takes a little practice, especially in a rolling sea. It's called getting your sea legs. Papa told me all about it."

Orville rose to his feet, holding out both arms to keep his balance. He grinned at Sophia. "It's not as hard as it looks, and I can see where we're going when I'm standing. We're about thirty feet above the ground and it looks like the aqueduct is passing over some kind of weird forest. It's too dark to see exactly what it is. I don't know why there would be trees down here though." Orville turned to the front of the boat, trying to get a better view of the forest. He had time for one terrified shriek before they hit the sharp curve and he was hurled from the boat, disappearing over the edge of the aqueduct into the dark forest below.

Chapter 19

So Cute

"Is it dead?"

"No, I'm sensing a strong life force."

"Why did it collapse when it looked at us?"

"Uncertain. Maybe the fall from the aqueduct damaged it. We may have frightened it. Sometimes little creatures like this collapse when they get scared."

"It was surrounded by a small energy field. That should have protected it from the fall."

"It's moving again."

Orville groaned, opening his eyes. He looked up at the two enormous insects towering above him. "Uh…uh… are you going to eat me? Is this a dream? Am I dead?"

"It talks! It's so cute, all covered with fur like that. We should keep it."

Orville was still dazed. "Have to think… giant insects… I can understand what they're saying, so this must be a dream. I must be sleeping."

One of the insects made a low buzzing sound, shaking all over. "That is so darling, it thinks it's

128

having a dream."

"Precious. Where do you think it came from?"

"It fell off the aqueduct. It must have wandered down here from the surface and gotten lost."

Orville frowned. Maybe this wasn't a dream. "Stop calling me it! I'm not an it, I'm Orville Wellington Mouse, and I can hear everything you're saying."

Both insects began buzzing and shaking. "It said it's not an it!"

"Are you laughing? Is that what you're doing when you buzz like that?"

"Are you lost, little fellow?"

Orville studied the tallest insect. Standing over twelve feet tall, it had a strong resemblance to a praying mantis, but was a mustardy yellow color. The shorter insect was the same dull yellow but was also covered with small irregular splotches of orange. "What are you? What is this place?"

"We should keep it. It's so cute. It wants to know where it is."

Orville was beginning to get angry. "Stop talking about me like I'm not here and saying how cute I am! I can hear everything you're saying, you know."

"It can sense our thoughts. Surprising for such a little furry fellow. We could build a cage for it, feed it and take care of it."

"That sounds like a lot of trouble. We'd have to feed it every day, give it water, clean its litter box."

Orville jumped to his feet. "I'm not using a litter box! Don't say litter box again. I'm not a pet. I'm Orville Wellington Mouse and I'm a member of the Metaphysical Adventurers. My friends will be worried about me, and just so you know, one of them is a powerful and terrifying Rabbiton."

"It's trying to scare us!" The two insects began buzzing and shaking.

Orville was now livid. "That's it, I'm gone." He shot up the most powerful sphere of defense he could muster and took off running. Much to his dismay after two steps he collided with an invisible wall.

"Don't hurt yourself, little fellow."

"Is it all right? It ran into the air wall. It couldn't see it, I guess. That's odd."

A brilliant orange light shot out of the insect's left eye, scanning Orville. "It's fine, just scared, that's all."

"I'm not scared, I happen to be a very powerful shaper, just so you know."

"A shaper, why didn't you say so? What kind of things do you like to shape, little one? Funny toys and tasty little snacks?"

Orville glared at the enormous creatures. They were definitely more amused than afraid. He flicked his wrist and a deadly looking black dagger appeared in his paw. He raised one eyebrow, trying to look as threatening as possible.

The two insects looked at each other, once again buzzing and shaking.

Orville growled, "I wouldn't be laughing if I were you. I'm not afraid to use this."

The taller insect looked at the dagger and it vanished from Orville's paw. "Seriously, it's not safe to play with sharp things like that, someone could get badly injured. We're not going to hurt you, I promise. We'll take really good care of you."

Orville's mind was racing. This was bad. Whoever these creatures were, they had shaping powers far more advanced than his. His eyes darted around, searching for an escape route. The trees he had seen from the aqueduct were not trees at all, but gigantic ferns. It was these soft pliable jungle ferns which had broken his fall, possibly saving his life.

Orville almost kicked himself. How could he have forgotten blinking? He would blink up to the aqueduct and leap into the raging water. An airtight sphere of defense would keep him afloat and eventually he would catch up with Sophia and Proto. He flicked his wrist but nothing happened. "Why can't I blink?"

"It's trying to turn into a thought cloud and escape. It really is scared, isn't it? We're not going to hurt you, little one, we'll take the best care of you and feed you whatever you like to eat."

"I've got news for you, bug eyes, no one is keeping me for a pet!" Orville raised both paws and a brilliant force beam blasted out at the insects, powerful enough to knock them both over. Unfortunately, halfway between Orville and the insects the force beam froze, the light transforming into a cloud of red dust which drifted slowly to the ground.

One of the insects picked Orville up, cradling him in its arms. "There, there, little friend, no need to be afraid. Time to take you home. You'll be nice and safe there, I promise."

There was a small flash of light and Orville found himself still in the arms of the praying mantis, but now in an enormous circular room, rectangular panels of swirling light covering the walls, tall curved gold metallic consoles peppered with small blinking lights circling the room. "Where are we? What is this place?"

The huge insect set Orville gently on the floor.

"Let's see what it does."

A low humming sound filled Orville's ears. This was very bad. He recognized the sound, having heard it on Varmoran when he was reliving the memories of an attack ship pilot. He dashed over to one of the consoles and hopped up onto it, peering out through a round viewing port. His knees grew weak. All he could see was the infinite blackness of space filled with glittering stars and galaxies. Orville sank to his knees with a moan. They were in an interstellar craft somewhere in dark space. Sophia and Proto would never find him here. His parents would never know what happened to him. Tears welled up in his eyes.

"Hide him, quick!"

One of the insects grabbed Orville, flipping open a storage compartment panel and stuffing him inside. The door snapped shut, leaving Orville in darkness. He tried to shape a light orb but couldn't. "They're blocking my thought clouds somehow. Who are these creatures? They're not from Tectar, not if they're flying around in an interstellar ship like this. What do they want? Why would they kidnap me?"

Twenty minutes later the panel door flipped open and one of the insects peered in. "Sorry, little one. Come with us, but be very quiet, not a sound, okay? If they hear you, it would be bad. Really bad."

Orville was now beyond terrified. Who were they afraid of? What kind of creature could scare these two huge insects? "I feel sick. I think I'm going to throw up."

"Shhh, no throwing up. Hop into this box and don't make a sound. We have to get you to a safe place before they find you."

"Before who finds me?"

"Quiet, no talking."

Orville climbed into the box and the lid slammed shut. He slumped down, burying his head in his paws. All he could think of was how worried Sophia and Proto must be. When his paw touched the top of his head he let out a groan. He'd lost his adventuring hat.

Chapter 20

Searching for Orville

"ORVILLE!!" Sophia screamed when she saw Orville fly over the side of the aqueduct, their boat careening wildly down the turbulent roaring river. She knew she could blink down to the forest floor, but that would leave Proto alone in the boat.

"Proto! We have to stop the boat! We have to go back and find Orville!"

Proto nodded. "I will slide off and hold the boat still while you climb out."

"The current is too strong, it will knock you over!"

"A highly unlikely outcome. I have calculated precisely the forces involved and my plan has a ninety-seven percent chance of success. Hold on tight!"

Proto slipped off the stern of the rocking craft, his massive silver hands gripping the outer rim of the boat. Much to Sophia's surprise, Proto's calculations were proven correct. The rushing water was up to his chest, but he was standing solidly in the pounding turbulence, water foaming and roaring around him. Using his incredible strength he maneuvered the boat out of the raging water and onto the flat outer wall of the aqueduct. Sophia hopped onto the stone ledge, joined a moment later by a dripping wet Proto.

"You did it! You're amazing!"

Proto grinned. "It is always a pleasure to rescue you."

Sophia's grin disappeared. "We have to find Orville. I can blink down, but how will you get down?"

Proto hopped off the aqueduct, landing on the soft ground below with a resounding thud. "I'm fine! It looks safe, not a dreadful creature in sight."

Sophia popped down next to Proto. "I've never seen ferns this big. Can you scan the area for Orville?"

A wide beam of yellow light from Proto's eyes traveled across the jungle. "I am finding no life forms other than plants, it should be safe to–"

"You're sure? There's no sign of Orville?"

Proto hesitated. "My scan does have limited range. Perhaps he wandered off in a different direction."

"He would have followed the aqueduct, he would have come this way. I know he would have."

"That is a logical assumption, of course, but perhaps the fall left him slightly disoriented. He did have his sphere of defense up, so he couldn't have been hurt badly. Nothing to worry about, we'll find him."

The pair of adventures set off through the steamy sweltering jungle, pushing their way through dripping foliage and past the gigantic ferns. Sophia stopped to listen. "There's not a sound, not a bird or buzzing insect. Jungles are usually teeming with life. This is very strange."

"It is peculiar. Did you happen to notice the sky?"

"Sky? How could there be sky?" Sophia looked up

to a starry night sky set off by a lovely crescent moon. "That's not possible. We're below the surface of the planet, how could we be seeing a night sky?"

Proto studied the twinkling stars above them. "The stars and the moon above us are stationary. We know from your shadow experiment that Tectar makes one complete rotation approximately every twenty-one hours. If we were seeing the night sky over Tectar, the stars would appear to be moving relative to our position on the planet. We are looking at an artificially created night sky."

"That's incredible. Who could have built something like that?"

Proto shook his head. "It is a most remarkable feat of engineering."

"Let's go, it will take us at least a half hour to reach the spot where Orville fell. Keep scanning for life force. We have no idea what might be roaming around down here."

Sophia's heart skipped a beat when she saw the purple feather sticking up from a cluster of small ferns. "No, no, no!" She raced over to it, terrified of what she might find. It was Orville's hat, but there was no sign of Orville. She mutely held it up for Proto to see.

Proto did his best to reassure her. "No need to fret, I'm sure he's quite all right. He lost his hat during the fall, quite a common occurrence. At least we know we're searching in the right area. He'll be quite pleased when we present him with his lost hat, quite pleased indeed."

Sophia barely heard Proto's words of encouragement. She grasped the trunk of a great fern, afraid she would collapse. Orville would never leave his adventuring hat behind. Never. Something bad had happened. She took a slow breath, gathering her thoughts and emotions. "Have you spotted anything? Any sign of him?"

"Nothing yet, I'm afraid, but there is a rather interesting electromagnetic field ahead of us. It seems an odd place to find such a strong energy field, in the middle of a dense jungle."

Sophia fought her way through a heavy thicket of ferns. "Maybe Orville found something there. Maybe that's where he is."

Ten minutes later they broke through a wall of vines and vegetation into a small clearing. In the center of the clearing stood a fifteen foot tall dark green dome.

Proto scanned the mysterious structure. "There is a powerful energy field surrounding it. I will scan it using electromagnetic and thermal vision."

Proto gave a laugh and strode over to the dome, tapping his finger on a barely visible disk. A circular opening appeared in the side of the dome, light flooding out into the shadowy jungle.

Proto hunched down and stepped through the entryway. "It appears to be a control center of some kind." He eyed the wide silver console covered with dials and tabs.

Sophia entered the dome, studying the array of controls. She tapped a small green button and a holo screen popped up, displaying an image of the night sky above the jungle. "This could be what regulates the artificial night sky. The symbols on the holo screen match the symbols on this dial." She twisted a large blue dial and the sea of stars transformed into a brilliant blue sky.

Proto looked out of the dome. "That's it, there's blue sky over the jungle, it's daytime now."

"I wonder what this one does?" Sophia twisted another dial and was rewarded with the sound of a torrential rainstorm spattering and pounding against the top of the dome. "That one's for rain. Someone put enormous effort into the creation of a fully functioning artificial environment."

Sophia turned another dial and the wind began to howl, the ferns outside flailing wildly. She turned the dial back and the wind stopped. "Why would someone create a subterranean environment with its own weather system?"

"Perhaps at one time the surface of the planet was not capable of supporting life, forcing the inhabitants to live underground."

"There are no lifeforms here now, except for the plants. Where did they go? We need to keep looking for Orville. I was hoping we'd find him here." Sophia shut off the rainstorm, but left the blue sky on.

"This is much better, we can see quite clearly now. I'm certain we'll find him shortly. This artificial environment really is quite remarkable. Millennia have passed since the creation of the jungle, and yet it is still vibrant and alive. Hold on, I'm picking up a secondary energy field a few hundred feet to the south. We should investigate."

Proto and Sophia pushed through the tangles of vegetation, soon discovering a huge metal cylinder protruding up from the jungle floor.

"What is that?"

"I am uncertain, but the cylinder is not the source of the energy field." Proto walked over to the base of a large fern and picked up a small rectangular object. "This object is emitting quite a powerful energy field."

"What is it?"

Proto examined it closely. "I believe it is a communication device, but unlike any I am familiar with." He pressed a small tab on the device. "Nothing."

"A thought cloud just came out of it!"

"Remarkable. Were you able to read its content?"

"Press the tab again." A pale yellow thought cloud emerged from the device and Sophia drew it to her. "It's empty, there's no information in it."

"Could it be a communication device utilizing thought clouds?"

"That could be it. That's incredible, a device which allows the owner to send and receive thought clouds. We'll take it back and show it to Mirus Mouse. He might be able to figure out how it works."

"The presence of the this enormous pipe is quite puzzling also."

"There's a ladder on that side."

Proto stepped over to the ladder and scaled the massive pipe. "The opening to the cylinder is covered with a stout wire mesh." He peered down into the pipe. "It goes straight down, too far to see the bottom."

Sophia scooped up a rock and tossed it to Proto. "Drop this down the tube, see how long it takes to hit bottom."

Proto tossed the rock into the cylinder and listened carefully. "Nothing. It could go down for miles."

"Maybe it's for ventilation. Bringing fresh air from the surface down into the planet?"

"It's possible. There is a small control panel next to the ladder. Shall I press one of the tabs?"

139

"Try it, but be careful, don't get sucked into the tube."

"Nothing to worry about, the wire mesh looks quite sturdy." Proto tapped the small violet disk. Much to his surprise he was instantly hurled backwards across the jungle floor from the titanic blast of air exploding out from the mammoth cylinder.

Sophia screamed, wrapping her arms around the base of a great fern, fighting against the monstrous cyclonic forces threatening to pull her up into the sky. "Shut it off! Proto, shut it off!" The surrounding foliage was being ripped out of the ground by the howling squall that screamed up from the pipe.

Proto crawled across the jungle floor to the metal ladder, climbing rung by rung until he reached the control panel. Clinging to the ladder with both hands, he used his nose to tap the yellow disk. The stupendously violent rush of air from the pipe stopped.

Sophia gasped, sliding down the side of the fern. "What was that? What just happened?"

"It would appear the cylinder's function is precisely the opposite of what we had hypothesized. It does not draw air in, it expels vast amounts of air out from deep within the planet. I have no explanation for this. Haukesworth Mouse was quite right about Tectar, it is a deeply mysterious world."

"Let's go, we have to find Orville."

Chapter 21

Light Worms

Orville's lip was curled in complete and utter disgust as he watched the two enormous yellow insects pluck wiggling blue worms from a large bowl, tossing them into their mouths, munching and chewing and chomping.

"Oh, barf, how can they eat squirmy worms?"

Orville grimaced as he watched them stuffing the wiggly blue creatures into their mouths.

Over the course of his stay in the ship he had come to call his two captors Yellow and Orange. Yellow stepped over to Orville and set down a bowl of the wiggling blue worms in front of him. "You really need to eat something. These are good for you, and they're really tasty. They're called Light Worms. Yummy. So good."

Orville eyed the churning, wriggling mound of blue worms. "I think I'm going to throw up. How can you eat live worms? Gakk."

"They're Light Worms, not real worms. That's disgusting, nobody eats real worms. These are snacks that wiggle when light shines on them. Watch." The lights in the room dimmed to near darkness.

"They stopped wiggling."

"They're not alive. Why would you eat something that's alive? Are you trying to make me barf?"

Orville snorted. He had to admit, Yellow was kind of funny. He picked up one of the blue wormy snacks and sniffed it. "It smells okay. You're sure it's not a real worm?"

"Try a bite, you'll like it."

Orville popped the wormy snack into his mouth, ready to spit it out or throw up. "Whoa, these are tasty. Really tasty, like candy. Yum." He grabbed a pawful of the blue worms and began eating. "Mmmm... good."

"I told you, little one. I knew you'd like them. They're really good for you, they have a very high nutritional value."

"Why do they wiggle when light hits them?"

"I don't know, they're just funny snacks my mum buys. It's fun to eat them when they wiggle."

Orville froze. "Did you say your mum buys them?"

Orange began buzzing and shaking. "Now you did it."

"He's still our pet, we just have to hide him from Mum."

"This isn't your ship? You don't fly it?"

"Of course not, I'm not old enough to fly something like this. It's way more complicated than flying a Light Runner."

"Your mum is the pilot?"

"I just said that. We're on vacation, Tectar is one of our favorite spots to visit. Mum lets us go down and explore the planet. The underground jungle is really fun, and it's safe because there's no dangerous creatures there."

Orville's mind was racing. Yellow and Orange were clearly highly evolved beings with astonishing powers, but they were young, maybe even younger than he was. "Do you bring many pets back to your ship?"

"We're not supposed to. We get in trouble if we get caught." Yellow looked at Orange, who started buzzing and shaking.

Orange made a curious clicking sound. "What will you give me not to tell Mum about the little one?"

"You helped bring him back. You'll get in trouble, too."

"Not if I tell her first and say it was your idea."

"You can fly my Light Runner for three hours."

"Okay. Want to go explore that ocean with the creepy fish?"

"Sure." Yellow looked down at Orville. "We'll be gone a day or so. I'll leave you plenty of food and water. Lots of Light Worms."

Orville's mind was racing. He had to get back to Tectar, had to find Sophia and Proto. Yellow and Orange seemed like good hearted creatures. Maybe he could persuade them to take him back. He looked as sad as he could, pretending to wipe a tear from his eye. "My mum doesn't know where I am. She'll be so worried."

"What do you mean, your mum?"

"I was exploring Tectar just like you. I told my mum I'd be back in two days."

"Your mum is waiting for you?" Yellow looked nervously at Orange.

"We should probably take him back to the jungle.

143

How would you feel if Mum was missing us?"

"I was with my friends when I fell out of our boat going down the aqueduct."

"Whoa, you went down the aqueduct in a boat? That sounds really fun. We should do that. Where did your friends go?"

"They were still in the boat when I fell out. I don't know where they are now. My mum will be really upset, maybe even crying." Orville gave a sad little sniff.

Yellow made the curious clicking sound.

"We have to tell Mum. She can do a time whip. I don't know how to do one yet."

"She'll clobber us for bringing him back to the ship."

Orville said, "I'll tell her I sneaked here in your pack without you knowing it."

"Clever. That will work. Here, hop into my pack and we'll go up to the bridge. I'll set the pack down on the floor and when you jump out we'll act really surprised. Mum will send you back."

Orville climbed into Yellow's enormous pack. "All set, I'll crawl out and act confused. Then I'll tell her I climbed into the pack because it looked like a good place to sleep. I'll look really scared so she'll feel sorry for me."

"Perfect, let's go."

Yellow grabbed his pack and a split second later they appeared on the bridge of the ship.

"We were thinking of exploring that ocean with all the really weird fish. Is it okay if we go?" Yellow casually placed his pack on the floor, giving it a kick with one leg.

Orville wriggled out of the pack, trying to look as though he had just woken up. The next part of his plan was to look scared and lost, but when he saw the bright blue twenty foot tall praying mantis looking down at him with glowing orange eyes he gave a small moan and sank to the floor.

"What did I tell you about pets?"

"It must have climbed into my pack to take a nap. I didn't know it was there."

Yellow's mum buzzed, her upper torso shaking. "Really, he climbed into your pack without you noticing?"

Orange was looking down at the ground, shuffling his legs back and forth.

"No. More. Pets. You can't take a living creature out of its natural environment, away from its own kind. Every living creature, no matter the level of awareness, should be treated with kindness and respect. Look at this poor little fellow, he fainted away at the very sight of me. I don't want to see another pet in this ship ever again, do you both understand me?"

"Yes, we're sorry. I was really nice to him, he liked the Light Worms, he said they were really tasty."

"I thought you said you didn't know he was in your pack?"

Orange began buzzing and shaking. "Busted."

Yellow's mum picked Orville up, holding him gently in her arms. "He is kind of cute, all furry and soft. Look at his cute little clothes. He's so sweet."

"He said he was going down the aqueduct in a boat and fell out. His friends are looking for him."

Yellow's mum scanned Orville's thoughts and memories. His eyes popped open, a shriek bursting from his lips.

"Shhhh… no need to fear, little one. I will send you back before you fell out of your boat. You won't remember anything about your visit to our ship, but you will remember not to stand up in the boat. Never stand up in small boats, very dangerous. You'll be fine, I promise."

Chapter 22

Sailing, Sailing

"This isn't so bad. It's a lot better than walking along that ledge." Orville slid down into the boat, leaning back against the smooth curved surface. "I kind of the like the way the boat bobbles and sways. It's a little like riding in the back of a hay wagon. I bet I could stand up. It's not as rough as I thought it would be."

"That sounds like a very bad idea."

A long forgotten memory came flooding back to Orville. Someone had told him never to stand up in a small boat, it was very dangerous. Was it his mum? "You're right, it's a bad idea. We should strap ourselves in." Orville shaped canvas harnesses for everyone. "Buckle in, it could get rough."

Orville gave a screech when the boat shot around a sharp turn in the aqueduct. "Whoa! Good thing I wasn't standing up!"

Sophia sat up, her ears turning. "Do you hear that crashing sound?"

"What is it?"

"I think we might be heading for a waterfall."

Orville gave a yelp, tightening his harness. A brilliant light shot out from his paw, illuminating the tunnel ahead of them. The crashing had become a dull thundering roar.

Sophia cried out, "Hold on tight!"

Before Orville had time to react, they shot off the end of the aqueduct, sailing through the air above an enormous lake. Orville covered his eyes, the deafening roar of tons of water crashing down from the aqueduct reverberating in his ears.

With a bone jarring smack their little craft hit the surface of the lake, the sudden jolt almost knocking Orville unconscious. "Unnghh…" The metal bowl rocked wildly at first, finally settling down to a gentle swaying motion as it drifted away from the falls.

Sophia groaned. "Oww! Is everyone all right? Orville?"

"I'm okay, I'm pretty sure all my bones are broken though. Hey, it's not dark down here. Where's the light coming from?"

Proto looked up. "Great heavens, it's coming from tree roots! We must be directly beneath the Forest of Thorns."

Orville and Sophia looked up at a broad sky of brightly glowing roots stretching out as far as they could see. "There's millions of roots dangling down into the lake. This is where the Forest of Thorns gets water, not from the aqueduct."

"Why are their roots glowing?"

Proto shook his head. "I have read about undersea creatures who use bioluminescence as a means of communication, but I've never heard of bioluminescent roots. I suppose the trees could store sunlight in their roots, using it to create food on dark and cloudy days."

"Wait, if the sunlight travels down through the tree during the day, when it's nighttime up above it will get dark down here."

"Perhaps the Forest of Thorns was engineered for that very purpose, a means of bringing sunlight to a dark subsurface world."

Sophia frowned. "I wish we knew who built this underground world, and why they built it."

"How are we going to cross the lake? It's still a long way to the Obex Mountains."

"We could shape some paddles."

"It's way too far to paddle. Besides, it's nearly impossible to paddle a round boat."

"If there was wind we could shape a sail."

"That gives me an idea, remember how we linked minds to create the whirlwind on Varmoran? We could do the same thing here, but this time shape a small windstorm that trails along behind the boat."

"Brilliant! I'll shape a mast, you shape the sail."

"We'll need a rudder, too."

An hour later Orville and Sophia had converted the metal bowl into a reasonably functional single masted sailboat. Orville hoisted up a bright yellow square sail and tied it off. "That should do it. We don't need to turn the sail since we'll be traveling in a straight line across the lake, and the wind direction won't change."

"I attached the rudder. All we need now is wind."

"Hey, Proto, maybe you could swim behind us and blow on the sail." Orville let out a cackling laugh.

Sophia snorted. "Okay, Master Funny Bones, we need to link our minds and create a windstorm. We don't need a big cyclone like the one on Varmoran, just a nice steady wind blowing directly east that will carry us across the lake to the Obex Mountains. Once we reach the other side we'll make our way to the surface, probably through one of those stone huts."

"What about all the roots hanging down into the lake? How do we get past them?"

"I have a feeling that won't be a problem. Ready?"

"Ready." Orville took Sophia's paw and closed his eyes, letting go of this thoughts, concentrating deeply, merging with his inner self, leaving his physical form behind. It felt as if the universe had become his body, as though he was connected to all things. He became aware of Sophia's inner self merging with his, their deepest thoughts and memories intermingling. It was a strange feeling to know everything about Sophia and to have her know everything about him. There were no secrets between two mice who linked minds, each mouse aware of every event which had occurred in the other's life, and how it had affected them.

A thought from Sophia blossomed in Orville's mind.

"Okay, here we go, we need a nice brisk wind heading directly east."

Proto looked on with fascination as the two shapers sat silently in the boat. The process of merging minds lay outside Proto's scientific understanding, but he found it intriguing, a scientific puzzle worthy of a solution. Small ripples appeared in the water behind them, breaking up the reflection of the golden glowing roots, turning the water a warm amber color. The sail flapped wildly for a moment, then billowed out, pushing the ship forward.

"They did it. Astonishing, using the combined power

of two minds to create a windstorm."

Sophia let go of Orville's paw and opened her eyes. She looked up at the taut yellow sail and grinned. "Good job, Orville!"

It took Orville a moment to regain his focus on the world. "It's a weird feeling to link minds like that. I could see all your memories from when you were growing up. I can't believe those mice made fun of you and called you names because you were so smart. That was really mean of them."

"They were afraid of anyone who was different. You went through the same thing, that's why you never told anyone about the objects you shaped in your sleep, or how you spontaneously blinked into your front yard when you were just a mouseling. You didn't want other mice to think you were different, you were afraid they wouldn't like you."

"It was easier for me to hide my shaping skills than for you to hide how smart you were."

"I knew why they were making fun of me, but it still bothered me a bit. They were just afraid, that's all. Most mice are afraid of things they don't understand."

Orville gave a yelp and grabbed the rudder. "Duck! We're going to hit the roots!"

Sophia did not move, keeping her eyes on the rapidly approaching roots. She knew when the boat moved forward it pushed against the water, creating a wall of pressure which was transmitted through the water toward the tree roots ahead of them. Much to Orville's surprise the roots moved out of the way, avoiding any contact with the boat.

"Just as I suspected. The trees interpreted the increased water pressure coming from the boat as an approaching predator, and moved to avoid it. We can sail directly east with no interference from the roots."

"That makes it a lot easier, all I have to do is hold the rudder steady." Orville leaned back against the side of the boat, holding the tiller with one paw. With a small flash of light a large oatmeal cookie appeared in his other paw. "Mmm…. nothing tastier than a warm oatmeal cookie while you're sailing across a mysterious subterranean lake on a weird planet inhabited by walking trees."

Sophia smiled. Her adventures with Orville were some of the happiest moments of her life.

Three hours later Proto was guiding the ship while Orville napped, curled up in a warm blanket. Sophia's eyes were drooping, her head nodding. Proto glanced up at the roots. The light from the roots had been decreasing for the last hour. He gave Orville's foot a nudge. "Orville, I believe your theory regarding sunlight traveling directly down through the trees to the roots has been proven correct. The sun is going down on Tectar and the roots are dimming. In a few minutes we shall be in total darkness."

Orville sat up, rubbing his eyes. "Total darkness? How can we see where we're going? The lake is too big to light with orbs."

A sphere of light shot out from Sophia's paw. "I'm sending this orb directly east, traveling at the same speed as the wind. Just follow the light and we'll be fine."

"Good idea."

As the roots faded to darkness, Proto held the rudder steady, following Sophia's guiding light as the wind pushed them ever closer to Castle Caligari and

Mendacium the Dark Wizard.

It was Orville who spotted the curious glow coming from the murky depths of the lake.

Chapter 23

Sophia's Lost Ring

Orville flicked his wrist and the wind storm which had been propelling them across the lake stopped, the surface of the water becoming a vast and silent mirror.

"What are you doing? Why did you stop the wind?"

"Look down below. There's a glowing light running along the bottom of the lake."

Sophia and Proto peered over the edge of the boat. "What do you think it is?"

"I don't know, but it's not natural, it's perfectly straight and has–"

Orville heard a small splash followed by a shriek. "My ring! I dropped my ring into the lake!"

Orville had never seen Sophia cry before. His stomach twisted. "You dropped your ring? What ring?"

"I dropped Papa's ring! His Metaphysical Adventurers ring slipped off my paw. I lost his ring."

"Maybe we can find it."

Proto's eyes were wide. He was uncertain how to respond to Sophia's tears. "Orville is quite right, there must be a way to find it. No need to cry. Perhaps you could shape one just like it?"

Sophia wiped the tears from her eyes. "I can't shape

another one, it wouldn't be the same. It's my fault, I shouldn't have put my paw over the edge of the boat."

"We'll find it. If we can find Tectar, we can find a ring at the bottom of a lake. One of us will dive down and look for it." Orville gave Proto a significant look, raising his eyebrows.

"Of course I would be the logical choice since I don't need air and I can utilize my thermal sensors to locate the ring. My only concern is how I shall return to the boat once I recover the ring."

"I'll shape a rope, fifty feet should do it. Once you find the ring we'll pull you back up."

With a flash of light a sturdy rope appeared in Orville's paws. "Tie this around your waist and give a couple of quick tugs when you're ready to come up."

Sophia put her paw on Proto's arm. "You don't have to do this. I don't want something to happen to you because of a lost ring."

"I am more than happy to help. Don't forget, I am quite indestructible."

Orville held the rope taut as Proto slid into the water. "Two tugs means I've found the ring. You shouldn't have any problem raising me up due to the upwardly directed buoyant force produced by the water, decreasing my subjective weight."

Orville nodded politely. "Sure, sounds good." He glanced over at Sophia to see if she understood what Proto had said.

"It means he'll weigh less when he's underwater. It's just physics."

Proto released his grip, slipping beneath the surface with a small splash.

"He turned on his ear lights, I can see him." The

155

rope ran through Orville's paws as Proto continued his descent.

"He's hit bottom, the rope stopped. I can just barely make out his lights, but he's walking around down there. He's next to that long glowing thing. I don't know what he's doing, though. How will he find the ring if it's buried in mud?"

"He said something about thermal optics, so maybe he's scanning for infrared radiation."

"Um, that's probably it. Whoa! He's tugging on the rope! Let's pull him up."

The pair of adventurers pressed their feet against the side of the boat and began hauling the rope in. "Creekers! How much does he weigh? I thought he said this would be easy."

Orville's muscles were burning by the time Proto's silver hands grabbed the side of the boat and his head popped out of the water. He triumphantly held up Sophia's ring. Sophia took the ring and gave Proto a hug. "Thank you, thank you so much!"

"It was far easier to find than I had expected. The lake is an artificial body of water, the bottom flat and smooth, constructed from Morsennium. Your lost ring has proven to be quite a fortuitous event. If you hadn't dropped it, I would not have made a most remarkable discovery." Proto raised one eyebrow.

Orville's eyes narrowed. "What kind of remarkable discovery? It's not a cave, is it? Or creepy creatures living down there?"

"No need to fret, it's not a cave or a trapdoor, and the good news is you don't need to know how to swim, just how to hold your breath."

"Wait, are you saying we have to dive down to the

bottom of the lake?"

"Precisely. It will be as easy as falling off a log, or in this case, falling off a boat. I'll hold both of you and we'll sink like a stone to the bottom of the lake. Nothing could be simpler."

"Sink like a stone? I don't really like the sound of that."

Sophia slipped her papa's silver ring onto her paw. "What's down there?"

"The long glowing light Orville spotted is nothing less than an enormous transparent tube running along the bottom of the lake heading east. Even better, I watched a cylindrical car pass through this marvelous subaquatic tunnel, and I located an airlock we can use to gain entrance. Once we're inside, we simply take a transport car to the end of the tunnel, which may even take us past the Obex Range."

"How do you know the tunnel goes where we need to go? It might just go in a big circle."

"Oh my, did I forget to mention what else I found? There was a rather peculiar symbol scratched into the airlock door. Let me think now, what was that? Oh, I believe it was the image of a coiled serpent." Proto let out a great laugh.

"Whoa! Haukesworth was down there? How long do I have to hold my breath?"

Sophia said, "You don't have to hold your breath. Shape an airtight sphere of defense around you and fill it with fresh air. If you need more air, you can shape more."

"And your sphere of defense will also protect you from the pesky little creatures with the big snappy teeth."

Orville's whipped around to face Proto. "There are pesky little creatures swimming around down there with big snappy teeth?"

Sophia snickered. "Come on, let's go for a swim. Don't let a few little fishies scare you."

Sophia blinked up a powerful sphere of defense and leapt into the water. "See? I'm not even getting wet."

"You said the creatures with the snappy teeth are little, not big and scary?"

"Quite small, indeed. No need for concern."

Orville flicked his wrist and a glimmering sphere of defense popped up around him. He took a deep breath and jumped off the boat, bobbing around inside his airtight sphere.

"All right, one of you on each side of me, please." When Orville and Sophia were in position, Proto released his grip on the boat, quickly wrapping his arms around them. Orville did his best not to shriek as they sank beneath the rippling waves. He did, however, let out a screech of horror when a huge scaly creature with rows of long spiky legs smashed into Proto.

"AGGHH!! What was that thing?? You said they were little!"

"Oh my, did you get a good look? Quite terrifying indeed, those fangs looked dreadfully sharp, more than likely filled with deadly toxins. It could be some sort of giant underwater carnivorous centipede. Quite frightening."

Moments later they were on the bottom of the lake. Proto flicked on his ear lights, illuminating the Morsennium lake floor. Orville studied the glowing transport tube as Proto pushed his way through the water.

158

The huge school of small blue fish with oversized teeth came out of nowhere, smacking into Orville's sphere of defense. He instinctively jumped back, the fish gnawing wildly at the invisible field of energy surrounding him.

"Stop wriggling around, please. If I lose my grip you'll float back up to the surface of the lake."

Orville tried to slow his breathing, tried to fight the feeling that he was running out of air, that the fish were going to eat him. "Lots of air, plenty of fresh air to breathe, I can shape more if I need to. Fish are gone now. No more blue fish with snappy teeth. No more giant creatures with spiky legs."

Orville had calmed himself by the time they reached the airlock. Proto tapped a control panel and a transparent door slid open, water rushing into the small room. Holding Orville and Sophia tightly in his arms, he entered the room and tapped a yellow disk. The door slid shut and pressurized air was pumped into the room, expelling the lake water.

Proto set the two adventurers down. "Safe and sound, just as I promised."

Orville blinked off his sphere of defense. "What was that giant thing that crashed into you? You said there were pesky little creatures, not giant scaly things with a million creepy legs."

"A marvelous stroke of luck, wasn't it? It's not often you get to see a terrifying beast in such close proximity. Its resemblance to the giant carnivorous centipedes on Periculum was quite uncanny."

Proto tapped the violet tab next to the inner door, stepping back as it whirred open. The three adventurers stepped into the transport tube. Proto pointed to the gleaming silver tracks running through the tunnel. "The car floats several feet above those tracks. I would assume the system is based in hyper-conduction magnetics or antigrav displacement units in the cars."

Sophia nodded in agreement. "That would make sense."

Orville had no idea what either of those things were. "How do we get the car to stop?"

"An excellent question. I believe the answer shall be found on that panel next to the airlock with the grid of colored tabs." Proto stepped over to the flat console and tapped a large yellow circle. "Violet is go, yellow is stop."

"What about the other tabs?" Orville reached over and pressed a bright red tab. Sophia let out a screech when the enormous yellow striped gelatinous blob appeared in front of her, the top half of it covered with wiggling green eyes on pale blue stalks. A sphere of defense popped up around her as she jumped backwards, bumping into the wall of the tube.

Orville was pressed back against the tube, his eyes wide.

Proto chuckled. "It's quite harmless, nothing more than a holo image. Perhaps this was once a great aquarium where visitors would come to view all manner of fascinating undersea creatures." He pressed another of the colored tabs and a school of small blue fish with enormous teeth appeared in front of Orville.

Orville reached out cautiously with one paw, swiping it through one of the fish. "You're right, they're not real. I didn't think they were, I was just surprised to see that big blobby thing with all the wiggly eyes."

Sophia was about to make an extremely humorous comment when she felt a powerful gust of wind, immediately followed by a blaring alarm.

"Here comes the car!" Proto pointed down the tracks to an orange light speeding toward them. The three adventurers stepped back against the airlock door, waiting until the cylindrical silver car came to a full stop, hovering silently in front of them. A wide curved door slid open.

"What do we do?"

"We get in." Sophia jumped into the car, followed by Proto and Orville.

Orville flopped down on one of the bright yellow padded chairs. "These seats are comfy. Maybe this won't be as scary as I thought it would be." He flicked his wrist and a plate of Proto's tasty little cakes appeared in his paw.

Sophia reached over and snatched four of the little cakes from Orville's plate. "Thanks for sharing, best friend."

Orville was about to offer his thoughts on Sophia's concept of sharing when the car shot forward, pressing him back against the seat, his plate of tasty cakes tumbling to the floor.

Chapter 24

Tickets, Please

"We passed another airlock, that makes six, and I saw another one of those big centipede things swim past. So creepy. How fast do you think we're going?" Orville's face was pressed up against one of the car's round viewing ports, watching as they flashed through the tunnel beneath the enormous lake.

"According to my Interworld Positioning System we are traveling precisely at seventy-nine miles per hour. It shouldn't take us long to reach the other side of the lake. I am assuming the train will come to a stop of its own accord and not—"

Proto was interrupted by an earsplitting explosion of sound blasting out from the front of the car. Orville later described the sound as a thousand angry parrots having an argument in a raging thunderstorm.

Orville's paws were pressed against his ears. "What's that noise?? What's happening?"

Proto hollered into Orville's ear. "I believe the car is announcing our next stop, but in a language I am unfamiliar with."

Proto was quite correct. Less than a minute later the car slowed to a halt, hovering in the center of a vast, brightly illuminated dome shaped pavilion. The passenger door slid open with a hiss, and the angry parrots in a thunderstorm voice screeched out again, followed by a shrill honking sound.

"Everybody off!" Sophia hopped down from the car, studying the enormous dome above them. "It's beautiful! Look at all those lovely murals of the green rabbits with short ears. They look like Aelric and Gemma. Proto, do you have any idea who those rabbits are?"

Proto eyed the exquisitely painted scenes covering the dome's ceiling, studying in particular the strange hieroglyphs running around the base of the dome. "If I am correct in my assessment, we have discovered something quite remarkable."

"What do you mean? What is this place?"

"I will need to do more research before I am one hundred percent certain, but I believe the images shown above are authentic portrayals of ancient Thaumatarians, more than likely the original inhabitants of this planet."

Sophia let out a gasp. "Thaumatarians? How could that be? They've been gone for eons. Their home planet was only recently discovered by the Quintarian Science Guild, and orbital scans found no life at all on their planet, no plants, animals, or even microbes. It had been abandoned for millennia."

"Wait, who were the Thaumatarians? The name sounds kind of familiar, but I can't quite…"

"Orville, you know this. Thaumatarians were the first inhabitants of our universe, their technology surpassing anything we have today. The Thaumatarians created the World Doors, interdimensional gateways to twelve different worlds."

"Weren't we trying to get back from Periculum through the World Doors?"

"Yes, Periculum is one of the worlds accessible through the World Doors. Earth is another."

Orville scanned the great domed hall. The rotunda had a diameter of over a hundred feet, the apex of the dome towering one hundred and fifty feet above them. The floor was inlaid with intricate designs created with an incalculable number of colorful ceramic tiles. Soft padded chairs sat in long serpentine rows, sweeping around the periphery of the room.

Orville whipped around at the sound of a blaring alarm, watching the silver car slip silently back through the tunnel beneath the lake.

"What do we do now? How do we get up to the surface?"

Sophia spotted an arched opening on the far side of the hall. "That looks promising, let's see where it goes."

"That circular symbol over the door must mean something."

"Maybe it's an exit sign." The three adventurers strode across the atrium and through the arched doorway, heading down an expansive corridor.

"Check out the pictures on the walls. It looks like the Thaumatarians were building something, but I can't tell what it is. A lot of the images show interstellar ships in dark space. Maybe this was a transport station. There might be more spectral doorways like the one on the Isle of the Serpent."

"Here's another set of doors with that same circular symbol you saw in the hall."

The doors whirred open at Sophia's approach. She

peered into a magnificently appointed room, the floors bedecked with luxurious maroon carpeting, lavishly illustrated panels lining the walls. "These paintings are beautiful. They all show the construction of some enormous structure."

As Orville was studying one of the panels, trying to identify the object under construction, three things happened. Sophia gave a loud screech, Orville gave a yelp, and Proto skittered backwards, colliding with the wall. A four foot tall dark green metallic rabbit had stepped out from behind a set of decorative freestanding panels, a cacophonous angry parrot thunderstorm voice blaring out from its mouth.

Spheres of defense popped up around Orville and Sophia.

"Why is it so loud??"

"I don't think he means us any harm."

"Proto, is that a Thaumatarian? His ears are short, and he's green."

"I do not believe so, but he does appear to be a robotic representation of a Thaumatarian, much as I was created in the image of the Elders."

"Can you talk to it?"

Proto stepped closer to the dark green robotic creature.

"Greetings, I am Proto the Rabbiton from the planet Earth. We mean you no harm."

The creature's voice thundered out again. Orville covered his ears. "I'm not deaf, but I will be if he keeps yelling like that!"

The green robotic rabbit studied Orville closely, then turned and disappeared behind the set of panels, reappearing moments later carrying three small golden discs. It motioned for the adventurers to approach him. The mechanical rabbit reached up and pressed a gold disk onto Sophia's forehead, then did the same for Orville and Proto.

Orville ran his paw over the disc. "It's stuck on my fur. What is this thing?"

The creature spoke again. "At no extra cost to our valued patrons, the Museum provides universal neuronic translator disks on an as needed basis. You should currently be hearing my voice in whatever language, and at whatever volume you are accustomed to. I am Copo, your host for today's showing, and I warmly welcome you to the History of Tectar Temporal Displacement Museum. May I have your tickets, please?" The green rabbit smiled pleasantly and held out his paw.

Orville stared blankly at the green rabbit. "What tickets?"

"Your tickets, please. The next show begins in five minutes. You purchased your tickets on Stellar Holowave?"

"Wait, what is this place? Why do we need tickets? There's a show?"

Copo's eyes blinked rapidly. "In order to view the History of Tectar Temporal Displacement Experience you must have tickets. Our patrons generally purchase them prior to their arrival, on Stellar Holowave, as I previously had mentioned."

Sophia smiled apologetically at Copo. "I'm so sorry, we're not from around here, and sadly we are quite unfamiliar with your lovely museum. The show is about the history of Tectar?"

"Yes, it is a Temporal Displacement Experience

revisiting the construction of Tectar."

"The construction of Tectar?"

"Is your translator disk not working properly? Should I speak louder? More slowly?"

"I'm so sorry, are you referring to the structures found beneath the surface of Tectar?"

"Where did you say you were from?"

"We are visitors from another planet, a planet called Earth."

"Ah, I see. You have been misinformed, I'm afraid. Tectar is not a planet, it is an interstellar ship created by the Thaumatarians nearly twenty thousand years ago. The Temporal Displacement Experience allows you to view first hand the creation of Tectar, the pinnacle of Thaumatarian interstellar engineering. The presentation is extremely informative and I highly recommend it, especially since you are unfamiliar with Tectar. As an added bonus, at the end of each show there is a drawing for a marvelous door prize."

"Tectar is an interstellar ship? That's not possible."

Copo gave a most gracious smile. "Today's showing may very well sway your position on that particular topic."

"How do we buy tickets for the show?"

"It could not be any simpler. Press your Transtar Credit Ring to the violet panel and the tickets will pop out of that little slot next to the window."

"Transtar what ring?"

Copo glanced at Orville's paw. "I see, you have no Transtar Credit Ring. This is not unheard of, no need to worry. Taking into consideration the great distance you have traveled to visit our fine museum, I have unilaterally made the decision to present each of you with a complimentary ticket for today's showing, courtesy of the History of Tectar Temporal Displacement Museum management."

Copo waved his paw and three tickets popped out of the small slot on the wall.

Sophia looked at Orville and Proto. "We should watch the show. The universe has brought us here for a reason, although what that reason might be certainly eludes me at the moment."

Orville plucked the three tickets from the slot. "I like shows. I hope there's lots of music. Can we shape snacks or do we have to buy them?"

"Your tickets, please?"

Orville presented the three tickets to Copo, who deftly tore off the stubs with one hand, dropping them into a large glass vase behind him. "The prize drawing takes place at the end of each show. Best of luck to you all."

"Are there many other patrons here for today's show?"

"You are currently the only attendees for this particular showing."

Sophia looked curiously at Copo. "When was the last time you had visitors here?"

"Seven hundred and thirteen years ago we had a visitor from a small planet called Nirriim. I believe his interstellar craft had gone rather disastrously off course."

"So it's been a while. How long have you been here?"

"We must hurry along now, the show starts in one minute, and you don't want to miss the opening sequence. Quite dramatic, I assure you. This way, please."

Copo strode across the thick carpet to a set of gleaming brass doors. He swung them open, revealing a small darkened room holding three ornate stuffed chairs.

"There are only three chairs?"

"One for each of you, of course. Have a seat please. Only thirty seconds left."

Orville flopped down in one of the chairs. "Comfy. Can I shape snacks?" Sophia and Proto took their seats.

Sophia looked at Copo. "What do we do now?"

"Relax, sit back, and enjoy the History of Tectar Temporal Displacement Experience. Don't forget the prize drawing at the conclusion of today's showing."

Orville raised his paw. "How long does the show last?"

Copo laughed with delight. "Ha ha ha, I see you have quite an elevated sense of humor. Do enjoy the show!" Copo stepped out of the small room, closing the brass doors softly behind him.

Orville let out a terrified shriek when he found himself floating in dark space surrounded by a trillion stars, galaxies, and planets.

"AGGHHHH!! I'm going to die in space!"

"It's part of the show, you ninny. Didn't you hear Copo say it was a temporal displacement experience?"

Orville turned to see Sophia and Proto floating in space next to him. "What are we doing here? Where's my chair?"

"Temporal displacement means you're experiencing something in another time. I guess we're going to watch the Thaumatarians build Tectar. It sounds really interesting."

"I'm not going to die? I'm in space, there's no air and it's a zillion degrees below zero. I won't freeze? What about snacks?"

"You're not really in dark space. Well, you are in dark space, but you're not really here. It's hard to explain, just watch the show."

"Fine. It seems like Copo could have warned us about this before the show started."

"Quiet. Look down there!"

Orville watched as a magnificent silver ship at least a mile long flickered into view. A soft mellifluous voice filled his thoughts.

"Tectar, a pinnacle of Thaumatarian engineering, the first interstellar planet ever created, and a technological marvel to this day unsurpassed by any other civilization. But why? Why build an entire planet capable of interstellar travel? The answer is simple. Thaumatarian scientists realized long ago that finding a planet of the correct size, in the precise orbit around the class of star needed to create a hospitable climate for colonists was more than a daunting task. That task became virtually impossible if they needed the planet to be in a particular sector of dark space at a particular time. Their solution to this vexing problem was the creation of Tectar, the first mobile planet. Designed and built by the finest Thaumatarian engineers, Tectar was fully capable of interstellar travel, powered by a bank of six Mark XVII Micronizing Distortion Thrusters, the most powerful space warping engines ever created. The construction of Tectar began in Dark Space Quadrant MBF062957, at a location nearly two light years from Thaumatar."

Orville gaped as a huge armada of massive

interstellar ships appeared in dark space, blinking out of nothingness. The melodious voice continued, describing the impossibly complex task of building a planet capable of interstellar flight. Massive engines deep inside the planet would warp the space around it, creating an artificial gravitational field identical to that of Thaumatar. The planet contained living space for three million inhabitants, including a wide variety of natural environments filled with a vast array of carefully selected Thaumatarian flora and fauna.

The three adventurers watched as stupendously massive Morsennium beams were offloaded from an endless stream of gleaming interstellar ships, then joined together like so many puzzle pieces to form the planet's spherical framework. Time sped up as they watched, the construction moving faster and faster, ships blinking in and out of view, the planet growing in layer after layer of depth and complexity.

Orville lost track of time, mesmerized by the process of Tectar's creation. A voice seemed to come out of nowhere. It was Sophia.

"How long have we been watching? It seems like a really long time but it might only be a few minutes."

Orville had no answer. "I have no idea, but this is amazing. I can't believe I'm floating in space watching the Thaumatarians build a planet. I wish I had snacks, though."

"The silver ships are gone. I think they're finished. It's beautiful! The outer surface is reflecting the stars."

"How come Tectar looks smooth on the outside, but we have mountain ranges and rivers and trees on the surface?"

"That's a good question. We can ask Copo."

"Something's happening! Look at the right side of Tectar."

"The stars are rippling, getting squished together. I think the Mark XVII Thrusters are warping space in front of the planet."

There was a sudden blinding flash of light and the planet vanished.

"Whoa! Did you see that?"

Before Sophia could answer she was back in her comfy chair sitting next to Orville and Proto. The lights above them blinked on and the door whirred open.

"My legs are wobbly." Orville saw Copo peering through the doorway, a cheery look on his face.

"Careful now, watch your step! I do hope you enjoyed the show? It was a very popular tourist destination when I first arrived at the Museum, visitors coming from every corner of the universe."

Despite his cheerful demeanor, Sophia sensed a sadness in Copo. "Where did everyone go, all the Thaumatarians who made the journey here?"

Copo shook his head. "I'm afraid I have no ready answer to your question. They were all here, then there was an event of some kind. I'm not certain what occurred, it was a rather confusing time, and I'm afraid I lost awareness for many years. When I regained consciousness, everyone was gone. I remember stepping into the Greater Tectarian Aquarium and seeing huge vines dangling down from above, vines I had never seen before. It was quite disturbing."

"Are you talking about the tree roots hanging down into the big lake?"

"No, not tree roots, vines. The vines were hanging down from the outer hull of the ship, only a few feet

172

above them. There are no trees on the surface, the entire outer shell of Tectar is constructed of gleaming smooth Morsennium."

Sophia looked over to Orville, then back to Copo. "When is the last time you were on the surface of Tectar?"

"I have never actually been to the surface, but I have viewed a great variety of holo images and have studied the planet's construction process in exquisite detail. No living being could survive up there, I'm afraid. There is no atmosphere, nothing to block the deadly cosmic rays. Such radiation would quickly bring an end to any creature attempting to survive on the ship's surface."

Sophia said gently, "Copo, things have changed a lot on the surface, although I don't really understand how it happened. There are mountains and rivers and sky, many creatures living up there, including villages filled with green short-eared rabbits."

Copo did not seem to hear Sophia's words. "The drawing! I almost forgot the prize drawing!" He strode over to the stand with the glass vase on it. "Who would like to pick the winning ticket? It's quite an honor."

Orville looked at the vase. There were three ticket stubs in it. It seemed obvious one of them was going to win, so why bother with the drawing?

Sophia volunteered. "I'll do it, I can't wait to see who the lucky winner is!" She smiled brightly at Copo as she reached into the vase, pulling out a single ticket stub. "The winning ticket is number 1232008!"

Orville looked at his ticket stub. "I won! I can't believe I won! I never win anything!"

Copo gave a cheery laugh. "Excellent! I'm so pleased. Just wait until you see the prize!" Orville rubbed his paws together. Maybe it would be something really valuable.

Copo stepped behind the colorful display panels, rummaging around in a drawer. He returned with a curious object in his paw, graciously presenting it to Orville. "Congratulations, and may you treasure this gift forever, a cherished memento of your visit to the History of Tectar Temporal Displacement Museum."

Orville studied the object he was now holding, a gleaming eight inch long gold cylinder. Protruding from the top half of the cylinder were several dozen small black cubes, each of them embedded with a tiny blinking colored light. Orville sensed the object contained enormous power.

"It's very nice, um... but what exactly is it?"

Copo gave an understanding smile. "You are from Earth, of course, so there is no way you could know. You are holding in your paws a perfect working replica of the key used to start the first Mark XVII Micronizing Distortion Thruster, one of the six interstellar engines which brought Tectar to this very location."

Orville did his best to sound excited. "That's amazing, a perfect replica of the key used to start the... um... big engine thing. Copo, thank you so much for the complementary tickets. It was an amazing show, and I have to tell you, this is the best museum I've ever visited."

Sophia grinned. This was why she loved Orville.

Copo couldn't stop smiling. "Oh my, thank you so much for your patronage. You will come back again if you have time? There are quite a number of other exhibits I'm certain you would find most interesting."

"We'd love to, but our plans are a little hazy just

now. We're trying to reach the surface of Tectar. Say, would you like to come with us? It might be fun for you to see what's up there. You said you've never been to the surface."

"Quite true, quite true. I do thank you for your kind offer, but I'm afraid with me gone, there would be no one to watch over the museum. I would hate for visitors to arrive, only to find the Museum doors closed."

"I understand. This is your home, it's where you belong."

"You said there are trees on the surface?"

Sophia nodded. Copo had heard her after all. "Yes, they're quite lovely, and they walk around during the night."

A faraway look appeared in Copo's eyes. "The Great Walkers from the jungles of Athne in southern Thaumatar. A lovely area, stunning natural beauty. Perhaps one day I shall take a quick peek out the door."

Proto was remembering the centuries he had spent hidden inside the Cube, too afraid to venture out. It had taken Sophia and Orville's friendship and encouragement to help him find the strength to leave the Cube, to move to Muridaan Falls. "It's really quite lovely up there. Nothing to worry about at all. You could pop out for a moment, then come right back in if you wanted to. Each day you could spend a little more time on the surface until you became accustomed to it. You'd be perfectly safe."

Copo studied Proto's face. "You are quite perceptive for a Rabbiton, quite perceptive indeed. Perhaps I shall venture forth upon the surface in the near future. I suppose I could put a sign on the museum door indicating the precise time of my return."

Sophia nodded. "That's a wonderful idea. I think you'd like it, it might even remind you of your days on Thaumatar."

"That would be lovely. I will confess there are moments when I become quite wistful, yearning for those long ago days when I roamed the jungles of Athne."

"You roamed the jungles? What were you doing there?"

Copo smiled. "I was the sole passenger aboard an autonomous transport ship which malfunctioned, crashing deep in the jungles of Athne. I was forced to fend for myself for over a year, until the day I was rescued by a gang of ruthless bandits. That was the real beginning of my grand adventure."

"You lived with ruthless bandits?"

"Indeed I did. The bandits made every attempt to recruit me, hoping I would join them in their rather unscrupulous activities, but of course my programming did not allow me to participate in such unsavory behavior. Instead, I became their cook, preparing three meals a day for over twenty bandits. It was a lovely time. After dinner they would bring out their bolaphones and play such lively tunes. I felt quite alive back then."

"How did you get home?"

"Another interesting story. I was picking wild scramberries for a birthday pie when a beam of violet light flashed down from above, transporting me to a recovery ship. The pilot had been scanning the jungle for a lost Flybot and found me instead. I never got to say goodbye to my friends."

"That's very sad. You grew to be friends with the

bandits?"

"Quite good friends. They treated me as one of their own, even though I never took part in any unlawful activities. They never hurt anyone, but they did take a great many things which did not belong to them."

"Well, it's good they didn't hurt anyone. You know, if you went up to the surface and asked around you might find a jungle just like the one in Athne. Who knows, there might even be some ruthless bandits living there."

Copo laughed. "It would be fun to sit around a roaring campfire once again, tapping my toes to a lively bolaphone tune. Such fond memories I have of those days."

"Copo, can you tell us how to get to the surface? We don't really know our way around Tectar."

"I would be more than happy to help you. Follow me and I'll set you off in the right direction." Copo led them out of the Museum and into the long hallway.

"To reach the nearest escape hatch, head down the hall and take your first left turn. You'll pass through five sets of doors, then you turn right, up the stairs, turn left again, straight for one hundred feet, turn right, tap the violet button, exit, veer to the left, through the transport doors, push the third violet tab, exit again, turn right, turn left and there you are. Press the violet tab to exit through the airlock."

Orville stared blankly at Copo. "We go down the hall, then which way?"

Sophia grinned. "Follow me, Captain Orville."

Chapter 25

Up, Up, and Away

The three adventurers emerged from the airlock into a bitter cold blast of blinding white snow.

"It's a blizzard! I can't see anything!" Orville tried to shield his eyes from the furious stinging flakes, Sophia blinking up a sphere of defense around them to block the ferocious winds and pelting snow.

"That's better, but I still can't see anything. Proto, do you know where we are?"

Proto studied their surroundings, his eyes glowing with a vibrant green light. "My sensors indicate we are in a broad valley surrounded by snow covered peaks, somewhere deep within the Obex Range."

"I don't understand how there can be mountains on Tectar. When they built it, it was a giant shiny Morsennium ball."

"Several possible explanations come to mind. The Thaumatarians may have purposefully directed asteroids and comets to strike the surface of Tectar, completely covering the outer shell and in the process creating mountain ranges. Another possibility is that Tectar passed through a dense asteroid field the Thaumatarians were unaware of. Thousands of asteroids and comets could have crashed into the planet over the millennia. Comets are composed primarily of ice, which would have melted on impact, forming the lakes and rivers on the planet. Such collisions could have been catastrophic events, possibly affecting the internal structure of the planet. Copo mentioned there was a long period of time when he was not conscious. Perhaps he was damaged during one of these events."

Sophia squinted, peering into the swirling blizzard. "However the mountains got here, we have to get past them. We'll have a better idea what we're up against once we reach the far end of the valley. If this blizzard is any indication of the weather we'll be facing, it's going to be a very dangerous climb."

"I'm not that crazy about mountain climbing, especially the part where you fall into a thousand foot deep crevasse."

Sophia laughed. "Proto will rescue us if anything happens."

Orville shaped heavy winter gear for himself and Sophia; snowshoes, thick woolen coats, gloves, snow pants, insulated boots and goggles.

Sophia pulled her hood tight, adjusted her goggles, and flicked off the sphere of defense. "Much better. Let's go."

The adventurers headed east across the broad valley, Orville on the alert for snow bears or any other dreadful beasts which might attempt to turn him into an afternoon snack.

After two arduous days of battling the frigid icy terrain, raging blizzards and pelting snow, the party of adventurers reached the western foothills of the Obex Range.

179

"Let's camp here for the night. I'll shape a fire and we can have dinner."

Orville shaped a sturdy tent while Sophia shaped a blazing campfire. Proto soon had a pot of tasty vegetable soup simmering over the fire, the delectable aroma permeating the chilly mountain air.

"Mmmm… that smells good, Proto, I was thinking of shaping some tasty little cakes for–" Orville stopped in mid sentence, his eyes on the roaring fire, watching the bright orange embers float up toward the dark gray sky. He was remembering the day his papa took him to the Muridaan Falls Summer Sun Festival. He was five years old, only a mouseling, but the memory of that day was etched forever in his mind.

"What's that big round thing, Papa?"

"It's called a hot air balloon. See the fire above the big basket? That fills the balloon with hot air, and hot air rises. What do you think will happen when the air inside the balloon gets hot enough?"

"The balloon will catch on fire?"

"Something else. What does hot air do?"

"It rises. The balloon will rise because it's filled with hot air? It flies? The mouse in the basket is going to fly??"

"Orville, are you still with us?"

"Oh, sorry, I was just remembering something. I think I know how we can cross over the mountains. We can shape a hot air balloon and fly over."

A dozen possible outcomes of Orville's daring plan ran through Sophia's mind, most of them involving fire and crashing into rocks. "I don't know, it could work, but it sounds risky, there's a lot of variables. Did you see the wind up there? It looks dreadful, the snow is whipping across the peaks. We'd be at the mercy of the wind. The balloon goes wherever the wind takes it, it's not like being in a Dragonfly or a blinker ship."

"I guess we could shape a small hot air balloon and test it to see what happens."

"Now you're thinking like a scientist."

An hour later Orville was holding up a six foot wide paper balloon while Sophia steadied the alcohol burner hanging beneath it. "This should work, the opening is wide enough to fill the balloon with hot air without setting the paper on fire."

Proto nodded. "If this test proves successful we can build a large scale version, perhaps with a duplonium powered heat exchanger, much safer than using an open flame."

Orville grinned. "The balloon is filling up and getting lighter! It's tugging, trying to rise. This was a good idea."

"It might work."

"Okay, here goes!" Orville released his grip on the balloon.

"It's going up!"

Sophia held off final judgement. "What matters is how the wind affects it."

Orville watched nervously as the balloon rose higher and higher. "It's a hundred feet up and looking stable!"

"Don't forget the mountains are seven thousand feet tall and the wind up there looks brutal."

Three minutes later the balloon was at five hundred feet and still rising. Orville could see the small blue flame beneath the balloon. When it reached six hundred feet a ferocious blast of wind grabbed the balloon, ripping it across the sky. Orville watched in dismay as his creation burst into flames, disappearing seconds later into a bank of churning gray clouds. "Oh, no!"

"It's okay, we'll find another way over the mountains."

"It was a dumb idea."

"If the weather was better it would have worked perfectly."

"I guess testing it first was a pretty good idea."

"A scientist learns from every experiment, especially if the results are unexpected. This experiment gave us the data we needed. We know we can't safely fly a hot air balloon over the mountains, so we'll find another way."

Chapter 26

Just a Thought

Orville rose early the next morning, grumbling to himself about his less than successful hot air balloon venture. "Dumb blustery wind." He gave a long sigh, imagining the three of them drifting triumphantly over the mountain peaks in a great colorful hot air balloon, beneath a clear blue sky. He could almost hear Sophia's voice. "This was the best idea ever, Orville!"

Orville directed his gaze toward the snowy peaks, the early morning light revealing the true ferocity of the winds tearing across the top of the mountains. His eyes traveled down the mountainous slopes to the foothills. "How are we supposed to climb a mountain with these crazy winds?"

Orville scanned the foothills, searching out possible routes for their ascent. "That's weird. That big black rock doesn't have any snow on it. It should be covered with snow."

Sophia was sleeping, and Proto was in the tent reading one of the many books he'd brought with him. Orville buttoned up his winter coat and pulled the hood tight, curious about the peculiar black rock. As he slogged through the deep snow, he was once again reminded that things are seldom what they appear to be.

"It's not a big black rock at all, it's the entrance to a cave." He groaned to himself. "I hate caves, especially ones filled with hungry snow bears. One quick peek, then I'll head back." A powerful sphere of defense popped up around him.

Orville approached the cave cautiously, listening closely for growling or slithering or the sound of snapping teeth. He crept up to the side of the entrance, peering around the rocks into the shadowy interior. The first ten feet of the cave was covered with windblown snow, beyond that lay dark and nebulous shadows. He sent an orb of light into the cave.

"It's Tectar's outer hull!" Orville stepped into the cave, his eyes on the pale green floor. He scrunched down and ran his paw across the smooth cool surface of the planet. "I can't believe they built a whole world out of Morsennium. It looks brand new, not a scratch on it. I wish I knew what happened to all the Thaumatarians who came here."

Orville pressed forward, deeper into the cave. "What is that?" He had spotted two glowing lights, one violet and one yellow. "It could be another airlock. Whoa, there could be a tunnel running under the mountain range!" Orville darted toward the lights, imagining Sophia's expression when he told her he'd found a secret hidden passage beneath the mountains.

Orville was correct, the two small lights belonged to an airlock identical to the one they had used to reach the surface of Tectar. He tapped the violet light and a six foot wide transparent cylinder telescoped up from the floor, the door sliding silently open.

"I should go tell Sophia and Proto about this." He

looked back through the cave entrance to their distant campsite. He could make out the tent, but saw no sign of either Sophia or Proto. Orville studied the lift, weighing his next move.

"Creekers!" On the rocky wall next to the airlock was a coiled snake carving. "Haukesworth Mouse was here!" Orville stepped into the cylinder and pressed the violet tab. The door whirred shut, the cylinder descending into Tectar.

Orville crept out of the airlock, scanning for danger, but found only silence. He was in an enormous brightly lit tunnel, a tunnel running directly to the east.

"Yes! A tunnel under the mountains! I can't believe I found it! They should call me Orville the Explorer. Orville the Explorer, the daring mouse who discovered the ancient passage lying far below the mysterious Obex Mountains. Maybe I'll call it Orville Tunnel." Orville froze when he saw the vaporous form floating out of a doorway fifty feet down the tunnel. The strange blue cloud was drifting toward him. His insides turned to ice. "What is that thing? I think it's looking at me!"

Orville turned and ran from the churning amorphous horror. He raced back toward the airlock, his pounding footsteps reverberating through the empty tunnel. When he slapped the violet tab the door made a painful whining noise, but did not open.

"No!! Open up! Open up!!" Orville pounded with all his might on the airlock door but it did not respond. When he glanced back at the formless blue monstrosity, an involuntary shriek burst from his lips. The shapeless mass was hovering only inches away from him.

"Don't eat me! Or… whatever it is you do. Wait, sphere of defense!" He popped up a wall of energy around him. "I can't believe I forgot my sphere of defense. Sophia would kill me." The dense blue cloud had not advanced any further, roiling and churning directly in front of him.

"It's not trying to eat me. Maybe it's not alive. It could just be some weird blue cloud, a weird blue cloud that stares at mice and follows them around."

Orville had a sudden and remarkable flash of insight. He knew what the terrifying miasma was. He had been thrown off by its size, not recognizing it for what it was, nothing more than a thought cloud. Granted, it was an enormous thought cloud, a gargantuan one, the biggest one he'd ever seen, but at least now he knew it wasn't going to eat him.

"Whoa, not even the Thirteenth Monk could create a cloud like this one. Maybe I can control it." He focused on the thought cloud, imagining it floating away from him, back down the hallway.

"It works! I can move it around like a regular thought cloud. That's not so scary." He pulled the cloud back until it was hovering several yards away from him.

"I wonder whose thought cloud it is, and why it's so big? I could draw it to me and find out what's in it, but that's kind of scary. Suppose it's some creepy monster's thought that turns me into a big moaning ghoul." Orville burst out laughing, imagining himself returning to the campsite as a big green ghoul, chasing Sophia and Proto around the tent, tromping after them with big green clawed feet and burning yellow eyes.

"Okay, there's no way that's going to happen. It's probably just some old thought that's been floating around here for centuries. It came out of that doorway down the hall. I should see what's in there, maybe there's more thought clouds, maybe some little ones that aren't so scary."

Orville stepped around the blue cloud, walking toward the open doorway. When he peered into the room he gave a start, his eyes widening. "Creekers!!" Lying on the floor was a creepy old skeleton wearing a tattered, partially disintegrated gray uniform. Orville tried to calm his racing heart. He'd seen skeletons before. It was okay, just an old skeleton, a pile of bones. It wasn't going to jump up, grab his neck with its bony paws and choke the life out of him. Unghh, bad thought, why did he think of things like that?? He forced himself to push his fear aside, just as Sophia had taught him.

"All right, the skeleton has to be a Thaumatarian. It has the same basic bone structure as a rabbit, and it's only four feet tall, just like Copo. I wonder how he got here?" Orville noticed a small round silver pin attached to the gray uniform. "This is a good clue, it's the same symbol we saw above the museum door. Maybe this was one of the engineers who built Tectar. Whoa, he could have been in that show we saw." Orville gingerly removed the pin from the skeleton's ragged uniform. "I wish I knew what the little symbol inside the circle meant."

Orville was studying the silver pin as he stepped out of the room. He didn't notice the enormous blue thought cloud until it was too late. He walked directly into it, gave a low groan and sank to the floor, his eyes closing as he fell.

Chapter 27

Chief Master Orville

Orville was gone before he hit the floor. As a shaper, he had drawn thousands of thought clouds to him and had a good idea of what to expect when they entered his mind. He knew what Sophia's thoughts felt like, he knew that Master Marloh's thoughts possessed slightly more power, and nothing compared to the power of the Thirteenth Monk's thoughts. Nothing until his encounter with this thought.

Orville was staring at a group of gray uniformed rabbits huddled in whispered conversation at the end of a stark pale yellow room. It was a peculiar feeling, both knowing and not knowing who they were. He had no idea how he knew this, but he was looking at a group of Thaumatarian engineers, and he was the Chief Master. He looked down at his body. He wore a gray uniform with a round silver pin attached to the front pocket, the pin designating him as Chief Master Engineer of Tectar.

Orville eyed the engineers, a flurry of thoughts whirling through his mind. "This is weird. Okay, I need to use logic, just like Sophia does. I walked into the blue thought cloud, but instead of the thought cloud being absorbed by me, my awareness was pulled into the thought cloud, and now I'm experiencing the life of an ancient Tectarian engineer. That's whose skeleton I found. That's creepy, I'm walking around in a dead Thaumatarian's skeleton. Wait, this is just like when I wore the memory ring on Varmoran. I'm experiencing an event from his life. Maybe it's something he wanted me to see, something the universe wants me to see."

Orville watched himself as he strode toward to the group of engineers. A few of them looked up. He turned to face a tall engineer, an old and trusted friend. "What do you have?"

"Our only chance is to create a habitable surface environment for the population."

"They're not going to go up. They feel safe down here. Safe from the asteroids."

"It's either that or…"

Orville gave a long sigh. "He's out of control. He'll destroy us all if we don't do something and do it quickly. If we're caught, it's a death sentence for all of us."

One of the engineers raised his paw. "The number of asteroid impacts has been decreasing every year, each time we pass through the field. There weren't any strikes last year. We have mountains and rivers and something resembling an ocean."

"What about the atmosphere?"

"Not quite enough to support life, but we're close. We have a plan. It requires the use of a Mark XVII Distortion Thruster."

Orville eyed the engineer. "That's not going to be easy."

"Who better than us to allocate one?"

"How much water will it take? How long?"

"That's the beauty of it, we don't use water."

"Wait, you're not thinking of–"

"It's the only way to get it done quickly."

Orville ran his paw over his chin, deep in thought. *"We need to think about this. It could go very wrong. We might not have time, you do realize that?"*

"What other choice do we have?"

"How do we get everyone up to the surface?"

"We make it impossible for them to stay down here."

"How?"

"Trobesium tactate vapor."

"The automatons aren't going to like that."

"They'll recover."

"After a hundred years or so. You're right though, we don't have the luxury of time. Using the Mark XVII carries a high degree of risk. How long to produce a sustainable atmosphere?"

"A week at most. Trobesium vapor will clear out the population in a few days. They won't have any choice. We'll do one sector at a time, starting with 113."

"What about the Consul? He'll know we're the only ones capable of conducting an operation like this. He has a lot of followers."

The engineer gave Orville a grim look. *"It's being handled. You don't need to know about it."*

Orville nodded. *"I hope we're doing the right thing. They'll be without tech. No automatons, no comms, no engines, no plantonium converters."*

"No one knows what happened back on Thaumatar. Everyone is gone. Everyone. How do you explain that? It had to be something the big rabs were working on, something that went wrong. That's where technology

has taken us. More tech isn't the answer, less tech is. We'll be giving them a fresh start. Maybe this time they'll get it right."

"Go ahead with your plans. We'll let the history books decide whether we were right or wrong."

Orville turned and strode out of the room. He headed down the long hallway toward the tunnel entrance. It was time for the second part of his plan, the part the other engineers knew nothing about, the part which would save their lives. Orville felt queasy. He knew what came next and there was nothing he could do to stop it.

He stepped into the small room near the tunnel entrance and took a seat. He wouldn't have to wait very long. He was remembering the day he had decided to become an engineer when he heard the footsteps. All his fear vanished. He knew enough about deep physics to know there was more to life than this world, more to a rabbit than its physical body.

The rabbit who entered the room wore a dark green cape and a furious scowl. "Did you think we were stupid, that we wouldn't discover your treasonous scheme? We found your papers, we know all about your pitiful little plan, the plan the other engineers all laughed at. How does it feel to know you failed, to know you lost, to know I won?"

The smile that appeared on the Chief Master's face filled the Consul with a blinding rage. He would suffer many insults, but to be laughed at was not one of them. Orville knew why the Chief Master smiled. He had seen through the Consul's mask of rage to the desperate fear hidden beneath it, seen through to the terrible aching emptiness the Consul could never fill, no matter how

191

powerful he became, no matter how many rabbits feared and obeyed him.

The Consul pulled a silver cylinder from his pocket, pointing it at the Chief Master Engineer. There was a brilliant flash of purple light and a terrible pain shot through Orville's chest. As he was falling he let go of his world, let go of his thoughts, merging with his true inner self. His last act on Tectar was to send a powerful thought cloud into the world, knowing that one day a young shaper named Orville Wellington Mouse would find it.

"ORVILLE!" Sophia screamed, racing down the long corridor. She blinked the last hundred feet, appearing in a flash of light next to Orville. He was unconscious but still breathing. She grabbed his arms, dragging him out of the blue thought cloud. "What did you do?? Why did you come down here??" She pressed her paw against his chest, sensing his vital signs. He hadn't been injured. She put her arms around him. "Orville, wake up! It's time to wake up! You need to come back to us. Please, Orville!"

Orville let out a low moan. "Unhh...what? He killed me. I can't believe he really killed me. Who does something like that?"

"No one killed you, you're fine. You need to wake up."

"The other engineers? Are they okay? Did the plan work?"

Sophia glanced at the swirling blue thought cloud. She'd never seen one like it. "Orville, it's me, Sophia."

"Sophia? Wait...umm... I was... I found a tunnel that goes under the Obex Mountains."

"I know you did." Sophia kissed Orville.

"What was that for?"

"You scared me. I was afraid I'd lost you. We need to go. Proto saw an entire village appear out of nowhere. Things are getting worse."

Chapter 28

Under the Mountain

Orville had a silly grin plastered across his face as they strolled down the long tunnel. "You didn't know where I was, and when you found me you were so glad to see me that you kissed me? So, if I ran off and hid for an hour, then came back, you'd–"

"I'd pound your arm till it turned purple, that's what I'd do. Tell me about the Chief Master Engineer. You said they were trying to get all the passengers up to the surface of Tectar, to live there. Why was that so important?"

"After they lost all contact with Thaumatar, everything changed. Over time their Consul assumed more and more power, until he had become nothing more than a ruthless dictator, killing anyone who opposed him. If the engineers could move everyone up to the surface, the population could scatter to the four winds and the Consul would lose his control over them."

"You said the Chief Master Engineer sacrificed his own life to protect the other engineers?"

"He planted information he knew the Consul would find, papers revealing him as the sole conspirator of a treasonous but fictitious plot. He made it clear the other engineers wanted no part of his treacherous plan. I was there when the Consul killed him. It was awful."

"I can't imagine what that must have been like. There must be some reason why the universe sent you down here to find the Chief Master Engineer's thought cloud. You're certain he knew you would be the one to find it?"

"I'm sure of it. As he was falling, he merged with his inner self. I was a little disoriented, but he said my name, said I would be the one to find his thought cloud."

"I've never seen anything like this, it's incredible he knew you would find it. I don't know why you were brought here, but you were. All we can do now is continue on and let the events unfold."

The three adventurers pressed eastward through the tunnel beneath the Obex Mountains, the corridor illuminated by a warm ambient light emanating from the walls and ceiling. Other than the curious lighting and the tunnel's vast dimensions, the structure was relatively unremarkable.

"There's another door, a big one. I'm going to see what's in there. Maybe the room is filled with giant boxes of gold coins. It would be okay to keep them because we didn't shape them, we just found them."

Sophia looked at him curiously. "What would you do with a giant chest of gold coins?"

"I'd buy stuff. Anything I wanted."

"What kind of stuff?"

"I don't know, just stuff. I'd get Papa and Mum a lot of nice things, maybe a big house, and I'd probably get a really nice adventurers hat. One like Haukesworth's."

Orville took off the hat and held it up for Sophia to see. "It has the really long purple feather. Probably very expensive."

"You're saying you'd use your giant chest of gold coins to buy a new hat?"

"What's wrong with that? Every adventurer needs a snappy looking hat. I hope there's tons of gold." Orville dashed down the corridor and slapped the purple tab. The door whirred open, the interior lights blinking on. "Whoa! What is that thing? It has seats but no wheels."

Proto peered into the room, a grin appearing on his face. "I think you're going to like this." He stepped over to the oval shaped craft, reaching in and tapping a grid of disks on the control console. The sparkling blue metallic vehicle rose six inches off the ground, hovering silently. "I believe this will prove to be far more useful than a crate of gold coins."

"How does it work?"

"It is essentially the same technology as the personal floaters we used on Varmoran, but is a low level ground vehicle, using micro-grav displacers. It doesn't fly, it hovers." Proto hopped into the front seat. "Stand clear, everyone!" He pushed a small lever forward and the car lurched sideways, thumping into the wall. "Drat, wrong way."

Sophia and Orville scuttled away from the hovering car, Sophia whispering loudly, "You might want to pop up a sphere of defense until he gets the controls sorted out."

"I heard that! Rest assured I am in complete control of the craft at this time. I simply pushed the wrong lever, quite a simple mistake."

With a low hum the car eased out of the room into

the tunnel.

"All aboard!"

"Whoo hoo! No more walking!" Orville jumped into the car next to Proto and Sophia scrambled into the back, stretching out on the wide padded seat.

"Here we go!" Proto pulled back a silver lever and the car glided smoothly down the tunnel.

"How fast will it go?"

"We're currently traveling at top speed, about fifteen miles an hour. It's an indoor service car, not designed for speed."

"Well, it beats walking. How far till the end of the tunnel?"

"Barring unforeseen circumstances, we should reach our destination in about four hours."

Sophia flicked her wrist and a large puffy pillow appeared. "Just enough time for a nice nap."

"You take too many naps. You're going to miss something exciting if you're asleep. If I find gold coins I'm not sharing them with you."

"Keep your old coins, my amazing brain needs a rest. Wake me up if you spot a fancy restaurant where we can have lunch."

Orville rolled his eyes. "I guess it's just you and me, Proto. Keep your eyes open for treasure chests."

"Just out of curiosity, are you aware that gold is an extremely dense element, one cubic foot weighing approximately twelve hundred pounds? If we assume a traditional treasure chest has an internal volume of approximately two cubic feet, the resultant weight would be two thousand four hundred pounds, more if you factor in the weight of the strongbox itself. If we found only one such treasure chest, we would be forced to trek across the countryside carrying well over a ton of gold coins, a rather daunting task under any circumstance."

Orville had a hilarious reply on the tip of his tongue, but kept it to himself, saying instead, "Proto, you don't understand the nature of daydreams. When I'm daydreaming about finding a chest of gold coins, I'm not thinking about the practical aspects of finding them, I'm just thinking about the part when I open the chest, see all the shiny gold coins and scream 'Whoo hoooo!! I'm rich!!'."

"If that is true, it demonstrates a rather short sighted and illogical perspective. If you can't take them with you, what is the point of getting excited about finding them? Besides, why do you even want gold coins when you can shape anything you need?"

Orville heard Sophia snicker in the back seat. He frowned. "You're right, Proto, you have shown me the error of my ways. From now on, instead of daydreaming about gold coins I will daydream about discovering a thriving colony of friendly little creatures made of solid gold who will happily run along behind us so I won't have to carry them."

"Oh dear, I don't wish to be disparaging, but I'm afraid that is a highly unlikely prospect. I have read extensively on the nearly infinite variety of life forms inhabiting the known universe, but none have a physiology based in gold, or any other heavy metal for that matter. Most, of course, are carbon based creatures, although quite a number of small gaseous planets have been known to…"

Orville closed his eyes, leaning back in his seat. He was asleep before Proto had finished his sentence.

"AGGGHHHH!!"

The car lurched across the tunnel, scraping against the wall. Orville's scream had caused Proto to momentarily lose control of the vehicle. Sophia sat upright, her eyes blinking open. "What is it? Who screamed?"

Orville gave a sheepish look. "Sorry, I just had a bad dream about Mendacium. He was staring at me with those burning yellow eyes. So scary."

Sophia flopped back down on her pillow. "How many times do I have to say it? He doesn't have dark magical powers. There's no such thing as that and he can't hurt us, so stop having bad dreams about him."

Orville knew he would never convince Sophia that dark magic might really exist. "Fine, no more bad dreams. Proto, how much longer to the end of the tunnel?"

"We're almost there. We've been going uphill for the last ten miles. We should reach the surface in about fifteen minutes."

"Aelric said once we're on the surface we should head east for three days, following a big river until we reach Castle Caligari."

Sophia studied Orville's face, sensing his growing unease. She reached forward and squeezed his shoulder. "We'll be fine, we have Proto the Brave to protect us."

Proto grinned. "Here we are!" The tunnel had leveled off, the car gliding into a vast circular chamber with fifty foot tall ceilings.

"It looks like the Thaumatarians left in a hurry, everything is scattered all over. The engineers said they were going to use some kind of weird vapor to get everyone to leave, that they'd be forced to evacuate."

"What do you think this place was?"

"It appears to have been a maintenance center. There's an airlock in the corner, just like the one you found in the cave. That should take us up to the surface."

"Too bad the car won't fit. I guess we're back to walking again."

Proto switched off the motor and the car sank gently to the floor. "Even if we could get it up to the surface it wouldn't be of any use in the outdoors, it only floats six inches above the ground."

Orville wove his way through the cluttered chaos of the room. "I wonder what all these weird tools were for? Maybe they fixed vehicles here. There might be blinker ships like the one we found on Varmoran. We should look."

Sophia stood impatiently next to the airlock. "We don't have time to look around, we have to go."

Orville gave a groan. Every step he took was one step closer to his inevitable encounter with Mendacium the Dark Wizard.

Chapter 29

Village 113

The first thing Orville noticed when he emerged from the airlock was the gloriously radiant sunshine. "This is nice, so warm out, no snow. The tunnel took us a couple of miles past the mountains. That must be why it's so toasty."

"That must be the river Aelric mentioned. It's wide and slow, probably fed by melting snow from the Obex Range."

Orville clambered up onto a large boulder for a better view. "The river is meandering and really long. Aelric said we follow it for three days. We should keep an eye on the trees. I don't see any big thorns, so that's good news."

Sophia strode over to the closest tree, placing her paw on its trunk and sending a thought cloud into it.

"Hello, my name is Sophia." The tree did not respond. "We're okay. These trees are like our trees back home, they stay in one spot and they don't read thought clouds."

"More good news. I don't like the idea of trees strolling around in the moonlight, especially the ones with big stabby thorns."

"Let's head down to the river, we can walk along the bank."

The trio wove their way through several heavily wooded groves, Sophia spotting small patches of brightly colored wildflowers. "Hey, Orville, purple wildflowers, your favorite." She snickered, remembering the mutant purple flowers on Varmoran who had tried to eat Orville.

"So funny, ha ha, let's all tease Orville about the purple flowers again." Orville stepped through the trees, the great winding river before him, sparkling in the noonday sun. "The river is beautiful. It's really peaceful, kind of makes me wish we were just–"

"Get down!" Sophia dropped into the tall grass, motioning toward a wooden raft drifting downriver.

Orville hit the ground, his eyes on the slow moving craft. He could see three dark green rabbits, two of them steering the vessel with long poles. The craft was carrying dozens of baskets filled with fruits and vegetables.

"They look like farmers taking their produce to market. They don't look dangerous. Maybe Aelric was confused. The rabbits here look just like the rabbits on the other side of the range. Hey, I just thought of something. Aelric and Gemma must be descendants of the Thaumatarians who arrived here in Tectar. Isn't that weird?"

"Keep down, you can't tell if they're dangerous just by looking at them."

"I can't believe we met real live Thaumatarians. I wonder if they know who their ancestors were, and all the things they did? You know, like building Tectar and the World Doors?"

"Even if they don't know, they seem happy enough. Aelric and Gemma have a good life on their farm. Maybe the Chief Master Engineer was right, maybe too much technology was the downfall of the Thaumatarians."

"I liked the floaters on Varmoran. They were really fun. Even if you did fly like my old grandmum."

"Oh, please, you could barely keep up with me. Okay, the raft is gone, let's get moving. We need to find Castle Caligari and find out what is causing the Void to disappear. We can't forget why we're here."

The adventurers stepped out of the tall grass and headed down to the river's edge.

"Do you think Aelric was right about the rabbits on this side of the mountains being so scary? They looked like peaceful farmers to me, no different than Aelric."

"He must have had some reason for saying it. He did say he'd heard a lot of grisly tales about Castle Caligari."

"Who do you think built the castle? It seems too primitive for the Thaumatarians."

"Don't forget when they moved to the surface of Tectar they didn't have any technology, and Copo said they arrived here almost twenty thousand years ago. A lot of things can happen in twenty thousand years."

Orville was about to reply when a green thought cloud enveloped his head. "Excellent day for a brisk walk along the river."

Orville and Sophia whipped around to face an elderly Thaumatarian rabbit strolling behind them, a gnarled walking stick in one paw.

Another thought cloud flashed out toward them. "I walk every day, rain or shine. Good for the constitution.

You're not bandits, are you? You might scare some rabbits, but you don't scare me. Don't try anything funny, I know how to handle a walking stick."

Sophia sent a cloud back to the rabbit. "We're not bandits, but we are lost. We're looking for Castle Caligari. Have you heard of it?"

"You must be taking offerings to Mendacium. I should have guessed, it's the only way to prevent plague and pestilence. You're odd looking rabbits. Does everyone in your village have round ears?"

"We're mice, not rabbits. We're from a distant land and we're searching for Castle Caligari. We're trying to locate a friend of ours who was last seen near the castle."

"He didn't go inside the castle, did he?"

"What did you mean about taking offerings to Mendacium?"

"We bring him offerings in exchange for his services. We give him books, food, and gold, and in return he prevents plague and pestilence, a fair enough trade in my eyes. Our village has been doing it for as long as anyone can remember, and for hundreds of years we've never had a plague or an infestation."

"You've been making offerings for hundreds of years? How old is Mendacium? Do you know what he looks like? Does he practice dark magic?"

"Of course he does, only the darkest magic will stop plague and pestilence, everyone knows that. I've never seen him, but one of the elders in our village saw him when he was a bunny. He wandered off into the castle during an offering. Had dreadful nightmares for years after. Still claims Mendacium was twelve feet tall, wore a great purple robe with a long yellow sash, had burning yellow eyes and a flaming scepter. His voice shook the walls of the castle and he was surrounded by an eerie purple glow. Poor Rabidus was never the same after that. We leave our offerings in the gatehouse, no one ever goes inside the castle." The elderly rabbit looked around to see if anyone was watching. "You've probably heard some of the stories they tell about Mendacium? All those gruesome and grisly things he does to rabbits in the castle?"

"We've heard a few stories, but the rabbits we met didn't want to talk about it."

The old rabbit gave Sophia a sly wink. "There's a bit of truth stretching to be found in those tales, mostly to keep the bandits away from our village. They're terrified of Mendacium and what he might do to them if they harm anyone in our village. The bandits never bother us."

Orville realized he was clenching his paws. The old rabbit's description of Mendacium was identical in every way to what he'd seen in his dream. This was irrefutable proof that Mendacium was a real living being, not just a character in a three hundred year old book.

"It takes three days to reach the castle?"

"Only if you follow the river all the way around the big loop. I have a boat hidden up ahead I use to cross the river. Cuts the journey down to a few hours. The castle is two miles east of our village."

"Have you ever heard of the Thaumatarians?"

The old rabbit furrowed his brows. "No rabbits in the village by that name. Is that the name of your missing friend?"

"No, someone mentioned they might live around

here, but I think they were confused." Sophia smiled politely.

"You're welcome to come with me to the village. Plautilla runs a fine inn where you can stay, maybe ask around about your missing friend." The old rabbit eyed Proto with curiosity. "Never seen a silver rabbit before. Heard stories though. They say there's a big group of them living south of the range. Does it read clouds, or just talk? I heard they eat nails for dinner."

"No nails for dinner. Rabbitons don't eat or sleep. His name is Proto, and he talks but doesn't read clouds."

"Guess I've seen everything now. Boat's right here in this grove. You two can ride, but it's not big enough for your silver friend. He'll have to wade across. River's not too deep and the current's slow. I'm Serus, by the way."

Sophia and Orville dragged Serus' boat down to the water while he fetched the long pole to guide the boat.

Proto pushed the boat into the river, strolling along behind it as Serus poled the craft across the lazy current. Midway across the meandering waterway, only the tips of Proto's ears were visible above the water. Orville nudged Sophia. "A pair of scary silver ears is chasing us!"

Sophia snickered. "What's the name of your town, Serus?"

"Village 113."

"The name of your town is a number?"

"That's how we've done it for as long as anyone can remember. It's just our way. Maybe had something to do with ancient calendars, no one really knows."

"It sounds like a very practical idea." Orville was

remembering something the engineers had said, the first passengers they would force up to the surface of the planet would be from Sector 113.

When they arrived on the other side, Orville and Sophia hopped out of the boat and dragged it into the woods.

Proto had a wide grin when he emerged from the river. "Fascinating, I was able to observe a wide variety of colorful fish in the river, some of them quite frightening. Do you happen to know if they're poisonous?"

"Serus only reads thought clouds. How scary were they?"

"I would not recommend taking a leisurely dip in the river. Some of the fish had peculiar looking long teeth, and the creatures squirming around in the mud would not stop snapping at my feet and legs."

"And I forgot my swimming suit. Maybe next time." Orville gave a cackling laugh.

The adventurers followed Serus along a lovely forest trail, beams of warm sunlight flickering down through emerald green foliage, patterns of light and shadow rippling across the forest floor.

"What a beautiful forest. The rustling of the leaves is almost a melody."

"That's the song of the trees. Everything in the world has its own song, that's where music comes from."

Sophia looked at Serus with new eyes. Her papa always said most creatures have greater depth than is first apparent.

Orville pointed though the trees to a bright yellow farmhouse. "That looks like Aelric and Gemma's house, but without the big wall."

The adventurers emerged into lush farmland, the vast fields filled with innumerable rows of healthy vibrant crops. Sophia breathed in the rich earthy air of the countryside. "Mmm, that smells so good."

After a relaxing stroll past several farms they arrived on the outskirts of Village 113. Even Proto was taken aback by the beauty of the setting. "A lovely rustic village, almost like stepping into a fairy tale. Of course, fairy tales often have dark castles with evil wizards, not to mention dank musty dungeons filled with piles of old bones." Proto gave Orville a significant look.

Serus gestured for them to follow him. "Welcome to our humble village. As they say, 'See the village and know the heart of the villagers'. I'll take you to the inn, it's in the town square."

Two laughing young bunnies darted out from behind a low wooden building, its weathered sign swinging in the warm breeze. They stopped short when they saw Proto, thought clouds flashing between them, then ran over to Serus, their eyes on Proto.

"Whoa, a silver rabbit! Where'd you find him, Master Serus? Is he real? Is he going to help us with the crops? I bet he's really strong. He could fix our roof! Is he going to live here?"

Serus ran his paw across the young bunny's head. "You leave him be, he's a guest, not here to do your chores. They come from far away looking for a lost friend. He might be in Castle Caligari."

The bunny's eyes opened wide. "The castle? They're going into the castle? Can we go, too? I want to see Mendacium. Is he really twelve feet tall? I bet the silver rabbit wouldn't be afraid of him. Can we go?"

"You can both go home, that's where you can go. The castle isn't a fit place for bunnies or anyone else. When you're older you can help take offerings to Mendacium. The only rabbit in the village who's ever seen him is Master Rabidus."

"Papa says he's loopy as a six-eyed barnbird."

"You be nice. Just because you haven't seen something doesn't mean it's not real. Everyone knows Master Rabidus saw Mendacium when he was your age, and that's why he is the way he is."

Orville was reading the clouds as they flashed back and forth, his apprehension growing. If one look at Mendacium could change Rabidus like that, what would happen to him and Sophia?

Serus stopped in front of a white wooden building adorned with an array of lovely hanging flower baskets, the scent from the yellow and violet blooms filling the air. He pushed the front door open and strode inside.

"Afternoon, Plautilla. Got some guests for you. They're here to see the castle, looking for a lost friend who might be around these parts."

Plautilla was an instantly likable rabbit with a warm and friendly disposition. She eyed Proto, gentle concern crossing her face. A thought cloud flashed out to Sophia.

"Not sure we have a bed big enough for a silver rabbit. We could put two beds end to end, that might work."

Sophia smiled her thanks. "Our friend Proto doesn't need a bed, he doesn't sleep. Most of the time he stays up all night reading."

"Sounds like me." Plautilla gave a great laugh, highly amused by her own joke. "I'll show you to your

209

rooms. Dinner is in two hours, plenty of time to rest and freshen up. What does your big silver friend eat?"

"He doesn't eat or drink, but he is a marvelous chef. His tasty little cakes are famous where we come from. I bet if you asked him he'd share a few of his recipes with you."

"Knock me over with a barnbird feather, a silver rabbit who loves to cook? If he wants to help with dinner, you won't hear me complaining."

After Orville and Sophia had been shown to their rooms, Plautilla and Proto headed to the kitchen, soon filled with the delicious aromas of simmering vegetable stew and baking bread. An hour later Proto stood at the counter frosting a tray of freshly baked tasty little cakes. Plautilla was sampling her third little cake.

"Mmmm... so delicious! I have a proposition for you, Chef Proto. How about we call these *Chef Proto's Tasty Little Cakes* and I'll make them the inn's signature dessert? In no time at all you'll be the most famous chef in all of Tectar, and we'll both be rolling in silvers. What do you say?" She grinned as she shook Proto's hand.

Proto had no idea why Plautilla was shaking his hand, but he did know he had a new friend who loved his tasty little cakes.

Chapter 30

Castle Caligari

The following morning Orville woke with a severe stomach ache. The cause of his malady was not too many tasty little cakes the night before, but stemmed from too many thoughts regarding the day's impending activities, in particular their trip to Castle Caligari and his likely encounter with Mendacium the Dark Wizard.

"Sophia, can you use shaping to cure a stomach ache?"

"I can cure it without shaping. Stop thinking about Mendacium. There, feel better?"

"It's not something I can just stop thinking about or stop dreaming about. He had those burning yellow eyes and he was staring right at me. He wasn't staring at you, he was staring at me."

"Remember your dream about jumping into a volcano? Remember how terrified you were after you had the dream?"

"I wouldn't say I was terrified."

"You were definitely terrified."

"Maybe a little."

211

"Did we have to jump into a lake of molten lava?"

"No, not exactly."

"Did we survive our leap into Mount Ianua?"

"You already know we did. I see what you're saying, though, I shouldn't take the dream so literally, the real castle might be different from the dream castle."

"Orville, you have an amazing imagination. A lot of times it's your best friend, like when you're solving puzzles, but when it comes to Mendacium, it's your worst enemy. You're imagining all kinds of frightful things that are not going to happen."

"You're right, I know you are, I'll try not to worry so much. I do have one question, though. Do you think my adventuring hat will still fit after Mendacium turns me into a warty toad?"

Sophia burst out laughing, then leaned over and kissed Orville on the cheek. "That's for being the bravest mouse I've ever known. Come on, let's go find Proto. He said he'd meet us in the dining room for breakfast. Serus should be there, too. He said he'd take us to Castle Caligari."

When Sophia and Orville entered the dining hall there was no sign of Proto or Serus. Orville peeked through the round window into the kitchen. "Sophia, you have to see this!"

Sophia stepped over to the door and peered through the foggy glass. Proto was standing in front of a mammoth cast iron stove wearing a tall chef's hat, pouring flapcake batter onto a hot griddle. Plautilla stood next to him, dropping purple berries into the sizzling batter. She laughed and slapped him on the back. "Who knew Rabbitons could be so funny??"

Sophia grinned. " Proto makes friends faster than

anyone I know."

After a delicious breakfast of crowberry flapcakes and honey, Sophia announced it was time to leave. Plautilla gave warm hugs to the three adventurers. "You be careful now, don't go traipsing around that castle looking for trouble. Most of those gruesome stories about Mendacium got cooked up here in this kitchen, but he's not one to tangle with. He's got the dark powers and he's not afraid to use them."

"Thanks, Plautilla, we'll be careful. We've had some experience with things like this. We'll be fine."

Orville nodded in agreement, but thought, "We've had experience battling evil dark wizards?"

Serus tromped into the dining room, rapping his heavy walking stick on the floor. "Let's go, daylight's burning." He turned and strode out the door. With a quick wave to Plautilla the three adventurers set off after him.

Serus marched along the winding dirt road leading to Castle Caligari. "You'll see the castle clear as day once we top that next hill. Didn't want to say this in front of Plautilla, but you need to hear it. There's something wrong about Castle Caligari, so be careful. I'll go as far as the gatehouse, but that's the end of it for me. You're on your own if you go into the castle."

"What do you mean there's something wrong about the castle?"

"It's off. Not right. Makes you feel crazy. Can't describe it. One thing, the trees near the castle aren't dead, but they aren't alive either. It's always winter for them, they have no leaves but they don't wither and die, even in summer. There's other things, but there's no words for it, the way you feel when you're inside the castle. Master Rabidus always talked about it."

"Has anyone besides Master Rabidus gone into the castle?"

"Just told you, the castle is wrong, it's a place to stay away from. I shouldn't have brought you here, Plautilla begged me not to. She likes you all, especially fond of Proto."

Sophia was the first to crest the hill. "I see it!" Serus had been right. Even at this distance she could sense an ominous force emanating from the towering black edifice. When Orville approached, she whispered, "It's just like your dream, the castle has a lake and a dock next to it. It even has the same boat tied to the dock."

Orville shivered. "How is it possible I dreamed about this place when we were on Varmoran? How could I know it existed? How could I know about Mendacium?"

"Master Marloh says dreams don't all come from the same place. Most come from day to day life, things that worry you, like being late for work or forgetting to study for a big test."

"I have one dream where I'm walking around Muridaan Falls in my underwear."

"Yes, dreams like that. He said there are other dreams, important ones, that come from a deeper place, the part of you that exists outside of space and time."

"But how could I know about the castle?"

"I just told you, those dreams come from your inner self, and your inner self exists outside of space and time. It's not constrained by time and space the way our physical bodies are. It can visit any time or any place it wants to, then it sends you a dream. A dream is like getting a postcard from your inner self."

214

"Why did it choose to send me that particular dream?"

Sophia shook her head. "No one knows the answer to that question. What I do know is you should pay careful attention to the dreams that are sent to you by your inner self."

Orville gazed at the monolithic stone fortress, a sudden truth rolling through him. "I know it now. We have to go inside the castle. That's where we'll find what we're looking for, where we'll discover what's destroying the Void."

A thought cloud flashed out from Serus. "Less talk, more walk."

Sophia laughed. "You sound a lot like a friend of ours named Mirus Mouse. I think you'd like him."

Two hours later Orville and Sophia stood before Castle Caligari's massive gatehouse. "Creekers, the stone is really black, scarier looking than it was in my dream." Orville ran his paw over one of the huge stone slabs used to build the castle's impregnable outer wall. "Serus, do you know who built Castle Caligari?"

"They say the ancients built castles like this to protect themselves from marauding bandits and warring tribes. The world was not always as peaceful as it is now."

"What about Mendacium? Does anyone know where he came from?"

"Impossible to say. He's been a mystery for as long as anyone can remember."

"How do we get in?"

"We raise the gate. This is where we leave our offerings. No one has entered the main castle since Master Rabidus wandered in."

"One last question, do you happen to know exactly where Master Rabidus saw Mendacium?"

"He says he wandered down two sets of stairs below the main castle floor, down into the dungeons. Says it was as dark as night when Mendacium appeared."

"Okay, thanks." Orville gave a weak smile. It was the same place he had found Mendacium in his dreams.

Serus strode across the broad wooden drawbridge to a massive gate constructed of stout timbers and black iron strapping. He wrapped both arms around a heavy iron lever, pushing down with all his might until it finally gave way. With a great grinding and shaking the immense gate rumbled open.

"Hard to tell you this, but if your friend went into the castle he is lost to our world. You will not find him."

Sophia nodded. "Thank you for being so honest with us. You are probably right, but we have to try. We truly appreciate the kindness you have shown us."

"I've done my best to warn you, can't do any more. Our prayers follow you on your journey." Without another word Serus turned and headed back down the dirt road toward Village 113. The three adventurers were alone, standing before the open gate of Castle Caligari.

"Serus was right about the trees near the castle. Every tree is bare, like it's winter. How could that be?"

"We should go." Sophia stepped through the arched stone entryway into the gatehouse.

Orville gazed around the structure's interior. "I can't imagine how long it took to build this, how hard it must have been without modern technology. It seems a little sad the rabbits have forgotten their Thaumatarian ancestors who built fleets of interstellar ships."

216

"They seem happy enough. They live in a peaceful village and have plenty of food and everyone seems to get along. What more could anyone ask for?"

Orville pointed to the far wall. "They must leave their offerings on those two big tables." He stepped over to one of the heavy wooden tables, running his paw across the ancient timbers. "They're worn smooth, must be really old. Whoa, look what I found wedged between the boards!" He pulled out a shiny gold coin for the others to see. "My lucky day! This is worth about fifty silvers!"

"So now you like Castle Caligari?"

Orville rolled his eyes and dropped the coin into his pocket. He stopped, pointing to a symbol carved into the table.

"A coiled serpent! Haukesworth Mouse found the castle. The serpent is pointing through that archway."

Proto stepped over to the stone doorway leading into the castle. "While you two have been snoozing away at night, lost in the world of dreams, I have been reading a number of highly informative volumes expounding on the surprisingly practical purposes lying beneath the design of ancient castles. As you might surmise, castles all served a similar purpose, something reflected in their construction. They were built to keep the inhabitants safe from external threats such as invading armies or marauding bandits. They possess one main entrance, the gatehouse. The gatehouse leads to the outer wall, the castle's first line of defense. Within the outer wall of the castle lies a second wall called the inner ward. Within the inner ward is where we find the castle keep, and within the keep are the stairs which take us down to the dungeons."

Proto rubbed his hands together. "I will lead the way since I am indestructible. I do hope we don't encounter any dark and forbidding creatures possessing vile and unnatural powers, monstrous beasts ripped from the very fabric of ghastly nightmares, abominations existing only within the shadowy and malevolent realms of Mendacium the Dark Evil Wizard."

"Proto! Seriously, why do you have to talk like that?? I'm already terrified, and that's making it a lot worse."

"Oh dear, was that too dramatic? I was trying add a little excitement to our adventure, make it seem a little more dangerous. The only remotely frightening creature we've encountered so far was that big clunky crab on the Isle of the Serpent. I suppose the creatures swimming in the great aquarium were somewhat frightening, especially the giant marine centipede."

"Have you forgotten the shiny blue creatures with four arms? The creepy things in the river biting your legs? And the Forest of Thorns? This adventure has plenty of danger, I don't think you need to make it–" Orville stopped.

"What is it? What's wrong?"

"Does anyone else feel kind of weird?"

"What do you mean, kind of weird?"

"Something's not right, but I don't know how to describe it."

"You're just worried about Proto's dark and forbidding creatures. We'll be fine, let's go."

Proto stepped into the outer ward of the castle, a wide grassy corridor separating the walls of the inner and outer wards.

"Whoa, that outer wall must be fifty feet tall, and it

has the big walkway along the top. I bet the warriors up there could make short work of you with their arrows."

"Not if you had your sphere of defense up." Sophia blinked up a powerful sphere of defense.

"Oops, good idea." An energy field popped up around Orville.

Proto turned, striding along the outer ward. "The entrance to the inner ward is at the opposite end of the outer ward, and that's where we'll find the keep. The keep is the huge stone tower located inside the inner ward."

"What do we do if we see Mendacium?"

Sophia stopped, turning to Orville. "Everything has been leading us to this castle. Your dreams, the hat you found, your capricious shadows, Madam Molly, Haukesworth Mouse's journal, the coiled snake symbols, all these things have led us here. This is where the universe wants us to be, this is where we are supposed to be. You said yourself that this is where we will find what is causing the Void to disappear. It's why we're here. If Mendacium is real and if he is behind all this, then we will face him. We will face the fires of life head on, and we will face them together. The fate of a thousand worlds depends on us. We have no choice. The universe has chosen us to fight this battle."

Orville looked at Sophia, then at Proto. "You're right. I was just worried that he's–" A light blinked on in Orville's eyes. "I know what's so weird about this place! I just figured it out. How long have we been here?"

Sophia looked puzzled. "What do you mean?"

"Tell me how long we've been inside Castle Caligari."

Sophia gave a snort. "That's silly, we've been here for... um... since..." Her eyes seemed to lose focus. "A few days maybe? It could be a week, I guess."

"Or it could be a hundred years, or a thousand years. There's something wrong with time in here. That's what Serus was trying to tell us." Orville took out his pocket watch and held it up in front of Sophia. "Watch the second hand and count how many times it goes around."

Sophia kept her eyes on the ticking silver hand as it marched around the dial. She blinked several times. Finally she turned away. "I can't do it. As soon as I start watching it I forget when I started watching. I forget how many times it's gone around. It could be once, it could be a thousand times. You're right, there's something wrong with time here. It's not slow, it's not fast, it just doesn't exist. There is no time inside Castle Caligari."

Orville nodded. "It's like being in a dream, with no past and no future, there's only right now."

"I can see why Serus said the castle wasn't right. It's a very peculiar feeling. I'm not sure I like it."

The adventurers pressed on, making their way along the outer ward. "Look at those wooden walkways running along the wall. They must have shot arrows through those vertical slots. Hard to believe that's all they had, no heavy beam particle disruptors."

"I daresay if they had disruptor beams they wouldn't have needed a castle." Proto turned left at the end of the outer ward. "That's the entrance to the inner ward, those two doors open up to the keep."

Orville gazed up at the ominous black tower. "Creekers, that's scary looking. Do you think

Mendacium lives up there? I wonder how they lifted the giant stone blocks that high?"

Proto replied, "I believe they used a complex system of ropes and pulleys to raise the great stone slabs, quite a remarkable feat, considering the primitive tools they had. Shall we go in?" He grabbed one of the massive iron rings bolted to the huge wooden doors. Much to his surprise, when he pulled on the ring the doors did not budge. "Odd. They must be locked from the inside."

"Who would have done that?"

Sophia gave Orville a sideways glance. "I think you know the answer to that question. What we really need to know is how to get in."

"What about the vertical slots on the tower used by the archers? Maybe we could climb in through one of those."

"I have a better idea, let's make our own doorway." Sophia stepped back a few feet and a blinding purple light shot out from her paws, blasting into the massive wooden doors. The heavy timbers glowed brightly for a moment, the glow quickly fading.

Sophia frowned. "That should have burned a big hole right through the doors. Something absorbed the energy. Proto, can you scan the doors for defense fields?"

A pale green light panned across the entryway. "You are quite correct, there is a powerful defensive energy shield covering the doors, protecting them from damage."

"Let me think for a minute." Sophia gazed up at the rectangular archer slots. "They're too narrow for us to fit through." Orville watched as Sophia paced back and forth in front of the doors, her mind racing. She stopped, a curious smile on her face. "I can't fit through an arrow slot, but a glowbird could."

"A glowbird? How does that help us? What are you talking about? Are you feeling all right?"

"Formshifting, that's what I'm talking about."

Orville's eyes bugged out. "Formshifting? That's really dangerous, Sophia. Have you ever done it? It doesn't sound like a very good idea."

"Master Marloh has been instructing me for over six months."

"You never told me about that. Why didn't you say something?"

"I didn't want you to worry. You know how you get."

"I still wish you would have told me. You really know how to do it?"

"I've formshifted into a glowbird at least fifty times. Master Marloh said I was ready to use it in the field if I needed to."

"How does it work exactly?"

"It's simple enough. When I blink somewhere, I turn my physical body into a thought cloud, travel for no more than two seconds, then use my inner self to convert the thought cloud back into my physical form. Formshifting is the same process, but I don't travel anywhere, and instead of converting back to my mouse body, I convert myself into the physical form of a glowbird."

"That's kind of weird. You can still think okay, even with... a bird brain?" Orville tried to stifle his laugh.

Sophia ignored his joke. "Of course I can, I'm not using the bird's physical brain to think, I'm using my inner self. I'm going to do it. It's our only way in."

Sophia stood silently, closing her eyes, then vanished in a flash of blue light. A split second later a glowbird blinked into existence at Orville's feet.

"Creekers! Sophia? Is that you? You're really a bird?"

The glowbird gave a loud squawk. A green thought cloud floated out of its feathers up to Orville. "It's me, I'm fine. Master Marloh said he would teach you how to formshift, if you want. I'm going to go through an arrow slot and unlock the doors from the inside. I'll pound on the doors when I'm done and Proto can pull them open."

With a flurry of feathers Sophia shot up into the air. Learning to fly had been far easier than she had originally thought it would be. When she took the form of a glowbird, flying was instinctive, as though she had always known how to do it. She let out a loud squawk. "This is the most fun ever!"

Orville watched as Sophia swooped and soared around the black tower. She shot straight up almost two hundred feet then blasted down, a shimmering blur, swooping past Orville with a loud screech. He jumped backwards. "Be careful, please!"

Sophia did a snap barrel roll, circled around the tower and flashed up to one of the rectangular slots. She landed on the stone ledge and peered into the tower. A thought cloud floated down to Orville.

"I see a circular stairway. I'm going in. Don't forget, have Proto open the doors when I pound on them." Sophia disappeared into the dark tower.

Chapter 31

The Dark Wizard

Sophia converted back to her mouse form once she was in the tower. She found herself standing on a narrow spiral stairway worn smooth from countless centuries of use, illuminated by a narrow shaft of light coming in through the arrow slot.

"Let's see what's down there." She sent out a bright orb of light, then cautiously descended the stairs, alert for any sudden sounds or movement. There was neither, only a heavy stillness and the musty smell of ages gone by.

She padded silently down the stone steps, finally reaching ground level, a circular room with the same diameter as the tower. The floor was covered with an elaborate mosaic created from innumerable brightly colored tiles.

"It's beautiful, a Thaumatarian rabbit wearing silver armor battling a big blue lizard. The lizard could be a mythological creature, or maybe even one they brought with them from Thaumatar. That would make Proto happy."

It was readily apparent why the doors had refused to open. A massive wooden beam ran across them, held in place by four stout iron brackets.

Sophia tried to lift the beam out of the brackets. "Too heavy. A little shaping should fix that." She backed away from the doors and extended both paws. A brilliant red light shot out, cutting the beam in half. "That should do it." A heavy stone blinked into her paw she and pounded on the doors.

The iron hinges squealed as the massive doors opened, Proto and Orville stepping into the keep.

Orville recognized the room instantly. "This is where I entered the castle in my dream! It had the same design on the floor, that rabbit fighting a big lizard. We took that staircase down to the dungeons."

"Are you ready for this? Ready to meet your dark wizard from ages long lost?"

A powerful sphere of defense blinked up around Orville. "Ready."

Proto headed down the long spiral stone staircase.

Sophia flicked her paw and a sphere of light flashed out. Within seconds the orb dimmed to the brightness of a single candle.

Orville whispered, "That's what happened in my dream. My light orbs dimmed down to almost nothing. It was really hard to see."

Proto flipped on his ear lights. "This should help. An unknown force is dimming your light orbs, but perhaps only shaped energy fields are affected."

"That's better, we can see the stairs."

The adventurers continued their descent, Orville gingerly feeling for the edge of each step, his eyes searching the darkness ahead. The light from Proto's ears dimmed, just as their light orbs had.

"What happened to your ear lights?"

"I am uncertain. The amount of light energy being emitted from my ears has not diminished, but it is being absorbed by an unknown force. This is reminiscent of the sticky green ball creatures on Periculum who surrounded themselves with perpetual darkness."

Orville knew dark magic when he saw it, but kept this thought to himself. "Okay, I'm at the bottom of the stairs, ground level. In my dream we turned left." Orville held out both paws and a dozen blazing white orbs shot out across the vast room. The lights dimmed, but not before Sophia had gotten a glimpse of their surroundings.

"I saw the stairs. You were right, we turn left and go straight for about fifty feet."

Proto's ear lights were now casting a barely visible glow around the party of adventurers. Step by step they crept across the uneven rocky floor.

Sophia touched Orville's shoulder, whispering, "The stairs are straight ahead."

"Do you hear it?"

"Hear what?"

"That dull pounding sound. It was a lot louder in my dream, like a giant heart beating."

"I hear it, but we're not supposed to go toward the sound, we go down the stairs. That's where we'll find Mendacium."

"I know." Orville concentrated deeply, letting go of his fear, becoming an objective observer.

"Let's go." Sophia took the lead. Proto's ear lights had gone dark, forcing Orville to run his paw along the rough castle wall so he wouldn't lose his balance.

Sophia whispered, "Orville, take my paw so we don't get separated." Orville gripped Sophia's paw, then reached back for Proto's hand.

Proto stopped short. "Hold on, I may have a solution for this peculiar darkness. Something is absorbing the light energy, but perhaps I can see using light outside the visible spectrum of electromagnetic radiation."

"What does that mean?"

"Your eyes use only a small portion of the electromagnetic spectrum to see, the segment we call visible light. I will adjust my optical input system to sense infrared radiation, which lies outside the range of visible light. What I will be seeing is the heat energy emitted from surrounding objects. If something is warm, such as you and Sophia, I will see glowing white forms. The warmer the object is, the brighter the image appears. Ah, it's working nicely, I can see the steps quite clearly now, since they are cooler than the air which surrounds them. Three more steps and we're there. I see a set of enormous doors."

"Is there a gold medallion above them?"

"I see a round object, but I am unable to make out any details."

The adventurers pressed on, creeping silently across the room.

Orville whispered, "There's a purple glow coming from between the doors, just like in my dream."

"Oh, dear." Proto stopped in his tracks.

Orville had a dreadful sinking feeling in his stomach. He could hear the doors groaning open. "What is it? What do you see?"

"The good news is my thermal vision is working exceptionally well, far better than I had anticipated."

Orville gulped. "What's the bad news?"

"The bad news is we are not alone. There is a

glowing white form about thirty feet in front of us. It's rather tall, I'm afraid."

Orville's voice was barely audible. "Mendacium?"

"It's quite possible."

"Sophia, what should we do?" Orville's breathing was fast and shallow.

"We face him head on. We are Metaphysical Adventurers, we are powerful shapers, and we are smart."

"Okay, let's go."

Sophia grabbed Orville's arm. "Wait, think about it, why is Mendacium keeping the room so dark?"

"Because he's a creepy dark wizard who wants to kill us?"

"Think, Orville. He's keeping it dark because he wants to scare us. Why would he want to do that?"

"So we'll run away screaming like little mouselings?"

"And why would he want us to run away?"

Something clicked in Orville's mind. "Because he's not as powerful as we think he is. If he was, he wouldn't need to frighten us, he would just destroy us."

"Bingo. Either he can't destroy us or he doesn't want to. I think we should find out exactly why Mendacium the Dark Wizard is afraid to show his face." Sophia strode forward across the ancient stone floor.

Orville gave a low gasp. "Look! Just like my dream, a purple glow surrounding a black silhouette."

"Whatever Mendacium is, he is producing a great deal of infrared radiation, especially his upper half. I am seeing his form quite clearly with my thermal vision."

"Did you hear that, Orville? Mendacium is not some

ethereal dark wizard, he has a warm body just like we do."

"Giant carnivorous centipedes have warm bodies, but that doesn't mean I want to stand next to one."

"The light around him is getting brighter." The three adventurers watched in silence as Mendacium's glowing aura slowly revealed the form within it.

"It's him, it's Mendacium."

Sophia's eyes locked onto the tall gaunt creature. It was indeed Mendacium, twelve feet tall, draped in a flowing purple robe, his face hidden deep within the shadows of a large floppy hood. His eyes glowed with a fearsome burning yellow light.

Orville could scarcely breathe.

A gnarled wooden staff topped with a crackling fiery orb appeared in Mendacium's hand. Three times he raised the staff and three times he brought it down with a thundering crash, the impact shaking the castle walls.

A hissing whisper slithered through the darkness toward them. "You stand on the border of nothingness, the land of the dead, the world of the lost. Leave now, while you are able."

"Sophia, I think we should– wait, that doesn't make sense." Orville frowned, taking a step forward. "You said this is the land of the dead?"

There was no reply from Mendacium.

"Just to be clear, you're saying that you're dead, and this is the land of the dead?"

The voice shook with rage. "You try my patience, mouse! Leave now or you shall join me forever in eternal darkness!" A brilliant blast of red light shot out from Mendacium's staff, exploding a few feet away from Orville.

"Just a few more questions then I promise we'll leave you alone. Are you Mendacium the Dark Wizard?"

"YOU DARE SPEAK MY NAME???" Orville's bones rattled from the thundering blast of Mendacium's voice, but he was sensing something quite curious about Mendacium. "No need to yell, we're not deaf, you know."

"SUCH INSOLENCE!! MY ARMY OF SPECTRAL DEMONS SHALL DESTROY YOU!!!"

"Orville, thought cloud coming our way!"

A large blood red thought cloud flashed across the room, surrounding Orville and Sophia. Orville screeched when he saw the horde of pale slithering serpents undulating across the floor toward them, their narrow red eyes glowing brightly, orange flames sprouting from their long yellow fangs.

"They're not real, they're from his thought cloud."

Orville flicked his wrist and Mendacium's thought cloud shot back across the room. The horde of approaching serpents vanished. "He's starting to make me mad."

Orville marched forward toward the towering purple figure. "Why are you trying to scare us? Do you really think I don't know what a thought cloud is? Did you think I'd be afraid of your silly slithering serpents?"

Mendacium let out a terrible roar of maniacal rage, his yellow eyes in flames. A gigantic purple beam of light shot out from his staff, streaking toward Orville. When the blast of light reached him, however, it was absorbed by Orville's sphere of defense.

Mendacium vanished in a blink of light. The room was filled with a terrible silence.

"Where did he go?"

Proto scanned the room using his thermal vision. "I'm afraid he is presently standing directly behind us." Orville and Sophia whirled around.

An unexpected voice came out of the darkness. "You are shapers?"

"What?"

"A simple enough question, I asked if you were both shapers?"

"Yes?"

Sophia added, "We're not only shapers, we're Metaphysical Adventurers."

The room was flooded with daylight. Orville covered his eyes, squinting up at the twelve foot tall creature, its face still hidden in the dark folds of a great purple hood.

"You are Metaphysical Adventurers?"

"Yes, we're here on a mission."

"I suppose I should not be surprised. Who else would dare enter such a frightening place as this?"

Sophia smiled pleasantly. "You're exceptionally tall, aren't you? It must be hard to find clothes that fit properly."

"One must keep up appearances." Mendacium's heavy purple robe slid off, falling to the floor in a heap.

"Creekers!"

Orville was gazing up at a rather handsome mouse sporting a blue striped vest and dark green pants, a handsome mouse who was perched atop a pair of tall stilts. The mouse hopped down, the stilts clattering to the floor.

Sophia smiled pleasantly. "Stilts? Really?"

"If you could show me your rings? Just to verify

your claim?"

Sophia and Orville held out their paws, showing Mendacium their Metaphysical Adventurer rings.

"Righto, they look authentic. So, what brings you to Castle Caligari?"

Orville was trying to process this unexpected turn of events. "Who *are* you?"

"I'm Mendacium the Dark Wizard, I thought I had made that abundantly clear. Now, if you would please answer my question. Why are you here in the land of the dead?"

Orville gave a start. "Wait, we really are in the land of the dead?"

"In a way. Not precisely the land of the living, and not precisely the land of the dead."

Sophia said, "It's the land of the dead because time does not exist here."

"I'm impressed, truly I am. Most visitors don't pick up on that. They get disoriented and confused and can't run away fast enough."

Orville was filled with a burning curiosity. "We know you're not a twelve foot tall dark wizard, so who are you? The villagers said they bring you offerings and in return you prevent all plague and pestilence."

Mendacium shrugged. "Give me a hundred gold coins and I'll keep the Nirriimian Purple Skrilly Beasts from nibbling at your toes while you sleep."

Proto frowned. "I've never heard of such a creature."

"My point exactly. There are no Purple Skrilly Beasts, and likewise there is no plague or pestilence on Tectar. The Thaumatarians were quite meticulous in their colonization practices."

"You know about the Thaumatarians?"

232

"Of course I do. Mendacium the Dark Wizard knows all." He waved one arm with a great flourish.

Sophia rolled her eyes. "It looks to me like you're nothing more than a common crook, tricking villagers out of their gold and food and books. I am curious about the books, however. Why books?"

"Follow me, if you would." Mendacium strolled across the vast hall to a set of elaborately engraved bronze doors. He waved his arm and the doors swung open.

Orville stepped cautiously into the room. "Whoa!" The breadth of Mendacium's library was staggering. Two wide wooden walkways circled the room, connected by a series of sliding ladders. Bookshelves lined every inch of the walls. Orville could not begin to guess how many books were in Mendacium's library.

"As of yesterday there were seven hundred twenty-nine thousand and seventeen volumes, and I have read them all."

Sophia looked at Mendacium in disbelief. "That's not possible. No one could read that many books." She stopped. "There is no time here. You just read."

"I just read."

Orville walked over to one of the shelves, studying the myriad of titles. "What language is this? I've never seen characters like this. Are they hieroglyphs? The book next to it is in a different language."

"The seven hundred thousand books you see here are written in over three thousand separate ancient archaic languages."

Orville gave a snort. "Now I know you didn't read them. No mouse alive could understand that many languages."

Mendacium focused his gaze on Orville. It was the same look the Thirteenth Monk used to give him. It felt like a gentle breeze was rustling through his thoughts and memories.

"Let me ask you this, Orville Wellington Mouse. Have you ever heard the expression, 'putting your thoughts to paper'?"

"Of course I have, it means you write your thoughts down on paper. My teachers used to say that all the time."

"So the words you write down are…"

"They're my thoughts. I write them down. On paper."

"So your thoughts are on the paper?"

Orville was beginning to think Mendacium was not quite as clever as he first appeared to be. Orville smiled politely. "I'm afraid I don't quite understand the point you're trying to make."

"When you are reading the words in a book, you are essentially hearing the thoughts of the writer in your mind, wouldn't you agree?"

"I think we've already made that very clear." Orville glanced over at Sophia. Her eyes had narrowed slightly.

"Indeed you have. Now, suppose when those thoughts were put to paper, the thoughts really were 'put to paper'. Suppose somehow those thoughts were embedded in the written words, and suppose there was a very clever mouse who could see through the words to the pure formless ideas held within them? Wouldn't this clever mouse be able to know the thoughts of the writer without having to interpret the words, without having to understand the language used to put them to paper? A mouse who could do that would certainly be able to read seven hundred thousand books in a world without time."

"You can do that? I've never heard of anything like that, and I know a lot about shaping. You're a shaper, right?"

Mendacium did not reply, his gaze moving from Orville to Sophia and back to Orville. A smile flickered across his face. "I see you found my hat."

Orville glared at Mendacium. "Your hat? I found it, and besides it's not yours, it belongs to... to... Haukesworth Mouse." Orville's eyes grew very wide.

Mendacium took a deep bow. "A pleasure to make your acquaintance. Although I have temporarily adopted the pseudonym of Mendacium the Dark Wizard, a notable character from one of my favorite old books, I am none other than Haukesworth Mouse, Metaphysical Adventurer. I welcome you to the land of the dead."

Chapter 32

Mendacium's Tale

Orville and Sophia were stunned by Mendacium's revelation. It strained credulity, and yet after some thought it became quite plausible. Because Haukesworth had spent the last three hundred years in a world without time, he had not aged a day since his arrival. A hundred questions filled Sophia's head. Orville, however, had only one question.

"I guess you'll be wanting your hat back? It got kind of mashed when we were riding a big bowl down a giant aqueduct. It's not an aqua duck, by the way, in case that's what you were thinking. Water splashed all over your hat when we went around this really sharp turn and I–"

"The hat is yours. It suits you, and I no longer have a need for it."

Orville grinned. "Really? Thanks, it's the nicest hat I've ever owned. I promise I'll take better care of it. Um… should we call you Haukesworth or Mendacium?"

"Haukesworth will do nicely. Using Mendacium was simply a tool which provided me some much needed solitude. The villagers stayed out of the castle because they were terrified of Mendacium the Dark Wizard, and they had no desire to cause me harm because of our agreement regarding plague and pestilence. Twice a week they left their offerings in the gatehouse. That's where this library came from, and all the gold."

Orville's eyebrows jumped up. "Gold?"

Haukesworth shrugged. "It seemed like a good idea when I arrived, but I have come to realize how superficial my thinking was back then. I have a room filled with gold coins, but I seldom even open the door. You can't eat gold, you can't read gold, you can't sleep on a pile of gold, you can't talk to gold, and gold doesn't comfort you when you are lonely."

"You could buy stuff with it. You know, stuff you wanted."

"I have everything I need."

Sophia asked, "Why were you looking for solitude?"

Haukesworth smiled. "A simple question, but one deserving of a rather complex answer. To be honest, I have no idea how long I have been here. I have read over seven hundred thousand books, but I could not tell you if that took ten minutes or ten thousand years. Within these walls it is impossible to gauge the passage of time in the outside world."

"Over three hundred years have passed since you left Muridaan Falls. It was your journal that led us here, through the gateway on the Isle of the Serpent."

"Three hundred years…"

Sophia felt a deep sadness coming from Haukesworth. "All your friends, all the Metaphysical Adventurers you once knew, they're all…"

"Gone, all of them. It is a great and terrible sacrifice I have made, trading love for knowledge. I would not do it again, but it is done and cannot be undone."

"I don't understand. Trading love for knowledge?"

Haukesworth motioned them toward a cozy sitting area in the corner of his grand library. He slid into a soft padded sofa with a sigh. "Sit, I will tell you my story, then you will tell me what has brought you to this distant castle, though I suspect I already know the reason. Perhaps the story of my encounter with the Others will answer some of your questions."

Orville's anxiety spiked sharply. "The Others? Who are the Others? They live here in the castle?"

Haukesworth leaned back, his eyes half closed.

"When I was a young mouse, life was far simpler, my purpose in this world abundantly clear. I was a powerful shaper, an esteemed member of the Metaphysical Adventurers, a mouse destined to save the world time and time again, a mouse ordained to a life of great adventure. You have read my journal, so you know in these endeavors I was successful, saving this dear world of ours on numerous occasions, all the while being fortunate enough not to lose my life.

"On my eighth year as a Metaphysical Adventurer, two seemingly unrelated events occurred within a few weeks of each other.

"The first event was a question put to me by my inner self. As the great questions of life usually are, it was deceptively simple, and yet it proved to be a query which haunted my thoughts for years to come. *'When you save the world, what is it you are saving?'*

"A simple enough question, which at first blush appeared to have a simple answer. I was saving the world. What else would I be saving? Months passed, but the question perpetually nagged at me. Perhaps

238

there was more to it, the question went deeper than I had originally thought. Perhaps it was asking me to define more clearly the true nature of the world I was saving.

"The second event to occur was my discovery of a tattered journal in a subterranean cavern on a planet called Periculum."

Orville let out a yelp. "We've been to Periculum! They have those creepy giant centipedes there. So scary!"

Haukesworth made no reply, his thoughts a lifetime away. "I found myself in an eerie cavern illuminated solely by a deadly form of bioluminescent moss, face to face with a colony of angry spiral headed Montrovian poker worms. With my life in dire jeopardy, a curious thought came to me. If I died before discovering the answer to my question, would my life have been for naught, my daring adventures held meaningless?

"That was the day I found Parzifal Mouse's journal, and within its pages his reference to a mysterious 'land of the dead', a world without time, a world existing within a dark castle on a lost planet called Tectar. I repeated the phrase over and over, 'a world without time'. I could think of nothing else. In such a place I would find the solitude I so longed for. In such a place I could contemplate my question for as long as I wished. When I had found the answer, I would pack up my belongings and leave the world of the dead behind, returning to the world of the living.

"The path to Tectar was revealed to me in Parzifal's journal, a gateway to be found on the Isle of the Serpent. Twice I journeyed to Tectar and twice I returned, vanquished by its unfathomable mystery. A few of its secrets were revealed to me, one of them being its connection to the ancient Thaumatarians. Still, I had failed to locate the dark castle and the timeless world within it.

"I would make one last attempt. As I stepped through the Tectarian gateway for the third and final time, I vowed I would not return to Earth without the castle's location. Seven grueling months later I was having a quiet meal in a small village tavern when I chanced to overhear a pair of traveling merchants discussing a castle they had passed on their journey to the inn. I remember it as if it were yesterday. They were brothers, their last name being Skeezle. An odd name, but they proved to be congenial and informative, taking the time to draw a map marking the castle's location. Four days later I stood before the gates of Castle Caligari.

"Were you scared?"

"I was not. My inner voice assured me this was where I needed to be. This was where I would find the answer I was seeking. What it failed to mention was this was also the place where I would meet the Others."

Orville glanced nervously at Sophia, then back to Haukesworth. "Um, these Others, the ones you met, they live here in the castle? Would you say they're scary?"

"I moved into the castle the day I arrived. It was dark, gloomy, cold, ominous, and generally uninviting, but it was now my home. As fate would have it, a few of the local villagers spotted me entering the gatehouse and came to investigate. When I heard them moving about, I knew they would find me if I didn't act quickly, and I craved solitude, not the company of others.

"Acting on impulse, I let out a terrible wailing moan followed by a bloodcurdling scream, then listened to the scrambling footsteps as the villagers fled the castle. It was then that I decided to adopt the persona of Mendacium the Dark Wizard. He was the most fearful character I could recall, plucked from a frightening book I had read as a mouseling. On several occasions I purposefully allowed the villagers to catch sight of me disguised as Mendacium, proof positive of my dark and dreadful presence within the castle. I delivered a letter to them during a magnificent display of my terrifying dark powers, a proposed contract for my services in the prevention of plague and pestilence. A few days later I received their reply. They agreed to my terms and would provide the items I had requested.

"I am uncertain where the villagers acquired all the books they delivered, but I would suppose they came from some dusty Thaumatarian library deep within the planet. In any event, twice a week they left dozens of volumes in the gatehouse. Many of the books I was unable to decipher, and those I set aside, hoping one day to understand the language in which they were written. I lost track of day and night in my dreamlike timeless world. I read, I ate, I slept, I thought, my awareness of the world around me steadily increasing. The more books I read, the more I thought, and the deeper those thoughts became. At times I was able to merge with my inner self, able to access information existing outside of space and time.

"I roamed the castle day and night, exploring every nook and cranny, coming to believe it no longer held any secrets for me. I was wrong, of course. I had not yet encountered the Others.

"There is a vast room on the first sub level of the castle which I called the Machine Room. You must have heard the great pounding engine on your way to the dungeons. The first time I dared enter the room I was completely baffled by what I saw. Pushing up through the stone floor was a silver machine of gargantuan proportions. The sound from the mechanical behemoth was deafening, and yet I could see no moving parts, could discern no purpose for this monolithic metallic creation. More perplexing and concerning than the machine was the fearsome swirling blackness behind it, terrifying to behold. I had not the slightest understanding of its nature or purpose.

"The answer was revealed to me in a volume chronicling the design and construction of Tectar, a dense and technical tome penned by one of the original Thaumatarian engineers. I learned the silver device I had seen in the Machine Room was one of the six massive Mark XVII Distortion Thrusters which propelled Tectar through dark space on its interstellar journey from Thaumatar. Some cataclysmic force had driven the engine up through the castle floor from the interior of the planet, and in the process had activated the machine. What this meant for the future of Castle Caligari I could not fathom, and consequently I made no attempt to interfere with it, fearful I might inadvertently cause the destruction of my timeless haven."

Orville leaned forward, his eyes wide. "When did you meet the Others?"

Haukesworth gave a curious smile. "You don't meet the Others, they meet you."

"But you saw them?"

"I did. Numerous times I entered the Machine Room during my stay in the castle, gazing upon this magnificent engine. The sound of its rhythmic pounding became a source of comfort to me, the steady heartbeat of the castle. In my mind the castle had become almost a living thing, an entity within which I existed. Perhaps I was going mad, perhaps not. In any event, when the heartbeat of the castle changed, so did my life.

"The rhythmic beating of the great machine diminished, becoming slower, quieter. I panicked, fearing for my personal safety and the safety of the castle, my refuge from the vagaries of time. Racing through the stone corridors to the Machine Room, I swung the doors open and was stunned by the sight which lay before me. The familiar stone chamber was gone, transformed into a vast sunlit pasture extending out for miles, rivers of soft green grass waving gently in a warm breeze, swaths of glorious wildflowers blooming in radiant golden sunlight.

"Whoa, where did the meadow come from?"

"I had no idea, and strangely enough, it did not matter. The meadow was the most profoundly beautiful vision I had ever encountered, filling me with a deep and infinite joy. I stepped into the pasture and sat on the soft grass, finding it to be more comforting than my own feather bed. I have no concept of how long I sat in the meadow – days, months, years. My thoughts came and went, my dreams came and went. My consciousness deepened, spurred on by the beauty and depth of that enchanting otherworldly meadow. I was close to finding my answer. I could feel it, almost touch it, taste it. That was the moment four distant white forms blinked into the meadow. I was looking at vaporous white clouds, yet the mere sight of them filled me with an inexplicable, unfathomable joy.

"I jumped to my feet and raced toward these shifting clouds of white. I ran until I could not, collapsing to the ground, realizing the glowing white phantasms were no closer to me than when I had started. I was brought to tears, I wanted to be near to these creatures. My inner voice spoke to me. *Sit. Listen. Do not chase after such things, for they will come to you in time.*"

"I obeyed my inner voice, sitting in the midst of a thousand glorious blossoms, their colors swirling and changing with my every thought. My eyes grew heavy. I may have slept, or may not, I could no longer distinguish between dreaming and wakefulness. When I opened my eyes, I was surrounded by the Others."

Chapter 33

The Others

Orville almost slid out of his seat. "What were they?"

Haukesworth paused, attempting to frame his answer. "It was not their appearance which stunned me, it was their presence, it was how I felt when I stood before them, feelings which defy all attempt at description, much like describing colors to a blind mouse. When I opened my eyes and saw them, I was immersed in an ocean of love, I was there, I was not there, I was part of the ocean, I was all of the ocean, I was seeing the Others, I was the Others, I was lost, I was found. To be in their presence is simply indescribable. You asked about their appearance. At times they were with form, at times without, at times they had wings, and yet they floated above the ground, their wings silent, motionless. Their faces were fluid, ever changing, one moment resembling mice, the next rabbits, then muroidians, then a hundred forms unfamiliar to me. They are not like us, they are ethereal, more thought than physical in nature, not confined to a single shape as we are. The power they have at their command is beyond comprehension."

"Why did they come here?"

"Their presence shall restore balance to the infinite chain of events which is our existence. They are here because of the great machine, they are here to see me, they are here to see you, to see Sophia, to see your friend Proto."

Orville stared in horror at Haukesworth. He didn't want to be one of the reasons the Others had appeared in Castle Caligari. "How do you know the Others want to see me? I just got here."

"They told me this moment, as you were asking the question."

"Why do they want to see us?"

"They did not tell me that."

"Why did they want to see you?"

"They were the spark which ignited my awareness, helping me find the answer to the question long ago posed by my inner voice. I sat in the meadow surrounded by the Others. When their wings brushed my shoulders I had the answer to my question. They did not give me the answer, but helped me realize what I had always known. I knew what I was saving when I saved the world."

"What was it? What were you saving?"

Orville recognized Haukesworth's expression. It was the same one Papa used to give him when Orville asked questions with impossibly difficult answers. What is time? How big is the universe?

"The answer lies beyond words, beyond thought."

"You understood it though?"

"I did. I was a fish swimming in the ocean who

suddenly realizes it is surrounded by something called water. The answer had always been in front of me, around me, and in me, but I had not seen it."

Orville gave Sophia a sideways glance. She looked as baffled as Orville.

Proto had been listening to their conversation with intense curiosity, trying to formulate the science which lay beneath the presence of the Others. "Do you think they arrived here from another dimension, a parallel world?"

"I suppose so. The meadow is unlike any world or dimension I have ever visited, and the Others are unlike any creatures I ever encountered during my years as a Metaphysical Adventurer."

"You're certain they wish to see me? It is curious that such highly evolved beings should take an interest in an ancient Rabbiton like me. I am simply a mechanical creation of the Elders, ultimately of little consequence."

Haukesworth shook his head. "I have no answer to your question, only the Others can tell you. You have heard my story, now it's time I hear yours, why you have undertaken your long and perilous journey to Castle Caligari."

"It all started when Orville saw your hat blow past him on a dirt road in Muridaan Falls. He rescued it from a tree and a few days later noticed its shadow wasn't behaving properly. After some research, a sundial experiment, and help from Madam Molly and her Book of Shadows, we discovered the shadow from your hat was being cast by Tectar's sun."

"I am not surprised to learn this. A lengthy portion of dirt road appeared some months ago in one of the dungeons, the landscape illuminated by an unseen sun. Uncertain if it existed in this world or another, I tossed my hat onto the phantom road, a test of its nature. Much to my surprise, a spirited wind caught my hat, carrying it out of sight and apparently into Orville's paws. I could only surmise the two worlds were overlapping. Is that why you are here, our two worlds are overlapping?"

"That's exactly why. Orville had a scary dream about Castle Caligari and Mendacium the Dark Wizard. Mendacium said *'the great darkness shall vanish, taking with it a thousand worlds'*. He also told Orville those left behind would face his wrath and hordes of spectral demons."

Haukesworth gave a puzzled smile. "I'm afraid I have no wrath for anyone to face, and no hordes of spectral demons at my command. As for the great darkness which will vanish, I am at a loss to explain the meaning of that phrase."

"We believe the 'great darkness' refers to the Void, the space between all worlds. If the Void vanishes, the worlds will overlap and destroy each other in the process."

Orville added, "Maybe I was seeing you in my dreams the same way the local villagers see you, as a scary dark wizard."

"An interesting thought. Sophia, do you know what is causing the Void to disappear? I assure you it is not me. I am a competent shaper, but such a feat as that lies well beyond my modest abilities."

"What about the Others? You said the power at their command was incomprehensible. Could they be responsible?"

Haukesworth shook his head. "When you meet them you will understand why that is not possible. Their thoughts and actions are motivated solely by love. For the Others to commit such a monstrous transgression as the destruction of worlds is not within the realm of possibility."

Orville wasn't sure what a transgression was, but he was pretty sure Haukesworth was saying the Others weren't responsible. He made a mental note to look up transgression in his dictionary when he got home. "If it's not you and it's not the Others, then who's doing it?"

Proto replied, "If the Others are as evolved as Haukesworth says they are, perhaps they can provide the answer to your question. It could be one of the reasons they are here. Sophia always says everything is exactly where it should be at every moment in time."

"That's a good thought, Proto. Haukesworth, can you take us to meet the Others? Is that possible?"

"More than possible, they are waiting for you in the meadow. They will speak with each of you separately."

Orville's eyebrows jumped up. "I have to go in alone?"

"Any fear you might be feeling will vanish the moment you step into the meadow."

Orville gave a weak smile. He was finding it very hard to believe that big floating ghosty creatures from another dimension would not be scary."

Chapter 34

The Road

The three adventurers trailed behind Haukesworth as he strode down the long stone corridor past the ancient dungeons.

Haukesworth stopped, pointing to the light spilling out from beneath one of the dungeon doors. "It must be daytime in Muridaan Falls." He twisted the iron latch and swung the door open, the brilliant sunlight blinding Orville for a moment. When his eyes had adjusted, he saw Haukesworth had been right, the dungeon's floor had been replaced by lengthy section of dirt road.

Haukesworth pointed up to a huge iron grate running along the ceiling. "Look up through the ventilation shaft, you can see the stars. It's nighttime on Tectar. The sunlight shining on this road is from Earth's sun."

"That's the road I take to work every day! I rescued your hat from a tree just around that bend."

"I stood here and tossed my hat onto the road, only to see it carried out of sight by an unseen wind."

A light of realization flashed in Orville's eyes. "If we stepped onto that road, we'd be back in Muridaan

Falls, like the hat! We'd be home again."

"You're right, we'd be home again, just in time to witness the destruction of our planet."

"That's a good point, we still have a lot to do." Orville swung the iron door shut. "At least we know it's here, in case we have to get home in a hurry."

They continued down the shadowy stone corridor, then up the enormous spiral staircase to the first sub level. Haukesworth stopped in front of an unremarkable dungeon door. He glanced over at Orville. "You might like this." When he swung the door open, Orville's jaw dropped. The dungeon was packed with stacks of small wooden crates, each one overflowing with gold coins, thousands of them spilling out onto the stone floor.

Orville was speechless.

Haukesworth shrugged. "The gold isn't doing any good here. If we are able to prevent the overlapping of worlds, you are free to take as much gold as you can carry. I have no need for it."

"Really? As much as I can carry?" Orville glanced at Sophia.

Sophia had hardly noticed the gold. "I can hear the big machine, the one that sounds like a heartbeat. We have to go."

A brisk walk down the stone corridor brought the adventurers to the heavy iron door of the Machine Room. Haukesworth's eyes were on Sophia. "The Others wish to see you first."

Orville took Sophia's arm. "Proto and I could go with you if you want. It might be dangerous."

"I'll be fine. I'm sensing a great force, but not a scary one. I'm ready."

Haukesworth pulled the door open enough for

Sophia to slip through.

Orville peeked through the open door. "Creekers!"

He sat on the floor with a sigh, leaning back against the wall, a frown on his face. He knew Sophia could take care of herself even in the most dire of circumstances, but he wished she didn't have to face the Others alone.

The first thing that struck Sophia was the immensity of the meadow, the second was the silence. She could feel the ground moving slightly from the massive Mark XVII Distortion Thruster, but she couldn't hear its pounding heartbeat. The scale of the machine was astonishing, the great silver engine pushing up through the floor several hundred feet above her, silhouetted against a brilliant blue sky. The original dungeon ceiling had become only a vague translucent shadow. She studied the wild swirling blackness behind the machine, but had no ready explanation for its presence. Possibly it was a huge thought cloud, or perhaps the machine was drawing power from the tenth dimension, the same technology used by the Elders to power Rabbitons and blinker ships.

One thing was certain, Haukesworth had been right about the meadow. No words could adequately describe it. It was stunning in its beauty, but it was also affecting Sophia on a far deeper level. "It feels like the dearest and oldest friend I have ever known, as though love has been transformed into a place, into a world."

Sophia was losing herself to the meadow, to a joy which was almost too much to bear. She sat on the soft grass, watching as a thousand delicate purple blossoms appeared around her. Violet was her favorite color, and the fragrance of the wildflowers was exquisite, calling up her fondest memories, bright sunlit days when she was a mouseling, when Mum and Papa were still with her. She could almost feel her mum holding her, telling her everything would be all right, telling her everything was as it should be.

The Others arrived the same way the sun rises every morning. Their appearance was not startling, their presence filling her with infinite hope. The moment was new, all things were possible. Neither was she startled when her mum and papa appeared. She had always known they were with her.

Sophia's mum helped her up and held her close. "I've missed your hugs. We see you often, but I have missed your hugs."

Tears were streaming down Sophia's face.

Her papa rubbed the top of her head. "We're glad you found Orville. We knew you would, you always do. He's a handsome young mouse and he loves you more than ever. I like his new adventurers hat, it's a lot nicer than the one I wore."

Sophia's mum laughed. "Stop, you loved that old hat. I can't count the times I offered to buy you a new one. You always said yours still had a lot of miles left in it."

Sophia wiped the tears from her eyes. "Are you real? Are you both real?"

"We are real. You are seeing us as you remember us, but we are real."

"I don't understand any of this. What is this place? Why am I seeing you? Why am I here?"

"The Others have given us this chance to be with you again. These moments are links in the infinite chain of events that is our universe."

Sophia didn't understand, but didn't question her mum's answer. It was enough to see them. "What is it like where you are?"

"Look around you. Our world is overlapping with the world of Tectar. You are in our world now, the world of the Others."

"You live in a giant meadow?"

Sophia's papa smiled. "It's not quite as simple as that. Look carefully and tell me what you see."

Sophia studied the horizon, seeing the world through the eyes of her inner self. A glimmering gossamer city appeared in the distance. She let out a low gasp. "It's beautiful, a city made of light."

"I told you she'd be able to see it."

Sophia's mum laughed. "Papa is always so proud of you."

Sophia's gaze moved from the sparkling city to the glowing forms of the Others, floating silently behind her parents. She could scarcely breathe, whispering, "What are you?"

"We are what you shall become."

"I don't understand. Will you let me visit Mum and Papa again? Are there spectral doors that open to your world? Orville and I have visited a lot of worlds, and if there's a doorway, I know we could–" Before she finished her sentence Sophia knew it would not be possible to visit her parents again. The universe held a greater depth and complexity than she could ever understand. A reassuring thought from the Others came to her. "There will come a time when you will see them again. Of this you may be certain."

A covered basket appeared in her mum's paw. "Let's have a picnic lunch like we used to. We can sit on that bench and visit for as long as you want."

Sophia looked behind her. A lovely white bench had appeared, sitting on the grassy banks of a sparkling blue river. The castle walls were gone now, the sky a deep and penetrating blue. Sophia listened closely. "The sound of the river is music, it's a song, a song of time passing."

Her papa grinned again. "Do you understand the song's meaning?"

"When I am in our world I am floating down the river of time, traveling as the river travels. In your world we stand on the banks of the river, no longer captive to the flow of time."

"That's it. In this world we can see the infinite chain of events, visit the past, the future, or the present."

"That's how you knew Orville and I would marry, that we would have two mouselings?"

"Yes."

"Do Orville and Proto and I stop the worlds from overlapping?"

Sophia's papa took her paw in his. "You already know my answer. Every mouse must face the fires of life without knowing the outcome. I saw you bring Draken Mouse to justice, prove he was responsible for my death. In doing that you changed the world in more ways than you can imagine, saved thousands of lives, each one of those lives going on to change the world in a thousand other ways."

Sophia's mum opened the picnic basket. "Time for lunch. I have some of those brimbleberry tarts you love so much, the ones Grandmum used to make." She held out a round tin filled with warm freshly baked pastries. "Let's start with dessert, then I want to hear all about

Orville. He's changed in so many ways since he last swam in the river of time."

Chapter 35

Three Questions

Orville gave a look of surprise when Sophia stepped out of the Machine Room. "They didn't want to see you?"

"What do you mean?"

"You just went in."

"What are you talking about? I was in there for hours and hours."

"It seemed like only a few seconds... but when I think about it, you could have been in there for a year. I don't like not having time, it's making me nummers in the head. I can't tell how long anything takes. What happened in there? Did you see the Others? What were they like?"

"I'll tell you all about it in a minute, right now they want to see Proto."

"Oh dear, I'm afraid this has me quite anxious. It's not frightening like the Anarkkian attack spiders once were, but it is worrisome. Did they seem nice? Were they pleasant? Did they happen to mention why they wish to see me? I didn't do anything wrong, did I?"

"There is nothing to worry about, I promise you."

"I hope I don't say anything which might be misconstrued as inappropriate. No jokes about deadly poisonous vegetables or crabs on the loose."

Sophia gave Proto a smile of confidence as he stepped into the brilliant sunlight.

When the door closed Orville turned to Sophia. "What were they like? Were they–" His question was interrupted by the creaking of the Machine Room door as it opened. Proto emerged, a dazed look on his face. He sank to his knees with a low moan.

Orville dashed over to him. "What happened? They didn't hurt you did they?"

Proto shook his head, trying to collect his thoughts. "No, they would never do that, but it was too much to process in such a short time. They showed me a tapestry woven from my actions in our world, each thread a choice I had made, each thread spanning across time, connected to all events, past and future. I saw the family of Elders I lived with when I was first created. I cannot explain it, but we stood on the edge of a river and I spoke with them. They cannot be alive and yet they stood in front of me, as real as you are now. They had not aged a day since I last set eyes on them. One of the bunnies told me I had inspired him to become a master scholar of deep physics. He said he was the one responsible for the scientific discoveries which led to the creation of interstellar doorways like the one on the Isle of the Serpent."

Orville's mind was racing. "Proto, think about it, if you hadn't inspired that young rabbit fourteen hundred years ago, we wouldn't be standing here on Tectar. Without his discoveries, the gateway on the Isle of the

Serpent would not exist. That's incredible. What else did you see?"

"They showed me thousands of events in my life which I had thought to be insignificant, but which had drastically altered the future, the present, and even the past. It defies all logic, but they showed me how an event in the present can change events in the past. My engineered intelligence was close to overloading, so they sent me back. I knew everything about our world, it was all so clear, but the moment I stepped back through the doorway the knowledge vanished. The loss was unbearable, I had known what the future holds for all of us. I knew whether or not we would prevent the worlds from merging, I knew the future, I knew the past. It's all gone now, I only remember talking to the young bunny responsible for the creation of the interstellar doorways."

Haukesworth tapped Orville on the shoulder. "I do hate to interrupt, but the Others wish to see you now."

Orville glanced anxiously at Sophia.

"You'll be fine."

Orville nodded to Haukesworth and the Machine Room door swung open for the third time.

The meadow was not what Orville had been expecting. He stood in silence, breathing in the fragrance of the glorious wildflowers, studying the great gleaming machine that sparkled above him in the warm rays of a golden sun. He tried to make sense of his feelings. "It's more than a lovely meadow, it's more real than my world, as though I have been living in an old faded photograph." He was becoming part of the glorious meadow when the Others appeared.

Their presence washed through Orville in great

pounding waves. He knew his intuitive mind was capable of sensing the true nature of other mice, whether they had dark intentions, whether they were honorable, whether they could hear their secret inner voice. The Others were beyond such description. He could not gauge their intentions, because they had no intentions. They were love and nothing more.

Remembering his lessons from the Thirteenth Monk, Orville brought his mind to sharp focus, doing his best to become objective and observant. "Why am I here?"

"You are Orville Wellington Mouse, Metaphysical Adventurer, that is why you are here. Who better to stop the worlds from overlapping than a brave and noble mouse such as yourself?"

"I'm not as brave as you think I am. I'm really scared of centipedes, and most anything with – sorry, I didn't mean to correct you, but I didn't want you to think I–"

"What was your least favorite class in school?"

"What?"

"Your least favorite class in school was…?"

"Um… science class, I guess, but that's because the teacher didn't like me. Master Osterous always called on me in class because he knew I didn't like science and he asked me harder questions than he asked anyone else. I never knew the answers."

"You say you don't like science and yet you have a great and eternal love for Sophia, a brilliant scientist."

"That's different, she doesn't make fun of me if I don't know something about science."

"Science Scholar Osterous made fun of you?"

"He didn't exactly make fun of me, but he always asked me questions I couldn't answer, and I know he did it on purpose."

A long stone table covered with curious scientific instruments appeared in front of Orville. Standing on the other side of the table was a tall gaunt mouse wearing the blue robe of a master scholar.

"Master Osterous??"

"Ah, Orville Wellington Mouse, one of my most memorable students. I welcome you to a land of infinite beauty and wonder. To be quite honest, I never expected to find myself in a glorious world such as this."

"What are you doing here?"

"I am doing the same thing I did in Muridaan Falls, I am learning."

"More science stuff?"

Master Osterous peered over his small gold glasses at Orville, a gentle frown crossing his face.

"Sorry, Master Osterous, I'm a little confused right now. I don't really know why I'm seeing you, or what this place is."

"Perhaps I shall be the mouse who shows you how to stop the worlds from overlapping."

"That would be great! How do I do it?"

"Oh, nothing is ever that simple, I'm afraid. Did I mention we'll be having a surprise quiz today?"

"What do you mean? I have to take a test? Why?"

"Nothing to worry about, I assure you. I will ask you three simple questions. If you are able to answer just one of them correctly, I will show you how to prevent the worlds from overlapping. Does that sound fair enough? You only have to answer one question correctly. Nothing could be easier."

Orville's heart sank. He was back in science class.

He clenched his paws together. "I guess so… if they're simple questions."

"Very well. First question, is there such a thing as magic?"

Orville breathed a sigh of relief. He knew this one. "That's easy, Sophia has told me a hundred times there is no magic, only science that we don't understand."

"Incorrect, I'm afraid. There is only magic, it is science which does not exist. We live in a magical world. When you bury a small seed in the ground, a beautiful flower soon appears. What could be more magical than that?"

"That's not magic, it's science. It's cells inside the seed multiplying and growing, using food that's stored in the seed. There's nothing magical about it."

"Incorrect, again. It's magic. It's all magic. Life is magic. The world is magic. Mice are magic. Our meeting in this wondrous world is magic."

"Wait, if you're saying the whole universe is magic, and Sophia is saying the whole universe is science, isn't that just two names for the same thing? Magic and science are just two different names used to describe how the universe works."

"Ah, that would have been a perfectly acceptable answer, but unfortunately it was not the answer you gave me. The next question is an easy one, a true or false question. True or false, when you were in my science class, I asked you very difficult questions because I didn't like you and I was trying to embarrass you in front of the class."

Orville froze. He had not been expecting a question like that. "Um… well, that was kind of true. Sorry."

"Wrong again. I purposefully asked you questions

you would be unable to answer so you would be forced to think, so you would try to discover the answers on your own. You are a brilliant mouse, whether you know it or not. A more creative mind I never saw in all my years of teaching. Great discoveries require innovative thinking. I had high hopes you would one day enter the world of science. We need minds like yours."

Orville was stunned. "You think I'm smart?"

Master Osterous stepped around the long table and put his paw on Orville's shoulder. "In this world I am able to see things from a far broader perspective than the world of Muridaan Falls. I did not realize it at the time, but I was learning a great deal about myself while I was teaching. I can see now my intentions were good, but my execution was lacking, my understanding of mice was lacking. I was never trying to embarrass you, Orville, I was trying to help you become the mouse I know you are."

"I should have studied more. I've learned a lot about science since I met Sophia. It's really kind of interesting. She's said a few times that I'd make a good scientist."

"This brings me great joy. Now, it's time for your third and final question. You have unfortunately given incorrect answers for the first two questions, but I have great hope for this last one. If you answer it correctly I will show you how to prevent the worlds from overlapping."

Master Osterous pulled a golden key from his robe. He stepped over to the stone table and unlocked the lid of a silver box, carefully removing a glass of bright purple liquid. He held it up for Orville to see. "A glass of delicious chilled brimbleberry juice. My question for

263

you is this – can I make it disappear?"

Orville tried to read Master Osterous' expression. His eyes narrowed. "Are you a shaper?"

"I am not a shaper."

"Do you have any weird magical powers in this world?"

"I do not."

"Then my answer is no, you can't make the brimbleberry juice disappear."

"I'm afraid that answer is also incorrect." Master Osterous raised the glass to his lips and drank the brimbleberry juice. He held the empty glass out for Orville to see.

"You didn't make it disappear, you just drank it. It's in your stomach."

"Are you certain? How can you know that for sure? The brimbleberry juice has clearly disappeared."

"Of course I'm certain, I saw you drink it!" Orville was suddenly very angry. "You're trying to trick me and I don't know why. It's just like being in science class again!"

Master Osterous set the empty glass on the table.

"Orville Wellington Mouse, you have incorrectly answered all three questions, but I am pleased to say that in the process you have learned everything you need to know in order to prevent the worlds from overlapping. You must now put your abundantly creative mind to work and solve this most vexing problem. Remember this, my brilliant young friend, we never stop making mistakes and we never stop learning from our mistakes, even in a glorious world such as this one. A wise mouse is simply a mouse who learns from his mistakes."

Master Osterous gave a great sweeping bow and vanished, the stone table vanishing with him. Orville stood before the Others, their thoughts filling his mind.

"A great mountain range in western Opar has vanished, replaced with a scorching desert. A storm of unparalleled fury is spreading rapidly across the Vesarak Sea, turning the waters blood red and moving relentlessly toward your home. You must act quickly or every mouse in Muridaan Falls shall perish, swept away by the raging sea."

"I don't know how to stop it! Why can't you just tell me? I don't understand what Master Osterous meant!"

"It is not our place to interfere in the affairs of your world. You possess everything you need to halt the storm. As Master Osterous said, you have a great mind, use it."

"Please, please, you have to–" The Others were gone. Orville stood alone in a vast and beautiful meadow. He fell to his knees.

Chapter 36

Brimbleberry Juice

Orville wiped the tears from his eyes. He was one small mouse in a vast universe. Why should he be responsible for the fate of a thousand universes, the lives of everyone in Muridaan Falls, the lives of everyone he loved?

Orville's inner voice spoke. "Remember the clockwork glowbirds, the blue marble that rolled uphill, the capricious shadows, all bewildering puzzles for which you found the solution. This is but one more puzzle to be solved, and who better than you to solve it? Let go of your doubt, let go of your fear."

Orville stood up. His inner voice was right. Sophia had used logic to discover the strange force causing the blue marble to roll uphill. He would do the same. The Others had told him he possessed everything he needed to prevent the worlds from overlapping. He emptied his pockets. Two silvers, a small pencil, half an oatmeal cookie, a piece of string, a wrinkled photo of Sophia, and the gold coin he had found on the gatehouse table. "None of this will help me."

He dumped the contents of his pack onto the meadow grass, studying everything carefully.

"Creekers. Double creekers." Orville froze, his breathing shallow. Master Osterous made the brimbleberry juice vanish by drinking it, but it had not truly vanished. The Chief Master Engineer had used a Mark XVII Distortion Thruster to create an atmosphere on Tectar. A brilliant light blazed inside him. He had solved the puzzle. He knew how to stop the worlds from overlapping. He also knew it meant a friend would have to die.

Sophia looked up when the door to the Machine Room opened and Orville emerged, his face grim.

"What is it? What's wrong?"

"I know how to stop the Void from vanishing."

"How? Did the Others tell you?"

"No, they made me figure it out." Orville turned to Haukesworth. "We know the great silver machine is a Mark XVII Distortion Thruster, one of the six engines which carried Tectar to its current location. The engineers altered the Mark XVII to create an atmosphere on Tectar, but something went wrong, just as the Chief Master Engineer had feared. There must have been a massive explosion which pushed the engine up through the outer shell of Tectar."

"What does that have to do with the Void and the overlapping worlds?"

"The Mark XVII works by continuously warping space in front of the interstellar ship. It takes a hundred thousand miles of space and compresses it down to a few inches. That is how Tectar could travel incredible distances in such a short time. I learned all this when I relived the Chief Master Engineer's memories. He knew I would be the one to find the thought he left behind. He knew the engine would be damaged, altered by the explosion. Instead of warping space, it has been warping the Void, compressing it. The Void has been shrinking since the explosion, but the change has gone unnoticed until now. With the Void almost gone, the worlds have begun to overlap."

"But if it's gone, there's nothing we can do."

"If I drink a glass of brimbleberry juice and show you the empty glass, does that mean the juice has vanished?"

"What?"

Sophia gave a yelp. "The Void isn't gone, it's inside the Mark XVII! We just have to shut off the engine and the Void will expand again."

"Exactly."

"How do we shut it off? If we damage the distortion thruster something could go wrong, it could kill us all."

Orville reached into his pack and pulled out his door prize from the History of Tectar Temporal Displacement Museum. "Copo said this was a perfect working replica of the key used to start the first of six Mark XVII Micronizing Distortion Thrusters. It's also how we turn off the machine."

Haukesworth was stunned. "The universe brought you to Tectar, led you to that museum, gave you that key, and led you to the Chief Master's thought cloud. How is it possible?"

"It's how the universe works, but we have to listen carefully to what it tells us, listen to the voice inside us."

"It doesn't seem possible, but I can't deny what I have seen."

"There's something else you need to know. It's not good news. The Chief Master Engineer said he was worried that if something went wrong they wouldn't have time. I misunderstood what he meant. He wasn't saying they wouldn't have time to get all the Thaumatarians to the surface of Tectar, he was saying time might not exist, they would not have time. He was right. The Mark XVII Distortion Thruster exists within a timeless bubble. If we shut the machine off, time will flow again. You will begin to age, you will be mortal, and one day you will die. If we don't turn off the engine, a thousand worlds will be destroyed but the castle will be unharmed, existing outside of time and space. We would be safe within Castle Caligari, but surrounded by nothingness, trapped in a world without time."

Haukesworth gave a long sigh. "Strangely enough, this comes as welcome news. I have lived in the castle long enough. I have always known that life is uncertainty, that life is adventure. Life is perilous. Life is learning. One thing that life is not, is sitting safely inside a timeless castle. I've had my fill of this land of the dead. We are Metaphysical Adventurers. We need to shut down the machine."

Orville nodded, turning to the Machine Room door. He pushed it open and they stepped into the sunlit meadow. There was no sign of the Others.

"How do we shut it off?"

Orville removed the golden cylindrical key from his coat pocket. "We have to figure out where the key goes." He strode over to the base of the monolithic silver engine and gazed upward. The machine was over a hundred feet tall, it's basic form a massive silver cone with a thirty foot wide golden dome protruding from one side. The huge black cloud swirled and pulsed next to the golden dome.

"The black cloud is the Void being compressed by the Distortion Thruster. I don't see any control panels where we could use the key, though." He stepped around to the other side of the Mark XVII and gave a yelp. He was standing face to face with a four foot tall green rabbit wearing a gray uniform, a silver pin on his lapel.

"You must be Orville Wellington Mouse."

"You're a Thaumatarian. Wait, you're the Chief Master Engineer of Tectar!" Orville looked behind him to Sophia, Proto, and Haukesworth, their eyes wide.

"You have a good memory for faces."

"Why are you here? How are you here? I saw what that rabbit in the blue cape did to you, shot you with some kind of beam weapon."

"He did indeed."

"So you were…"

"Murdered?"

"Are you a ghost?"

"The Others told me you were here, poking around the machine, trying to shut it off with that key you're holding. Did they teach you anything about icebergs in your science classes?"

"Huh?"

"Icebergs. Enormous chunks of ice floating in the ocean. What do you know about them?"

"They're cold… and only the tip of an iceberg is visible, most of it is hidden beneath the surface of the ocean."

"Precisely. Well done."

"You're saying we're only seeing part of the Mark XVII? Most of it is still below the surface of Tectar?"

"You are a very astute mouse."

"You sacrificed your life to bring the passengers to the surface of Tectar. Why did you do that?"

The Chief Master Engineer smiled. "If I told you that, I would be revealing life's greatest secret. How do I know you're ready for such knowledge?"

"The greatest secret of life? If you're talking about the secret of unlimited power, I already learned that from the Thirteenth Monk."

"This has nothing to do with power. It is a far deeper truth than that. Power means less than nothing. A single star has more power than a trillion shapers, a trillion armies. Power is nothing, a sad illusion. When you move to the world of the Others you will realize the truth of this."

"I know that already. I know that every event in the world takes place for a reason, that we are supposed to face the fires of life head on. The world is perfect as it stands, so there's no need to change it."

"I'm impressed. As a great Thaumatarian philosopher once said, the possession of great power does not necessitate its use. I sacrificed my life to bring everyone to the surface of Tectar because I wanted a better world for them, I wanted them to escape from the clutches of a brutal dictator who placed no value on their lives. I thought I was changing the world, but I was wrong. The world will never change. It is filled with brutal emperors and kings, creatures driven by insatiable greed and infinite lust for power. It is a world brimming with ignorance and violence and hatred for any creatures who are different from us. It is a world of mice fighting muroidians fighting rabbits fighting Anarkkians and on and on and on."

271

"Whoa, it's not *that* bad. I know a lot of mice who aren't like that at all."

"Of course it's not that bad. The world is also filled with loving creatures who spend their lives trying to improve the world. They bring light to the world, they bring love, they bring joy, they bring music and art and dance and humor. They feed the poor, heal the sick. And yet, despite their valiant efforts, the world remains much the same as it was a million years ago. They cannot change the world."

"That's kind of a gloomy secret. I don't think I like it too much."

The Chief Engineer laughed. "That's not the secret. The secret is a truth of infinite joy and eternal hope. Creatures who try to make the world a better place are not changing the nature of the world they live in, but in the process of trying to change their world, they are changing themselves. They are learning and growing, making personal sacrifices, their actions driven by love, not fear. They come to understand there is only one life force, no matter what physical form it takes. They come to understand we are all part of this life force, no matter what our current level of understanding might be. When the time comes, they move on to the world of the Others. Your world is a school, Orville Wellington Mouse. The school never changes, but the students come and go."

Orville was silent for a long time. "I wish you could have met the Thirteenth Monk. You would have been great friends. This is a good secret. Thank you for telling me."

"It is a good secret to those who understand the truth of it. Enough of such talk, it's time to shut down this infernal machine." The Chief Master Engineer pointed to a barely visible panel on the side of the Distortion Thruster. He tapped his paw on the panel and it slid open, revealing an entrance into the great engine, a silver ladder descending into the darkness below.

"Where does the ladder go?"

"It will take you down to the main control panel of the engine where you will find a hexagonal gold plate with an irregular shaped hole in the center. The key you are holding matches perfectly the shape of that hole. On the right side of the plate are two disks, one yellow and one violet. Once the key has been inserted, press the yellow disc and the Mark XVII will stop."

"Thank you for helping us."

"I didn't help you, you helped yourself by listening, by being aware, by thinking, by being here. Sometimes that's all it takes." The Chief Master rippled and vanished.

"I just talked to a ghost."

Sophia snorted. "He's just as alive as he was when he lived on Thaumatar."

"I guess so. He wasn't all spooky, but still. Either way it's time to shut down the machine." Orville stepped toward the silver ladder. Haukesworth grabbed his arm.

"Not so fast, my young friend. This is my job, not yours. I will be the one to shut off the machine."

Haukesworth took the golden key from Orville's paw. "You three will return to Muridaan Falls the same way my hat got there. Go back to the dungeon, step onto the dirt road and you will be home. I'll give you plenty of time to get there before I shut off the engine. The Void will expand, bringing to an end the overlapping of the worlds. When that happens, Tectar's connection to Muridaan Falls will be lost, along with our connection to the world of the Others."

A great sadness filled Sophia. She would not see her parents again.

Haukesworth's face softened. "You will see them again, but not today."

"I know you're right. How will you get back to Muridaan Falls?"

"I won't be coming back. There are a thousand worlds I should still like to visit. I've always wanted to see Thaumatar. It may take me a while, but I will find a way there."

Orville took off his adventurers hat and held it out to Haukesworth. "This belongs to you. If you're off on another adventure you'll need it."

"A new adventure calls for a new hat." Haukesworth flicked his wrist and a handsome adventurers hat with a bright yellow feather appeared in his paws. He deftly flipped it onto his head. "I believe farewell hugs are in order."

The adventurers hugged and said their good byes. As Orville shook Haukesworth's paw he said, "I'm going to write about Tectar in your journal back in Muridaan Falls. This might be your greatest adventure, and I want everyone to know about it."

"You mean my greatest adventure so far." Haukesworth grinned and tipped his hat, stepping through the doorway onto the silver ladder. "Back to Muridaan Falls with you. Some of us have to save the universe."

The three adventurers exited the Machine Room and headed down the long stone corridor to the great spiral staircase. Along the way they stopped at the dungeon filled with gold. "Haukesworth said I could take as much gold as I could carry."

Sophia smiled.

Orville continued, "The only problem is, it's not my gold to take, it belongs to everyone in Village 113." He reached into his pocket and drew out the gold coin he had found in the gatehouse, tossing it onto one of the wooden crates. A blue thought cloud flashed out of his ear and shot down the hall. "I sent Serus a cloud saying Mendacium was gone and the gold is here waiting for them. I also said Mendacium had put an end to all plague and pestilence on Tectar before he left."

Sophia put her arms around Orville and held him close for a long time.

"We should go before Haukesworth shuts off the machine."

Five minutes later the door to Muridaan Falls squealed open.

"Why is it so dark in there, and what's that weird flickering light? Wait, did Haukesworth shut off the machine already?" Sophia sensed a growing panic in Orville's voice.

"It's dark because the sun has gone down in Muridaan Falls. Maybe the flickering light is a campfire or something. Let's go."

They stepped through the doorway into a violent maelstrom, a ferocious blast of shrieking wind knocking Orville to his knees. Undulating sheets of pounding rain spattered wildly against Proto, blinding bursts of lightning crackling and sparking across the night sky. Proto raised one hand to shield his eyes. "Are you certain this is Muridaan Falls?"

Orville hollered, "The stormy red sea is almost here! The Others said the storm would destroy the whole town!"

Two things happened in the space of one second. First, Orville realized he was shouting, and second, he realized there was no need to shout because the storm had stopped, the air suddenly still and silent. He stood beneath a starry sky, breathing in the sweet fragrance of the towering spruce trees surrounding Muridaan Falls.

"We're home."

Sophia nodded. "Haukesworth did it, he shut off the machine."

Orville gazed up at the glorious night sky, an infinitely vast canvas of sparkling stars. "Is anyone else hungry? I'm starving. Mum said she was going to bake a snapberry pie. I hope Papa didn't eat it all."

Sophia gaped at Orville. "You're looking at this incredible night sky over our dear home of Muridaan Falls, and you're thinking about snapberry pie? Something is very wrong with you, Orville Wellington Mouse."

Chapter 37

The Silver Eye

"I'm kind of nervous, I've never gotten a medal before."

"Is there anything that doesn't make you nervous?"

"Snapberry pie doesn't."

Proto snickered. "My tasty little cakes don't cause you much trepidation either."

"Mmmm… tasty little cakes. So good."

"Quiet, the Supreme Counselor is getting up to speak."

Orville looked around the sprawling Hall of Metaphysical Adventurers, teeming with hundreds of members. This was the same hall where he and Sophia and Proto had brought Draken Mouse to justice nearly two years ago. A sharp rapping came from the front of the room. Orville turned to see a distinguished looking elderly mouse standing at the podium.

"Welcome, fellow Metaphysical Adventurers. Tonight's meeting will begin with a presentation of medals. I would request that Orville Wellington Mouse, Sophia Mouse, and Proto the Rabbiton please rise."

Proto turned to Orville in surprise. "Why did he call my name?"

"You'll just have to find out." Orville grinned. He couldn't wait to see the look on Proto's face.

The three adventurers stood up. The Counselor said, "I call upon Eldon Mouse to make the presentation." The Counselor stepped aside, Orville's papa appearing in a flash of blue light, three black velvet boxes in his paw.

Eldon stepped up to the podium and looked across the sea of adventurers. "There are moments in life you know will live with you forever. Your first kiss, the birth of a mouseling, the first time you realize you can shape a mug of ale."

The audience roared with laughter.

"This moment is one which shall live with me forever. Tonight I am presenting medals of valor to three of those among us, one of them being my son Orville, who have successfully concluded a dangerous and vital mission to the planet Tectar, a world created millennia ago by the Thaumatarians. As you well know, the purpose of their mission was to uncover the forces responsible for the vanishing Void, and subsequently to neutralize those forces, preventing the destruction of countless parallel universes. The terrible storms and flooding we have been experiencing in Muridaan Falls were an early sign of these overlapping worlds, the Vesarak Sea merging with the stormy world of Saevio. The lovely sunny days we are currently enjoying are irrefutable proof of their success. That being said, it is my great honor to present each of these esteemed Metaphysical Adventurers with the Silver Eye Medallion. Orville, Sophia, and Proto, please step forward and receive your award."

The three adventurers walked down the center aisle

to the front of the great hall, stepping up onto the stage. Eldon Mouse removed the first medallion from its box, placing the green ribbon around Orville's neck. "Well done, I could not be more proud of you."

Eldon stepped in front of Sophia, hanging the silver medallion around her neck. "Well done, Sophia. I suspect your mum and papa are watching from some distant realm." Sophia nodded, tears welling up in her eyes.

Before Eldon could present the third medallion, Proto leaned down and whispered something in his ear. Eldon nodded, turning to the audience. "Proto the Rabbiton has kindly informed me that he is not a member of the Metaphysical Adventurers, and as such is not eligible to receive the Silver Eye Medallion. I believe I have the solution to that particular dilemma right here in my pocket."

Eldon removed an extremely large silver ring from his coat. "Proto the Rabbiton, we have come to know and respect you as a true and loyal friend to Orville and Sophia, and now we shall know you as an honored member of the Metaphysical Adventurers." Eldon slid the great silver ring onto Proto's finger. Proto looked stunned, his eyes riveted on his new ring.

"Proto the Rabbiton, Metaphysical Adventurer, please accept your Silver Eye Medallion." Proto leaned down and Eldon placed the ribbon around his neck. "Congratulations, Proto."

The hall erupted in wild applause, the crowd cheering and stomping their feet. Orville grinned like a mouseling, holding up his medal for all to see. He glanced over at Sophia, who was also holding up her medal, tears in her eyes. It was Proto, however, who had the biggest smile of all.

Chapter 38

Ebenezer Mouse

The following morning Orville rose early. He grinned when he saw the gleaming silver medal hanging from his bedpost. He took it in his paw, studying it closely, feeling the weight of it. There were no words on it, only the image of a single eye, the ancient Thaumatarian symbol long used by the Shapers Guild. Papa had told him only another Metaphysical Adventurer would understand the true significance of the medal. Orville's name would not appear in the Muridaan Falls Gazette. He would be an unsung hero, his exploits and triumphs celebrated only by fellow members of the Metaphysical Adventurers. The citizens of Muridaan Falls would never hear about Tectar and the Mark XVII Distortion Thruster, about overlapping worlds. They only knew the terrible storms had ended, life had returned to normalcy.

Orville hopped out of bed, threw on his clothes and dashed down the stairs. Proto was standing in front of the iron stove wearing Mum's yellow flowered apron. He turned to greet Orville.

"A fine good morning to you. I have a special award winning breakfast today, snapberry muffins and red snackle flapcakes." Proto chuckled. "Did you catch my clever little play on words?"

"Got it, award winning breakfast. Funny. You're still wearing your Silver Eye Medallion?"

"Papa said I could wear it around the house but not out in public because mice would ask too many questions."

"That makes sense. I keep mine on my bedpost so I can see it when I wake up. Wait, you said red snackle flapcakes?"

"I did. Quite a treat, I assure you." He chuckled again. "I think you know how difficult it is to pick them."

"That's for sure, our cranky old neighbor Ebenezer Mouse was not pleased with my attempts to mimic the cry of the Gnorli bird. He shouted at me over the fence, said he was trying to take a nap."

"Perhaps you should take him a gift, a tray of tasty little cakes, for instance. They always seem to calm the waters, as they say."

"That's a good idea. I think he lives alone, maybe that's why he's so cranky. He was really nice to me when I was little and got lost. He found me and brought me home. I'll shape a tin of cakes and take them over to him."

An hour later Orville stood at the front door of a small yellow weathered cottage. "This place could use a coat of fresh paint, and the garden is really overgrown. Maybe Proto and I could paint the house for him."

Orville knocked on the door and waited, but there was no answer. He knocked harder and the door creaked open several inches. "The door wasn't closed. Maybe he's taking a nap." He nudged the door open a little wider, calling out, "Hello? Is anyone home? It's your neighbor, Orville Mouse."

The house was deathly silent. Orville felt a twinge of fear creep through him. "Maybe something's wrong, maybe he's sick." He peered into the house, his eyes gradually adjusting to the darkness. That was when he spotted a very curious object sitting against the living room wall.

"What in the world is that thing?" Orville studied the strange device, trying to identify it. "It looks a little like an old fashioned piano, or a parlor organ, but it has all those weird glass tubes and brass dials on the front. It has black and white keys like a piano, but there's way too many and the shape of them is all wrong." He stepped cautiously into the house. "Hello? Is anyone here? Hello?"

The house was silent, still. Ebenezer Mouse had not answered. Orville couldn't take his eyes off the peculiar wood and brass apparatus.

"That's weird, there's a blinking yellow light on the side panel. What in the world is this thing? Pianos don't have lights on them. Maybe it's some kind of ancient technology. I'll just take a quick peek then leave the tin of cakes on the kitchen table."

Orville stepped over to the mysterious contrivance, examining it closely. "It's definitely not a piano or an organ. It has six brass dials, but I don't recognize the symbols on them. It's seems really old, but it has a light on it so it must be advanced technology, maybe from some ancient civilization like the Thaumatarians. I wonder what the keys do? I guess it could be a weird kind of musical instrument."

Orville glanced around the room, making certain he was alone. He called out loudly, "HELLO? IS ANYONE HOME?"

Again there was no reply. "There is definitely no one home." He stepped closer to the device, touching his paw tentatively to one of the keys, then gently pressed down. Instead of the lovely musical note he was expecting, he heard the sound of distant drums.

"Creekers, what was that?" He pressed another key and heard the sound of a roaring wind shrieking through a canyon. The image of a vast red desert flashed before him. He was about to press a third key when something grabbed him from behind, yanking him away from the machine. Orville screeched, dropping the tin of cakes. He whirled around to see Ebenezer Mouse standing behind him, a furious scowl on his face.

"WHAT ARE YOU DOING IN MY HOUSE??"

Orville stammered wildly. "I... I... I was bringing you a tin of tasty little cakes but when I knocked on the door there was no answer so I–"

"So you thought you'd just break in and rob me blind? You thought you'd steal everything you could from an old mouse??"

"No! I wasn't trying to rob your house! I called out three times, I thought maybe something was wrong, that you needed help. I wanted to check on you and then I saw... um... that machine thing and I couldn't figure out what it was so I–"

"Never touch that again, do you understand me? NEVER TOUCH IT AGAIN!"

"I won't, I promise, I'm sorry, I didn't mean to

bother you while you were taking a nap.”

Ebenezer Mouse studied Orville's face closely. His anger seemed to be diminishing. “I was out taking a walk. You don't seem a bad sort, maybe a bit too curious for your own good. You'd best not be fooling with things you don't understand.”

“Sorry. What exactly is that thing?”

“You said you had a tin of cakes for me?”

Orville picked the tin up from the floor. “Here, they're really good. I hope they didn't get mashed when they fell. My friend Proto the Rabbiton made them and he's a really good chef. Everyone loves his tasty little cakes.”

Ebenezer took the tin from Orville. “Thanks. Practice your bird calls during the morning. I take a nap in the afternoon.”

“I will. Oh, I was wondering, it looks like your house could use a coat of paint. Proto and I could paint it for you if you'd like. We wouldn't charge you anything, but you'd have to pay for the paint.”

A curious look crossed Ebenezer's face. “Why would you want to do something like that?”

“You're our neighbor, and you're kind of… um…I mean…”

“Old? Crabby?”

“It just seemed like you could use a little help.”

“I'd appreciate that. I'm not very good with ladders anymore. Never liked heights anyway. I'll let you know when I get the paint.”

“Okay, sorry I bothered you.” Orville headed toward the door. He tried to hide his surprise when he noticed the tracks of snow on the wooden floor. It was the middle of summer and Ebenezer Mouse had tracked snow into the house. Orville darted out the front door, closing it behind him.

He dashed through the back door of his house. "Proto, you're never going to guess what just–" Orville stopped in his tracks. His mum and papa were standing at the kitchen table holding a large colorfully wrapped package. "What's that?"

"A present for you. Your papa thought it was time you had one."

"What is it?"

His Papa grinned. "Open it and find out."

Orville stepped over to the kitchen table and took the package from his papa. "It's heavy." He set it down on the table and tore the wrapping paper off. His eyes grew wide. In front of him was a large leather bound volume with gold lettering on the front cover reading:

ORVILLE WELLINGTON MOUSE
His Journal of Adventuring

"Whoa, my own journal? I have my own journal of adventuring? Wait, what about Sophia?"

"We have one for her and one for Proto, all courtesy of Master Marloh."

"I'd better get busy, I have to write about the clockwork glowbirds, the shattered Abacus and the capricious shadows."

"Capricious?"

Orville grinned. "What? I know a lot of big words."

Chapter 39

Every Word

"I should have been a king. What do you think?"
Orville leaned back in the ornate wooden throne,
raising one eyebrow, trying to look as regal as he
could.

"I don't think you'd like it. Being a king is more
than just having your subjects fetch your slippers and
bring you trays of tasty little cakes."

"How hard could it be? I'd just sit here and tell
everyone what to do. I'd be good at that."

Sophia's eyes wandered around Castle Caligari's
throne room, absently trying to decipher the symbols on
the tattered threadbare banners hanging from the
ceiling.

"There's a little game I like to play called 'what if'.
It goes like this. What if, one of your friends was chosen
to be the King of Muridaan Falls?"

"We don't have a king."

"That's not how you play. What if, we did have a
king, and your friend was crowned King of Muridaan
Falls. What if his first act as King was to command you
to fetch his slippers and a tray of tasty little cakes."

"He wouldn't do that because I'm his friend."

"He's King, he can do anything he wants."

"I wouldn't do it. I'd tell him to get his own slippers and tasty little cakes."

"They'd put you in chains and toss you into the dungeon for disobeying the King's order."

"That's not fair. I'd tell my other friends to clobber him."

"What if half of your friends thought you should bring the King his slippers and tasty little cakes, and the other half didn't think you should, and they wanted you to help them clobber the King? Do see where I'm going with this?"

"I guess so. I'd have to treat my subjects nicely so they wouldn't clobber me or get into a big fight."

"Exactly. It's not easy to be a good king."

"You're right. Besides, if I was king I couldn't go on adventures with you and Proto. I'd have to sit on this throne all day long signing important papers. So boring."

"Why do you think you're dreaming about Castle Caligari again?"

"I don't know. I like mysterious old castles, especially when they don't have creepy dark wizards living in them."

Sophia snorted. *"You were so wrong about Mendacium being a dark wizard. So wrong. I hope you learned your lesson about dreams. Hey, let's go check the Machine Room and see if the Distortion Thruster is still running."*

"Haukesworth shut it off."

"This is a dream, not the real world. It might still be running in your dream. Who knows, maybe someone opened a pastry shop in the meadow."

"We should check." Orville hopped down from the throne and the two best friends made their way down the spiral staircase to the first sub level.

Sophia stopped in her tracks, her eyes wide. She grabbed Orville's arm. "Orville! Did you hear that? It sounded like a ghost moaning!"

"A ghost?? Are you serious? You heard a ghost moaning?"

Sophia burst out laughing. "Woooooo wooooo! I'm coming to get Orville!!"

"That's not even funny. Besides, ghosts don't scare me anymore, not since my visit to the world of the Others."

"If you say so, Orville the Brave. Hey, there's the Machine Room." Sophia strolled through the wall into the room.

"How do you walk through walls like that? It's like you're a ghost. It's spooky." Orville pushed the door open and entered the huge room.

"It's not spooky at all. Think about it, we're in a dream, so there's no laws of physics, no laws of motion, no physical matter, no gravity. The wall and my body don't really exist, they're just thoughts in your dream. Our mind creates a thought image of the body we have in the real world. When I saw Mum and Papa in the world of the Others, they told me they appeared the way I remembered them so I'd feel comfortable talking to them. I think Master Osterous did the same thing for you."

"So did the Chief Master Engineer. What do you think they really look like?"

"They look like the Others. That's what everyone looks like in the world of the Others."

"It's a little spooky. I mean, I know they're still your mum and papa, but..."

"Whatever you're used to is normal. If we grew up in the world of shiny blue creatures with four arms, that would seem normal to us. If we grew up in the world of the Others, then the ghosty white cloud form would seem normal."

"Normal and spooky."

"The engine is off and the meadow is gone. It's just these old stone floors. I was kind of hoping the meadow would still be here."

Orville took Sophia's paw in his. He knew why Sophia was hoping the meadow would still be there.

Sophia's gaze traveled up the front of the towering silver engine. "Orville, look!" She pointed to the words scrawled across the side of the engine.

HAUKESWORTH MOUSE
WAS HERE

"That's weird, why would that be in my dream?"

"I don't know, but I have a feeling if we went back to the real Castle Caligari we'd find those same words written on the engine. Remember how Master Marloh said dreams are a mix of the real world and messages from our inner self? The hard part is telling which is which."

"Did your mum and papa say anything about you and me? You said they can see what's going to happen in the future."

"We talked about you a lot. They were really glad we found each other. They said they knew we would, that we always do."

290

"We always do?"

"They said this wasn't the first time you and I have gone swimming together in the river of time. They said we're old friends, eternal friends."

"I do feel like I've known you forever, and I love you more than anyone else. What else did they say?"

"They said we would marry and have two mouselings."

"That will be nice. Hey, I just realized something."

"What?"

"I'm going to remember this dream when I wake up."

"So am I. Every word."

If you enjoyed reading
*Orville Mouse and the Puzzle of the
Capricious Shadows*
please leave a short review or rating
on Amazon.com or on Goodreads.com
Reviews are the lifeblood of indie publishers –
we can't survive without them!

If you have any comments or suggestions
or would like to be notified of upcoming book
releases and Free Kindle book day promotions,
please email me at
BartholomewtheAdventurer@gmail.com

Best wishes until we meet again,

Tom Hoffman

ABOUT THE AUTHOR

Tom Hoffman received a B.S. in psychology from Georgetown University in 1972 and a B.A. in 1980 from the now-defunct Oregon College of Art. He has lived in Alaska with his wife Alexis since 1973. They have two adult children and two adorable grandchildren. Tom has been a graphic designer and artist for over 35 years. Redirecting his imagination from art to writing, he wrote his first novel, *The Eleventh Ring*, at age 63.